NOTHING
TO
REGRET

A NOVEL OF SUSPENSE

BELLAMY GAYLE

CALAMITY, DANGER,
AND LOSS

SAZERAC SERIES #2

AUTHOR'S NOTE

NOTHING TO REGRET is a work of fiction and any similarities between the characters of this book to any real persons, living or dead, is coincidental and not intended by the author. This book is intended to be historical in only a general way, though there are facts sprinkled throughout the story for readers to enjoy.

Vierville-sur-Mer does exist and is more famous because of Omaha Beach and the Allied landing in Normandy in 1944. The idyllic village is entirely fictitious as portrayed, though the French Resistance was firmly entrenched in the area.

For very sensitive readers, be aware this novel of suspense includes bits of the violence and death that war brings and alludes briefly to a miscarriage.

This content is the result of creative imagination and is not intended for use, reproduction, or incorporation into any artificial intelligence training or machine learning systems without prior written consent from the author.

CONTENTS

PART ONE

WAR WAS UP close now and personal. A young woman was on the run, breathing hard… sick of this stupid war… and way too tired to keep running.

Sunlight streamed through the forest canopy, its rays burrowing into the decaying leaves and mounds of mosses. She would have appreciated the loveliness of the forest, but the need for a frantic escape was all she could manage. She paused to rub cramping legs and get some air in her lungs.

She knew there was no way to outrun the men pursuing her. As a child she could run forever, but not today. She stopped and bent over, her tangled hair hanging in a mass almost down to her sturdy shoes, her breathing ragged, her lungs struggling, knowing these were the least of her worries.

The thud of heavy boots sent a new surge of stamina, and she was back on the run, crashing through underbrush, around trees, over roots. She ran for her life, her thoughts panicked as German shouts came near, knowing she wasn't as invincible as she pretended to be.

Merde, these Nazi pigs calling themselves civilized. It's 1940, for God's sake. How have I let my life become so twisted around?

Tree trunks blurred past, presenting their own threats to her safety. Thorns grabbed at her clothes and vines slashed her face and hands, leaving drops of blood trailing on the forest floor.

Could fear kill her? That would be ironic, but she almost wished it would. As blood whooshed in her ears, she heard a German sentry's command: *Halt, oder ich schiesse!*

She might not understand the guttural words the guard spat, but the man's intent was clear. Keep running, and he would shoot her. But run she did, and she didn't stop. She knew the alternative: torture, maybe rape, and *then* she would be shot. Stop running and the outcome was certain—she would be dead.

She pushed off with the last of her reserves, ducking and weaving through tangled woods, her muscles on fire.

Though not the speedy youngster she'd once been, she still had strength in her long legs. Her life depended on what speed she could muster. Salty sweat burning her eyes, her vision cloudy, she kept reminding herself how fast she'd once been able to run. Just ask old New Orleans playmates.

She skidded to a sudden stop at the rim of a deep *coulée*, a ravine, windmilling her arms for balance, teetering as the ground under her feet crumbled. The gap was too wide to jump across. The woman wavered, knowing she was a perfect target. She could hear a Nazi guard's footsteps close in behind her.

She heard a metallic click. During weeks of secret training with the French Resistance she'd learned the sound of a gun's safety disengaging. He was ready to shoot her. There would be no more warnings.

The back of her neck itched, prepared for a lethal bullet. Fear overwhelmed her. She'd never been so helpless.

But loose soil cascaded beneath her feet and she tumbled with it, her stomach briefly left behind before falling with her body.

Being shot was surprisingly painless. She'd heard the crack of rifle fire; the sentry could not have missed. She covered her head with her arms and tried to tuck into a ball as she fell.

She caromed down the steep incline, hitting bushes and saplings, her legs and arms jounced free and fluttered like tattered rags. She grunted an oath as she spotted a sturdy tree ahead.

A glancing blow knocked her unconscious, her inert body rolling to a stop, still as death. Cushioned by a mat of fallen leaves, she lay at the bottom of the deep ravine, surrounded by the beautiful flaming colors of autumn.

A second sentry caught up to the first and stood beside him. Peering down into the ravine, they spotted a barely visible body through the trees and bushes.

The latecomer laughed and clapped the shooter on the shoulder, one young man complimenting another.

The marksman was chagrined. "I didn't know it was a woman until she stopped. I shot too soon. She was running as fast as a man."

Sure of the kill, the men returned to their patrol of a small Nazi stockade, regretting lost opportunities had they captured the *fraulein* alive.

Hattie DeValcourt recalled the day she'd caught sight of Luke strolling down a mostly deserted cobbled street in Paris. It had been a mild and lovely June that awful summer of 1940.

Although constantly homesick and yearning for her family and New Orleans, Hattie DuMond had become thoroughly Parisian after four years there. Now she wondered if she might not live to see them again.

After graduating from Tulane University with a degree in biology in 1936, it had been an uphill battle to find a medical school that would accept her. Few women were admitted to American medical schools. It was not that medical schools didn't accept women; they would, but only in the absence of qualified males. Men always moved to the head of the line and that was just the way it was.

One admissions officer took her call, then laughingly suggested she try Paris. Oh, but of course, she'd have to speak French.

Hattie checked into it. The Sorbonne in Paris was indeed a possibility—they accepted men and women. But could her family afford it, and would her undergraduate coursework, even with excellent grades, be good enough? All classes would be in French and there would be no allowance made for the language limitations of foreign students. The Sorbonne's medical school was highly rated and gender-blind, its only qualifications aptitude and achievement.

Much to Maman and Papa DuMond's dismay, the Sorbonne had accepted Hattie into their medical program. And with generations of family from bilingual New Orleans, her adjustment in Paris would be to family separation and cultural differences, not language.

When Hattie arrived in Paris in 1936, her female classmates introduced themselves and clucked over her appearance. Already shy in the company of cosmopolitan French girls, she was dismayed to be told she dressed like an American colonial, hopelessly at odds with the fashion sense of Parisian women.

They took Hattie under their wing as their pet American girl—gradually introducing her to understated French elegance. Once that had been taken care of, the group was free to flutter along the pavements of Paris, like a chirping flock of black birds moving from one place to another.

They pronounced her name, "*Ha-tee*," and folded her into *la rive gauche* bohemian life, where she gained confidence and polish and began to bloom. By Hattie's final semester, her talent for fun and her unaffected laughter had made her popular with both young women and young men—but none understood why such a pretty girl remained chaste.

As a practical matter, nearly everything was acceptable by the *laissez-faire* policies of *l'université* created in 1257, long before Europeans had settled in North America. An American like Hattie found the Sorbonne ancient, of an age almost inconceivable.

Magnolia-scented heavy vellum carried the words of the long letters Maman wrote to her daughter. Beautifully written in a disciplined hand, receiving one was a high point in the week for Hattie. Maman would describe her flowering garden and enclose water colorings. With each delightful letter, Hattie rediscovered her mother's erudition and wit. She would stop reading just to press the pages to her heart for a moment, then read on of her brother's escapades and romances. Hattie smiled each time, knowing this was not all Jack did, only what Maman knew about.

It was in Maman's letters that she learned of Maman's concern for Papa's occasional health challenges. Hattie understood Maman's descriptions of his symptoms, and wished she were there to treat him. She believed she'd soon be home to do just that.

But lately the tone of Maman's most recent letters had changed. She and Papa had kept up with the news from Europe, and Germany's aggression was making her frantic to get her daughter home. She begged Hattie to leave the Sorbonne and flee Europe before it was too late.

Maman never wrote a word about Hattie's estranged friend, Luke DeValcourt, and rarely mentioned Hattie's fiancé, Karl Schmitzer, knowing Karl and Hattie kept in close touch. She did report Karl's rare visits to their home, always commenting on his good looks.

Before Hattie sailed off to France, she and Karl had announced their engagement as part of their long range plan. A plan, without Maman's or Papa's approval, that sounded just like the circumspect Karl, not something their Hattie would say on her own. The two lovebirds had agreed to set aside for now their passion and desire for a future together, in favor of completing their educations. Maman had said nothing, though it left a sour taste; she knew the plan as stated was completely at odds with Hattie's usual way of thinking: They would complete their educations thousands of miles and an ocean apart; Karl would finish his law studies and Hattie would begin four years of medical school in Paris; She would receive her degree, return, and they would get married; and then they would live a happy life together. *Karl's plan*, Maman thought. *Not Hattie's.*

Man proposes, God disposes, and fate had other plans in store.

Blending in, invisible in the black clothing favored at the Sorbonne, Hattie sat with other students in a *café*. Sipping from a tiny cup of strong espresso, she listened to earnest discussions that boomeranged around the smoke-filled, crowded room.

Most of the debaters were obsessing over Hitler's increasing authoritarianism and aggression. They argued over what the Nazi invasions of Czechoslovakia and Poland might portend for France, with the borders of those countries not all that far away.

A fellow speaking in a corner of the room was a friend of Hattie's. He was a bit pompous, which she thought was likely compensating for some insecurity. Like the other debaters, he was still young, not much more than a boy. As he gestured with a nicotine-stained hand, noxious smoke spewed from his nose and mouth.

"That invasion is the best thing that could happen to Poland."

It was a pronouncement, rather than a statement for discussion, and Hattie thought it ill-considered. Like some of the other students, his hygiene was questionable. Overall, he was very unattractive, even slightly repulsive, but Armand was Hattie's friend and she liked his company.

He pinched a worrisome speck of tobacco from his tongue and flicked it to the filthy floor to join dozens of cigarette butts lying there. Hattie grimaced, torn between amusement and slight disgust.

Holding his lit cigarette between the tips of his thumb and forefinger, Armand sucked in more bitter Gauloises smoke, then exhaled it into the choking air. A dirty black beret sat at a rakish angle over his lank, dark hair. Black clothing and the pasty pallor of his skin gave his cadaverous body an other-worldly appearance.

Having been born into an aristocratic French family, he believed the Poles needed a totalitarian government to lead them from serfdom into the modern age. He wasn't the only man to believe that—many young Frenchmen applauded Hitler and his actions. "Hitler believes Polish serfs deserve an education and a structured life. What's wrong with that? Maybe I should join the *German* army," he was saying.

Expatriate Hattie DuMond and others, though, were uncomfortable and concerned by Hitler's unprovoked incursions into sovereign nations, especially those so near France. A strong foreboding, as if holding one's breath, hung in the air, as France followed Switzerland's example and declared neutrality. With a typical Gallic shrug, the government thought this simplistic political posture would insulate them from invasion or other threats to their sovereignty.

So they believed.

Hattie beckoned Armand over, and challenged her friend. "*Comment?* What do you mean, Armand? Those people were living quiet lives. They didn't ask for change. Why should Hitler bother them?"

She shivered, unable to imagine life under the restrictive Third Reich—skewered like the specimen bugs she had studied in the entomology lab.

Armand, his head cocked to the side, enjoyed Hattie's pretty shiver and considered the winsome girl. He decided not to assault her sentimental statement with an acerbic retort.

Instead, he patted her hand, dismissive in a way she found insulting . Hattie's freckles stood out on her flaming cheeks. Her eyes flashed, furious under her lowered lashes. His response was that of the typical Gallic male, demeaning and indifferent, and not at all like her American men friends at home.

She wanted to punch Armand's shoulder, but scraped her chair back from the table. The sound went unnoticed under the conversational rumble.

"It's like you think I don't have good sense. So for a change, today *you* can pay for *my* coffee."

She stalked away, having flung those words over her shoulder, knowing it would hurt Armand where he lived—in his wallet. She slammed outside, smelling the stink of the *café* in her hair and clothes. She'd give a back tooth to talk to Maman right now, but that was impossible. She decided to buckle down and study for her final exams by going to a park.

The pocket park was a lovely place. Its narrow entrance was guarded by a curlicued wrought iron fence. Through the gate, a twenty-five-foot stroll across slate slabs ended in a grassy square that accommodated three large chestnut trees, each casting shade over its own wrought iron bench. In front of the benches, there were bare patches, evidence that the park was well used.

Hattie had the park all to herself today. An early exodus from the Sorbonne and, indeed, from all of Paris had begun, not for the annual summer holiday but from widespread certainty that Paris would be Hitler's next stop.

Opening her scuffed leather satchel, she pulled out a text on skeletal structure. Hattie had studying left to do, and finals were right around the corner. At this point in her studies, she was making hospital rounds and treating patients, but she was always on the lookout for the tiniest new details to absorb.

Studying was difficult, now that she was as anxious as her parents about the dangerous political climate, but she couldn't leave yet. Graduation was in May, in only two weeks. Hattie frowned in thought. *Just get past my exams and I'll have one of the Sorbonne's enviable 'gold-plated' medical degrees.*

Hattie hadn't heard back from her professor. She had requested a meeting to beg permission to take the final exams early. If he agreed, she could skip the ceremony and take her diploma on the first available ship home.

But things hardly ever work out as planned.

A few days later, Hattie found herself fretting, a heavy black telephone receiver against her ear. She had received her precious degree, but now Doctor Harriet DuMond was finding it impossible to book passage home to New Orleans. This most recent attempt had her sweating with nervous apprehension.

"*Mademoiselle, m'écoutez-vous?* Do you hear what I'm saying?" The frustrated sneer came clearly through the handset. To Hattie, sneers were the least endearing of all the unique French affectations. She sympathized with his frustration, and the man's tone more amused her than made her snicker. She visualized him as a cross-eyed functionary with oily black hair slicked back, making his long French nose seem even longer as it perched over a stylish, pencil-thin black moustache.

Hattie shook herself back to full attention. It had taken several attempts to get through to this officious booking agent. *Still,* she thought, *his dramatic skills would be very effective in the theater.*

"*Mais oui, m'sieur. Certainement.*" But amusement changed to alarm with the agent's next words. She blanched, not believing what she heard: Every cabin on every passenger ship to North America was fully booked for at least the next thirty days, if not longer. Foolhardy expatriate Americans and Canadians who had optimistically bet on stability in Western Europe had now decided, seemingly *en masse*, to flee the continent. And Dr. Harriet DuMond was stranded far from home.

Her shaking hand replaced the receiver as Hattie's heart accelerated, tattooing the inside of her rib cage. She was now as fully unsettled and apprehensive as the rest of Paris. The booking agent had frightened her, though he added Hattie's name and telephone number to his lengthy standby list. He confirmed a departure date, more than a month distant, on a small ship sailing from Calais to New York City. She'd then have to travel by train home to New Orleans, but she and her family had done that several times.

Only a few expatriate students remained in the strangely quiet dorm. Everyone else had scattered, anticipating a German invasion.

And now, a few days later, she wasn't sleeping well. Would she live to see her fiancé or her family again? Sitting alone in her dormitory room, she mooned over the day she and Karl had meandered to the end of Octavia Street, holding hands in the mild warmth of that late spring day. A sturdy stand of dense, secluded bamboo had grown at the base of the river levee. Exploration had been their excuse for pushing deep into the tall, dusty canes, rather than seeking more privacy. Karl was a twenty-one-year-old man. Hattie had just celebrated her eighteenth birthday.

Karl had taken her hand and pulled her into the massed growth. Hattie remembered carefully watching where she stepped, only to collide with Karl when he'd suddenly turned to ask if she wanted to retrace their steps.

He'd caught her as she stumbled by hooking his arms under hers, and his thumbs brushed her breasts. Realizing, he froze, powerless to move.

"I'm sorry," he sputtered. Hattie gasped, but didn't move away. She looked up at him, at the light in his beautiful amber eyes. Karl saw it as an invitation and folded Hattie into the circle of his arms, the two concealed by rustling bamboo canes.

She'd snuggled against his chest, inhaling his clean maleness and warmth as they touched along the length of their bodies. She heard his heartbeat thudding fast, strong and regular, against her ear. Thrilled at their contact, she pressed closer. The yielding softness of her breasts fit snugly against him.

Hattie sighed at the thrill of that day. She mourned that missing closeness with Karl, but with the Nazis now almost in Paris, she feared she would not survive to return home.

From her desk drawer, she withdrew a single sheet of white stationery and, with many pauses, wrote a letter to her fiancé, the ink crying across the page like indelible tears to match her weeping eyes.

It was not fair to keep him tied to her, Hattie wrote, and in her next sentence she broke their engagement off. She enclosed his ring with the letter in a heavy envelope. Later that day, she slid it across the counter to the postmaster. It turned out to be the last day before all French mail service ceased.

War had reached France… and Hattie. Neither of them ready.

Another week fraught with concern dragged past. Hattie's heavy feet trudged down the dormitory's ancient creaking stairs. Every day, she saw changes to neighborhoods where change had once been nonexistent. Buildings the length of her street seemed to sag and look bedraggled.

Today, her heart lifted when she saw that her favorite *café* was still open and busy, until she realized they were in the process of closing down for the duration of the war. Hattie was well known at the *café* from her years at the Sorbonne, and the owner personally set in front of her a large cup of steaming aromatic *café au lait*, paired with croissants, soft cheese, and a bunch of grapes, then refused to let her pay. His expression seemed to convey an uncertainty whether either of them would survive the coming invasion.

She remained sitting outside the *café* for a long time, staring at nothing and missing Karl's warm hugs, thinking of being stranded and alone. The *café*'s shutdown bustled about her, but no one suggested she leave.

Paris's cool spring evening was tucked under a protective shroud of darkness by the time she placed a stack of *francs* under her cup on the table as a goodbye gift. Hattie's table was the last one dragged inside the building.

A day could blur past, but more commonly it was hours inching by. The total male Sorbonne student population was gone, conscripted into France's army that was set to fight with Poland against the Nazis. It seemed ironic to Hattie that all the men were gone, and she, who had tried so hard to leave, had been the one left to attend a much diminished graduation ceremony.

Germany invaded France the same day the Sorbonne awarded Hattie DuMond a Doctorate in Medicine. It was May 10, 1940. She was twenty-six years old, a new young doctor, frightened and alone.

Even after undersea telegraph cables had been laid between the two continents, a robust postal business still crisscrossed the Atlantic by ship, sharing the information between Europe and North America that unreliable cables couldn't convey. Transatlantic mail service was slow and somewhat uncertain at its best during peacetime, but it became dramatically worse when the German rampages began. Ships became targets as they wallowed across the Atlantic waves to deliver mail to America, and the Germans bombed, torpedoed, and sank them so often that delivery became sporadic and finally ceased altogether. Later, once the war ended and armistice was signed by the warring nations, officials discovered warehouses full to the rafters with undelivered letters and packages, letters to Hattie among them.

May faded into June and Hattie's panic increased. Her father's bank stopped sending deposits to France and her funds dwindled. All her girlfriends had left Paris for the relative safety of the country.

The Sorbonne announced it would close its dormitories , and Hattie would soon be homeless. Even now her footsteps echoed in the empty halls and stairwells, all of the students' chattering laughter gone.

How would she survive? Paris was like a ghost town, nothing to indicate life except for gas streetlights that remained lit. Still wreathed in fogged haze, the wavering flames glowed on empty streets. Only a few vehicles rumbled and hissed along the cobbles, and few pedestrians strode the gritty sidewalks.

Colorful Parisian kiosks that had once been stuffed with exuberant, colorful blooms stood empty on street corners, their rustling canvas awnings now furled and casting silhouettes stark as daggers to pierce the sky.

Those who remained in the city by choice or by chance, as Hattie had, followed on the wireless as the Nazis crossed the French countryside. They were meeting little opposition, but annihilating what challengers there were. Like human locusts, they denuded family farms and quiet fields of anything edible, killing men and savaging women and girls as they passed. They emptied towns then burned them to the smoldering earth. Once picturesque thatched country roofs lit up the countryside in fiery conflagrations, only devastation remaining in the enemy's wake.

Hattie's narrow dormitory bed rested under the only window in her high-ceilinged room, the window standing open to capture errant breezes. She dressed for the day in her habitual black, then sprawled back across her mattress like a large ink blot. She gnawed her lower lip and stared vacantly at the ceiling. Heavy footsteps to a tune of pain-filled grunts sounded on the dormitory stairs, intruding on the silence.

Hattie sighed. It was either an overweight man or a very heavy woman. The steps stopped at her room. Hers was the only room still occupied on the floor. After one hard rap, the door cracked open far enough for the concierge to make her gravelly voice heard.

"*Chère*, telephone for you."

"*Qu'est que c'est?* What is it?"

"*Alors!* You wait for Calais, *n'est ce pas?* Your reservation? They are on the phone."

Hattie bounded to her feet. "*Ah! Merci.*"

A threaded needle in her lap, meant to darn a stocking, dropped to the floor. *A berth must've cleared.* She brushed past the concierge and hurtled down three flights of stairs, her black skirt flying.

Out of breath, she picked up the receiver and gasped, "*Merci, m'sieur, c'est* Hattie DuMond *ici.*"

"*Mademoiselle* DuMond," spoke a cold, officious voice in clipped tones, "we regret to inform you that your reservation for travel to *les États-Unis* has been cancelled. The government has taken all ships for government use."

Hattie went numb. An impossible heaviness kept her immobile. Her breath hitched. With great effort, she stuttered, "But…." The situation was incomprehensible.

"*Oui, oui,*" the impatient voice rasped, speaking quickly. Hattie pictured the man shrugging and waving his arms, Gauloises ash scattering around him. "You want to leave, but no, it's impossible. We can do nothing. *Au revoir, mam'selle, et bon courage.*"

He disconnected before Hattie could utter more than "but…." She dropped the heavy receiver into her lap to hear the broken connection buzz. *I'm doomed.* The concierge appeared a few moments later, and under her watchful eye Hattie dragged herself outside, closing the heavy door behind her. The concierge shook her head in compassion and clucked sympathy for the young woman.

Overwhelmed by fear and depression, Hattie wandered. She stumbled down a cracked sidewalk heading for the pocket park, only half-aware of her surroundings. The deserted street had an apocalyptic atmosphere without the sounds of conversation or traffic. The entire area felt abandoned. Unoccupied.

Once lively boutiques were dark and silent, their shades shut, their welcome mats pulled inside, and their doors securely locked. Their trimmed privet hedges were already unkempt.

Papers taped on window panes carried messages in the exquisite calligraphy Parisians loved. "*Ferme*," one said. Closed. "Our waiters forced into the army."

The waiters were grown men, but most of them were too old for this conflict. They were veterans of the Great War that had been fought thirty years earlier. Hattie knew that several of the men were debilitated by the injuries they'd suffered in that war to end all wars. Thrust into battle, they would be little more than a hiccup against able-bodied, well-trained Nazi troops.

The sign disturbed Hattie, and her depression deepened. Never had she experienced fear before, but she was now more frightened than she could have imagined. What would happen to her?

Hattie's throat burned with stomach acid. Goose bumps popped up under her thin sleeves and she sought refuge in the deserted park, nauseated by thoughts of the approaching carnage. She chose a bench that was warmed by pleasant sunshine. She stared blankly into space until the movement of a distant French soldier caught her eye.

The man sauntered closer, his uniform hat at a jaunty angle. She squinted in the bright sunlight. The way his arms swung—or something—was familiar. Armand? No. This man was taller than a typical Frenchman. His athletic stride and loose arms showed no cigarette, and Armand would have one in his fingers. And he was the only soldier Hattie knew.

Her imagination had been grasping at straws lately, working overtime. Her eyebrows knitted, frowning as the soldier's stride still held her gaze. She swatted at a gnat that thought her a juicy prize, while idly watching the man approach. Purple martins circled, zipping through the warm afternoon above her and devouring mosquitoes by the score.

Above her, serene gold-tipped, snow-white cumulus clouds drifted across a clear sky, unconcerned by the troubled world far below, and Hattie peered more closely at the approaching soldier.

She stumbled to her feet, astonished, and called out, her heart thudding. "Luke. My God. Luke DeValcourt!" Her throat was suddenly, painfully, tight with unexpected tears.

She ran then, her hair loosening from its pins and her arms outstretched. Her footfall echoed loud on the empty cobbled street, each step reminding her how badly she'd treated Luke so many years ago, hoping he didn't hate her. Hattie's heart plummeted when he halted to scrutinize the woman who was running recklessly his way.

She skittered to a stop and hesitated…until Luke flung his arms wide and ran to meet her. Luke's irises were a fascinating dark blue that was almost black, and his eyes shone with delight. Hattie's worry subsided, and she smiled. *Have his eyes always been so beautiful?*

"It's so good to see you, Luke. So good."

Hattie's warm pleasure was obvious, giving Luke license to move close. Their grins, wild as the childhood they'd shared, mirrored each other. She squeezed his hands, pulling him close for a big hug and a kiss on both of his smooth-shaven cheeks. Of all the things she could have expected, the sight of Luke was the least likely of them.

In a startling baritone that made Hattie tingle, and speaking in fluent, lyrical French, Luke softly touched her chin and murmured, "Beautiful Hattie, here you are." His deep voice resonated with joy, and Hattie blinked, her eyes damp.

Switching to ordinary southern-accented American English, Luke's voice vibrated deep in his chest, sounding warmly and deliciously foreign on the Paris street. His strong arms drew her close again, the way a man, not a boy, would, and the charged air crackled around them.

Astonished, Hattie whispered, "You're looking for *me*?"

They hadn't seen each other in years, but years evaporated as if only minutes, a *rapprochement* smacking of inevitability. Both were taller now, and leaner—and a decade older. There were other pleasant changes. Hattie approved of Luke's broad shoulders and strong chest. He had a handsome mouth and smile—*no*, she thought, *they're beautiful*—and the sweep of his long eyelashes gave her a visceral reaction she tried to hide.

Nor was Luke immune to Hattie's charms. Far from it. A spectacular body in shapely curves and the perfect height to snuggle under his chin, as he'd just learned. Hattie's abundant hair, the rich cordovan of ripe chestnuts, glinted with auburn highlights in the sunlight. Her full lower lip tilted upward at the corners, as though ready to smile. Those kissable lips held a fascination for him, as did the sparkling golden amber eyes he remembered so well, still framed by lush black eyelashes and naturally arched dark eyebrows.

Luke had often heard Hattie's family tease her that the freckles scattered across her nose were the family curse. Those freckles made the beautiful woman in front of him more approachable, and beneath the freckles a vaguely olive complexion hinted at the Mediterranean lineage of the DuMonds.

"Luke." Hattie's husky timbre took him by surprise and he shivered with sudden goose bumps. She was holding his hands, struggling now for her English after so many years in France.

"I've thought of you so often, and here you are—in a French Army uniform, of all things."

The physician's caduceus she saw pinned to each side of Luke's collar was a surprise, as were the chevrons indicating rank on his shoulders.

"You're a doctor now?" She pointed at herself. "Me, too. Brand new." He smiled his approval. Still holding his hands as they stood there in the street, she asked, "Why are you here?" then tugged him from the empty street to the sidewalk.

His eyes looked down on the graceful fingers entwined with his.

"I joined, just a regular officer, not a doctor, thinking I could help my relatives. We, you and I, we both have family here. Then your brother Jack told me *you* were here, too, marooned without a way to get home. So I took a furlough to find you." Because there was more than just *finding* her on Luke's mind, he had the good grace to blush.

Understanding that blush, Hattie said, "You are completely out of your mind" and dropped his hands like she'd been scalded.

At the edge of the sidewalk next to them, a window jalousie creaked open three floors above their heads. A wet, congested cough and an acrid plume of a *Gauloises* cigarette followed.

Hattie glanced up at an old man's unshaven face, his elbows balanced on the flaking blue-painted windowsill in a faded buttermilk-colored, stuccoed brick wall. A cigarette dangled between his fingers and an earthen pot of exuberant red poppies sat dangerously close to one elbow. He waggled his eyebrows and jutted his chin in salute.

She responded with a tiny wave and returned her attention to Luke. A brisk zephyr twined Hattie's long black skirt with Luke's legs as they faced each other on the wide brick sidewalk. Soft green, early summer growth leaves skittered, wrenched from the birch trees that lined the street and blown along the iron-red bricks. Embarrassed, Hattie gathered her skirt to her, releasing it when the breeze ruffled her hair free of its pins.

Hattie's thoughts scattered. She wondered vaguely why she felt the mighty happiness that fluttered against her breastbone.

As a teenager, an adult had always been in sight when boys visited her. This was different. Not a single soul walked past them, not that she would have noticed. Whenever Hattie heard trees rustling in a spring breeze even years later, she would recall the day she and Luke had held hands on a Paris street.

"Where are you staying, Luke?"

"Nowhere yet, but I'm here for at least two weeks. Know of a hostel nearby?"

She hesitated, then tugged his sleeve with a smile.

"My dormitory has vacancies. Let's talk to the concierge."

Luke's finger wormed its way under his collar that suddenly seemed two sizes too small. "What about your reputation? How old are you, anyway?"

Hattie flushed and stuttered, "Not *my* room, silly; your *own* room, just in the same building. And I'm almost twenty-six. I'm not a child."

That made Luke's cheeks flame as red as hers. The harder Hattie tried not to think of Luke in her room, the more she imagined it. She decided her inappropriate response was due to the unsettled times as she yearned for his embrace.

Luke and Hattie, who had known each other all their lives, were spending every idyllic moment together, reminiscing and sharing childhood secrets, laughing at and with each other. Their teasing grew more intimate and personal every day.

He told her once that she was beautiful, and tugged on her silk collar. In response, she tossed the loose chestnut hair that fell past her shoulders and brushed an invisible fiber from his cheek. She murmured that he was handsome, responding to his strong personal magnetism and chiseled jawline, calling him a "clever fellow." The more they laughed about their youthful escapades, the more their mutual attraction deepened.

As the days passed, they moved closer to each other. As they walked their shoulders grazed and their hips touched. Their clasped hands felt completely natural and the three-year disparity in their ages disappeared. So it was no surprise when, ten days after his arrival, Luke finally stole a kiss from Hattie's soft lips. His warm hand caressed the curve of her jaw and neck, and they sank into feelings that weakened them both.

"Mmm," she teased him as she straightened. "You taste like home."

Hattie absently tucked a few loose hairs behind her ears, moving unselfconsciously in ways that revealed her attractive body. Though she made no move to shrink from him, an odd expression crossed her face, and she added, "Somehow you make me yearn for Octavia Street. I'm as homesick as a child."

Her laugh bubbled with amazement, fizzing like seltzer. Privately, Hattie was conflicted. Though surely drawn to handsome, virile Luke, she was afraid that in some unconscious way she was responding to him as a provider of safety. She questioned whether her heart was in the right place.

Luke leaned back, his arms resting on top of the park bench's backrest. He didn't usually think very deeply, and he wondered what Hattie had meant by her cryptic remark. Still feeling the softness of her lips on his and basking in the warm June sunshine, he made a momentous decision.

She was worth taking another risk. He wanted more of her kisses. Hell, he decided, he wanted her kisses every day for the rest of his life and this was the day to tell her so.

He leaned forward and drew Hattie into an embrace. He kissed her again, but this time his kiss kicked friendship to the curb and deepened into an overt sexual advance. To his relief and great enjoyment, rather than retreat, she responded inexpertly, but eagerly.

Coming up for air, he gathered Hattie closer, enjoying her light citrusy scent. He looked down at the lovely girl who pressed against his chest, her arms reaching up to encircle his neck.

She'd hurt him before, but he was willing to risk his heart again. He scattered kisses anywhere he could—hair, forehead, eyes, cheeks—gently, gently nibbling her lower lip, breathing in her womanliness, and not quite sure what his next step should be. Despite his popularity with girls, Luke's romantic experiences had always been superficial.

"When my mother told me you were marooned, I had to find you," he murmured. "The fastest way was to join the French army. They needed more doctors and it was the only way to get into the country."

She leaned back, removing one hand to brush hair from her brow. "Luke! You put yourself in danger for me? What were you thinking?"

"I was thinking I love you as much now as I did when you stole that pie from Cook as a brave little girl, when you outran me in foot races, when you danced with me.

"You're a scary smart woman, and you have me dazed. It's hard to believe that I'm holding you. This has been my dream for years. All this week I lay on a cot with you close by. I thought of you asleep, luscious and vulnerable, and had to restrain myself from breaking into your room. It's been impossible to act normal.

"I want to tear off your clothes right now... and mine, too."

"Luke!" Hattie's ears felt hot, and warmth tightened the core of her body. She pressed closer, rather than withdrew, and squeaked, "That can't happen."

"If we get married, it can." Luke squeezed her tighter. "Marry me, Hattie. I love you. I want you to come live with me at the army base."

He held his breath, waiting to have his heart broken again, afraid he'd gone too far, too fast.

She grew still. His face lost its color when she shook her head from side to side. The wound she inflicted on him all those years ago reopened and began to bleed again. He had gambled again, and now he had lost for a second time. He never should have come to Paris.

Hattie tugged Luke's arm and began to speak.

"Karl and I were engaged for a long time. You know that, but you've been in my thoughts for weeks. I wondered if you were in love, where you were, even if you were married. I spent lots of time remembering my first ever date, with you at your graduation dance, and how perfect every part of that night felt."

Were? Luke had stopped listening when Hattie said "were engaged." Could she mean what he hoped she meant?

"You've been in my thoughts more than Karl. I wrote him a letter finally to break our engagement, and I enclosed his ring. That was just before the mail service shut down. I thought I might not make it home and I didn't want him waiting."

Hattie couldn't guess Luke's thoughts—he looked like he was about to explode. He'd known Hattie's family all his life. They trusted him, but the thoughts racing through his mind right now would scandalize them.

Crazily joyful laughter erupted from Luke, and he squeezed Hattie until she squeaked again. This… *this girl*… was the love of his life. She had once put love out of his reach. Was she saying it was a possibility?

His eyes glistened and Hattie sobbed in response to his joy. She regained control, pulled a handkerchief from her sleeve to dab her nose, and apologized.

"Sorry. Things have been so scary lately. That tipped me over the edge. I'm afraid I'll die without seeing my family again and I have to leave the dorm soon. Suddenly, here you are, almost like a mirage. It makes me feel like I can breathe again." She stroked Luke's cheek. He closed his eyes and leaned into her touch.

Hattie continued, "That's the long way of saying I'm already at least half in love, but I'm afraid. You're so impetuous. I don't want you hurt again, Luke, if I'm not sure."

He understood what she was trying to say. Even so, he rubbed her arms and held her tight.

His voice rough, Luke said, "Let me worry about that. I know exactly what I want and I've known it for years. I'm willing to take a chance, but I don't want to pressure you. This is a decision for you to make for yourself.

"I believe everything will work out for us. This might seem like a whirlwind romance, but it's not. For me it's a romance that was just delayed for a long time. Are you ready to take a chance, too? Will you marry me?"

Feeling a tug of emotion, Hattie brushed away her tears, laughed nervously, and threw away any hesitancy she may have had.

A strong feeling of certainty that this was always meant to be her future gave Hattie a *frisson* of excitement. She curled her fingers into his warm hand and looked into his gorgeous dark blue eyes. She nodded, giving her smiling, silent assent.

Love and emotions aside, the young couple knew their path forward would not be easy.

Hattie leaned against Luke and found her voice, "Marrying you will make me very happy." She paused. "May I call you my sweetheart?"

Grinning, he nodded, and she murmured, "Then let's get married, sweetheart."

Luke nuzzled the soft hollow of her neck, entranced with her fragrance as he nibbled and kissed her wherever opportunity permitted. Hattie surrendered happily, her eyes drifting closed, anticipating their wedding night.

By the end of Luke's furlough, they had been husband and wife for five days.

Their wedding had taken place in an exquisite small church, a few blocks from Hattie's dormitory. Her accommodating parish priest, *Père* Henri, one of the few chubby men left in France, officiated at the ceremony.

They stood at the altar, bathed in amber and cobalt sunlight pouring through ancient colored glass leaded windows. The quiet church smelled of sweet incense and beeswax polish. Dust motes danced in the air. The sound of their shuffling feet echoed off the vaulted ceiling and stone walls.

Hattie's dorm concierge, surprised to be pressed into service as their witness at the last moment, stared in wonder at everything in the building. It was the first time she'd ever entered a Catholic church. Except for a lack of music, the wedding was perfect. Immediately after the ceremony, *Père* Henri wrote down the particulars on a vellum sheet taken from a small stack kept in the sacristy. The prepared animal skin was translucent. It had a waxy finish that was embellished with vibrant, colorful curlicues and ancient designs on all sides. The four participants—*Père* Henri, the bride and groom, and their witness—added their signatures to the document.

Père Henri pursed his lips and blew on the glistening ink as it dried, gingerly holding the vellum by two corners, then rolled the vellum into a scroll and secured it with a satin ribbon that smelled of aromatic incense.

Holding Hattie's wrist, *Père* Henri gently placed the scroll in the new Mrs. DeValcourt's hand and whispered a fervent "Go with God."

Many young men from his small congregation had already lost their lives in the escalating war. He shuddered to think how brief this new union might be.

The newlyweds talked of everything and nothing every moment they spent together, touching, inhaling each other's warm breaths, and astonished by the unexpected delights of lovemaking and its satisfied afterglow. Pressed close to one another, they wore the flush of new lovers as they meandered through the streets of the deserted Left Bank. They touched as they loitered on low bridges, dangling their bare feet in slow-moving cool streams. They drank freely of water flowing from the pipe of an artesian well they found a long block away from their cozy nest.

Never getting enough of his bride, Hattie was always in Luke's thoughts. *This glorious girl.*

He soon discovered, however, that having a bride made travel, simple for him alone, far different when it came to getting Hattie and her gigantic trunk moved. He struggled to find a driver with a truck that had enough fuel to get them where they needed to go.

The last possible moving day arrived. Hattie's concierge sent Luke clear across Paris to Alphonse, a man she barely knew. The man, short in stature and nearly as wide as he was tall, had bushy black eyebrows. His shaggy hair was bushy, his black moustache even bushier. None of that mattered if he could help them.

To Luke's relief, Alphonse did own a decrepit truck, and yes, he had enough gasoline to haul Luke and Hattie plus her trunk to Nantes and the army base.

The man's fee was exorbitant and Luke felt robbed, though he grudgingly acknowledged it was just the law of supply and demand. And he knew his new wife was worth more than everything he owned, or ever would.

They'd need to pay Alphonse every *centime* the two of them had. Even so, Luke and Hattie were a few *francs* short. Alphonse, typical Frenchman, looked at the newlyweds and shrugged. It wasn't in his heart to deny romantic love. Furrowing his brow and throwing up his hands, he accepted what they had as enough, loaded his truck, and drove off through the French countryside with his three passengers—two humans and one gigantic trunk.

If one of them—Alphonse, Luke, or Hattie—could've seen into the future, they might have traveled to the relative safety of Switzerland to the southeast rather than into the dangerous life of a French soldier and his wife.

Luke, bouncing uncomfortably on the hard, gritty floor of the smelly truck's open bed, cradled Hattie in his arms. Despite the discomfort, he relished his bride's soft warmth and the clean sweetness of her abundant hair. Now with him, he wouldn't have to worry about her safety. A Paris overrun by Germans would be very dangerous for desirable women.

He roused from his thoughts and said, "We'll be so happy."

Hattie agreed and snuggled closer, enjoying her new status as a wife. They had bid a silent *adieu* to the old buildings and cloudless blue skies of Paris, and to whomever it was playing Chopin as they'd left the city— rare proof that at least a few souls remained in the emptying capitol.

Luke, fluent in both French and English, was asked to assist English troops that dribbled in small numbers across the English Channel to support the French army.

While quite a few Frenchmen could speak and understand German as a result of their common border, few Frenchmen deigned to learn English, regarding it as a guttural, barbaric language very much like the German they despised. The German army was aware of this Achilles heel, and so they often transmitted battlefield and other information in unencrypted English, knowing it would take quite some time, if at all, before the contents could be translated. France began to understand this was costing them dearly.

And so Luke's language skills made him more important to the army as a translator than as a doctor. His rank was adjusted to *capitaine*, and his commandant assigned him to translate English-language German intercepts, both written and spoken.

The drive to the Nantes barracks took longer than Hattie expected. Jolting over countless potholes on substandard roadways made for a miserable ride, though at first she found the fields of golden grains spread out under an opalescent sky remarkably beautiful, despite the discomfort.

1940s France had paved highways, but not many, and small roadways were often not much more than cart paths that meandered through a bucolic countryside. Alphonse's truck rumbled across a mosaic of green and gold fields, past stuccoed cottages with thatched roofs, and through an occasional village. Low walls of stacked stones gathered from the fields were everywhere, enclosing tidy orchards whose trees were heavy with young fruit.

Thick dust rose from Alphonse's churning tires, to float off over the fields. When Hattie looked at Luke, she marveled that his uniform still looked clean, and as pressed as the first day she'd seen him in Paris.

The truck bed held several sloshing containers of gasoline and fumes began to make Hattie dizzy. Usually she was the tough one, but she felt awful. The overpowering smell together with the constant juddering and jolting over washboard roads was making her nauseous. Pinching her nose didn't help. Neither did holding her head, or swallowing. She hoped they'd get where they were going soon—very soon.

Her family, and Luke's, too, knew this countryside. Before the war, both families often traveled to France, leaving the hot Louisiana summers for extended visits with relatives in a cooler climate. Her new husband's choice to join the French army was by no means impulsive or unusual—not for a New Orleans man with family in Europe. Hattie's own Papa had fought with France in the Great War —begun in 1914, the year Hattie was born—the war that was supposed to end all wars.

"We're here, wife."

Luke smiled at Hattie. She managed to smile, her eyes bleary, and very happy the truck had squealed to a halt. Luke looked tired and now was at least as disheveled as Hattie. She was where she wanted to be, beside her husband. She struggled to her feet, rumpled inside and out, and looked around.

With the difficult trip over, she was looking forward to her new life. The war felt far away, but she wondered if its violence would soon haunt them.

This is home? "This" was nothing like the home Hattie had envisioned in her romantic dreams as a young girl. For one thing, the pallid pink and blue sky of a sepia-toned French sunset differed dramatically from the glorious flaming red, orange, and yellow sunsets she'd known in Louisiana. In the waning daylight, two stark rows of hastily built, unpainted cabins squatted along an unpaved, rutted street. These were the officers' quarters, perhaps adequate for a single individual but hardly enough for a man and wife.

Hattie shook herself and tugged on Luke's sleeve, determined to be positive. She opened enthusiastic arms wide. "Our home. *Our* home, husband."

Home. The word rolled off her tongue, tasting like a savored, delicious dessert. She smoothed wisps of hair in place, then beat road dust from her clothing. With freshly energized deep breaths, Hattie relished the idea of creating her new marital nest even in the cookie cutter housing. Their doorways at least exhibited personal touches that gave clues to the tastes of their occupants—colorful doormats, a bright potted flower perched on a doorstep, a wreath twisted from twigs and pine cones hanging on a door. Little homey touches.

Luke kissed Hattie at her hairline before striding off to headquarters to report. That left Alphonse to help her unload the truck. Several soldiers' wives—her new neighbors—arrived shortly to offer welcome gifts of hot coffee and food. The women were curious, but had the good manners to stay only long enough to say "*Bienvenue!*" Welcome.

Few of the women wore skirts, fewer still gloves or court shoes. Their fashion statements confounded Hattie. One visitor—a gorgeous, petite woman about Hattie's age named Marie Chennault, stayed long enough for Hattie to ask about the odd mode of dress, certainly a marked contrast to the elegance of Paris and formal clothing of New Orleans.

Marie was quite lovely. Her curly dark hair sleeked into a low bun, her dark eyes flashed, and she smiled readily. She too wore trousers—an oversized pair of denim pants, rolled at the ankles and kept up with a length of rope around her small waist. She hesitated while talking to Hattie, surveying her new neighbor from head to toe.

"I'm sure the women here admire your clothes, Hattie. I certainly do—they're lovely. But clothes have to be different here on the base. Have you noticed we have no paved streets or sidewalks?"

Hattie had noticed, of course. Who wouldn't?

Speaking in a neutral tone, Marie sweetly suggested that Hattie store or give away her more delicate items and replace them with sturdier stuff.

"Life here is nothing like Paris."

Marie's suggestions were sensible and well-meant. Hattie had no desire to stand out by dressing differently and alienating herself. Marie and the other women likely would be her only friends while she and Luke lived on the base. Once Luke deployed, only these women would be her companions until he returned.

To fit in, Hattie appropriated a pair of her husband's civilian trousers and a button-front shirt to wear as her daily "uniform." Thank goodness she owned a pair of sturdy walking shoes, perfect to complete the outfit.

Hattie tied the apron sash and began cooking a big breakfast of coffee, fried ham, and poached eggs for Luke. She flipped the ham in a black iron skillet, then suddenly becoming dizzily sick—again. Every morning lately, the sight and smell of food sparked nausea. She had been rarely ill in her life, and couldn't understand why she felt so sick. It made no sense, but after suffering a week of nausea, she was ready to stay in bed and stop cooking altogether.

She dashed to the bathroom, flinging miserable apologies over her shoulder, her nightgown hem flying and the previous night's bedtime romp forgotten. Grateful they had indoor plumbing in the cramped cabin, she knew they were one of few French homes modern enough to boast an indoor bathroom. Stumbling back to bed, she crawled under the rumpled covers and squeezed her eyelids tight against the spinning room. What was wrong?

Hattie had never been a delicate flower. Her illness was mortifying. Would Luke decide he'd made a mistake in marrying a woman too weak to raise her head off the pillow in the morning.

Luke stood by their bed as he buttoned his tunic and looked down at his wife. His new bride had lost weight and looked more emaciated by the day.

"It was that bad artesian water in Paris. You'll feel better soon. Stay in bed and don't do too much," he cautioned, before bending to kiss her.

She couldn't detect warmth in his words, as though he didn't believe them himself. She cried after he left, afraid he regretted the day he'd found her in Paris.

Luke was leaving earlier each morning. His language skills gained greater importance as dozens of message intercepts, increasingly crucial to France's strategic defense, came across his desk, needing translation. They kept Luke busy long past dark each day, and Hattie was left alone and sick.

As an only child of wealthy older parents, Luke had never had to think of anyone other than himself. He had no idea how to help the wan Hattie, who seemed to be flailing helplessly, though he empathized with the way she felt.

One evening, he watched as Hattie slipped into a dress that had once clung to her curves. It now hung loose on her frame.

"Let's cancel dinner with the Chennaults. They'll understand you don't feel well."

"No, Luke. No, thank you," Hattie shook her head with a laugh. "If we did that, we'd have to scrounge up our own meal. I *want* to spend the evening with them. They're fun, and their food is always delicious enough to give me a big appetite. You know I somehow feel better at night than mornings, and I like them, especially Marie. They're smart, they're funny, and they make me laugh."

Luke was looking forward to the evening, too, so he shrugged and turned Hattie around to help button the unreachable buttons up her back. She smelled lightly of powder and perfume.

The faint scent stirred an immediate reaction in him. Luke hugged her to him from behind, sweeping her hair to the side to nibble her bare, slender neck.

"Let's hope you don't get sick while we're with the Chennaults," said Luke. "Cross your fingers their baby sleeps so we can visit in peace."

"You men—so spoiled," Hattie teased. She squirmed, trying to tug the bodice of her dark green faille dress into place.

"I don't understand this," she complained. "I feel crammed into this dress, but it's loose everywhere except at my chest. My breast feels bigger."

Luke's gaze swept over her. "I'll need to check that for myself."

He reached out and Hattie snorted, batting away his hands, but he gently pushed back until she fell onto the bed laughing, with Luke collapsing on top of her.

"I believe we have enough time to check out a few other things while we're here."

"Silly boy," she murmured, the words a caressing sigh as his dexterous fingers undid the garment whose buttons he had just secured. This was their happy life—a tumbling of two athletic young adults laughing breathlessly together. Nothing off limits, all impediments cast out of the way.

The Chennaults and the DeValcourts had quickly become close friends, having as much in common as any family would. The only difference was the other couple had a new baby to keep Marie busy.

At their first get-together, Marie said, "Thank goodness, finally two intelligent people who can carry a decent conversation. People we can enjoy." She had been astounded to learn that both DeValcourts were well-educated physicians.

Pierre Chennault, Marie's husband, held an important position as *aide-de-camp* to the base commandant. His work took him into every corner of the base, and Luke thought nothing of it when his friend developed a habit of dropping into the communications office unannounced.

The camaraderie of Luke's fellow officers and their families brought Hattie genuine enjoyment. Their lighthearted companionship was refreshing, so different from the dark intensity of her fellow students at the Sorbonne. This new circle of military friends, along with the fresh country air away from Paris, invigorated her.

As Hattie listened toLuke answering Pierre's questions about military communications, she learned more about her husband's responsibilities.

Officers' quarters were unlike the graceful classic architecture of Paris. The buildings were being put together quickly, somewhat magically flung into existence. Harried and hurried, construction workers jimmied doors and windows into approximate plumb with no regard for proper fit, openings forced to accommodate unwieldy and poorly measured insertions. This was all to the tune of colorful French curses, but no one dared to complain, certainly not in the presence of superior officers.

The small cabins were wooden, built on low supporting piers, leaving them barely suspended above the ground. The Chennaults' cabin was identical to that of the DeValcourts and to every other lucky officer's family.

Still, it was a luxury to share the roof over one's head with a mate during wartime, far better than bivouacking in a drafty canvas tent on bare, cold, uneven dirt—the fate of the fellow officers who were bachelors. Tents had been the norm for all officers and camp followers in the Great War only scant decades ago.

The two couples often shared an evening meal. Hattie never tired of listening to the men's conversation about their responsibilities. They held the same rank, though Pierre was in administration, while Luke worked in the top secret communications section where strategic information was received, processed, and sent on to the top echelon.

Marie and Pierre's kitchen/dining area was cramped, barely large enough for a smallish table and four narrow, painted chairs. Marie had used every ounce of her imaginative creativity to transform that room and three others into an extraordinary living space, filled with light and pleasant colors that attracted and invited the eye. Throughout the house, brightly colored sisal rugs were scattered underfoot, reflecting Marie's eclectic taste.

Both Chennaults were ingenious cooks whose excellent meals made abundant use of unexpected ingredients. Dinner this night was no exception. As soon as Luke and Hattie walked in, they'd smelled the delicious perfume of roasted capons stuffed with redolent spices, plus a delicious, mouthwatering, garlicky *cassoulet* as *lagniappe*.

Now Luke, with his fork paused halfway to his mouth, watched as Hattie cleaned her plate with gusto, washing the last bit down with a second glass of red wine. If she was suffering nausea, he thought with some surprise, she was certainly showing no trace of it.

After dinner, the men went outside, brushed grit from the doorstep, and sat to talk, the fretful baby bouncing on Pierre's knee as Luke used a shiny pocketknife to cut a few apple wedges.

Pierre juggled the baby to light a Gauloises cigarette. While its smoke snaked above them, he listened intently to Luke as he complained about his work.

"Everything is urgent, and that's the problem. There are more and more of these intercepted German messages every day. I have to translate them all from English to French before I can send them to headquarters.

As Hattie and Marie cleared the dishes and cleaned the table, they could easily hear the men's conversation.

"Do those translations really make a difference, Luke?" Pierre's tone was skeptical. He obviously thought the opposite until Luke corrected him.

"If I can believe what the commandant says, my work makes an enormous difference." Luke's attitude changed from complaint to bragging. "It's like having your opponent's chess moves laid out for you in advance, clear as night and day."

Pierre shook his head, but dropped the subject when Marie tapped his arm.

"You men," she chided. "Always talking business. What about us women? Don't talk shop, please. There must be something more enjoyable for us all to talk about."

Pierre strained to stand, holding his sleeping infant. Luke followed him and Marie back into the house, dusting off the back of his pants. Settling inside, the two couples conversed over snifters of cognac, covering a broad range of topics before they called it a night.

Hattie embraced Marie at the door. "Come over for coffee tomorrow and I'll bake a fresh apple tart."

Marie demurred. "Sorry, I can't. I hate to pass up a good apple tart, but tomorrow I have to go into Nantes on personal business."

In passing, Hattie thought, *How odd. What kind of personal business would Marie have in Nantes?* Hattie knew the base was set up to be self-sufficient and that Pierre and Marie had been there only a month longer than Hattie and Luke. *Probably something she couldn't find here at the base*, she thought.

Later, as they undressed for bed, Luke remarked how much he enjoyed Pierre's company, repeating some of their conversation. Hattie stared at him and stopped in the act of rolling down a stocking, reminded how surprised she'd been to overhear their conversation.

"Honey, Marie and I heard everything. You talked so openly about confidential matters that it surprised me. Does Pierre have clearance?"

Luke walked over and wrapped his arms around his wife, kissing each smooth, fragrant shoulder.

"Who's he going to tell, darling? By the way, I watched you clean your plate tonight. You must be feeling better. We should take advantage of that."

He gently cradled her breasts, so sensitive of late. Enjoying his caresses, she pressed into him, then pulled him down to her on their bed.

The stain of war was spreading across the ripening fields of France to penetrate her cities, burning and flattening buildings and trees—and the people—leaving poisonous heaps of smoking, fiery rubble. Ferocious battles raged between the well-equipped German war machine and the woefully underprepared French troops.

The Germans now began using more sophisticated codes. The army base outside Nantes saw far fewer messages in unencrypted English. Luke's usefulness as a translator waned and he was given new duties. He began treating wounded soldiers evacuated from the front, but then he was assigned to lead a squad to the front lines himself.

Hattie sank into a gathering of wives that was thoroughly entertaining. The women's chattering laughter and light conversation around her was a unique joy, she thought, as she snared another *canapé*.

She listened with amusement as a woman described how shocked she had been the moment she realized she was pregnant. She ticked off a litany of symptoms on her fingertips and Hattie's eyes widened.

She kicked herself mentally knowing she could well be pregnant. As a physician, perhaps she, more than others, should have recognized her own symptoms.

Back home, alone and excited, she counted the days back to her last period.

Paris. No wonder the truck ride made her feel so ill. It would take time for her body to adjust to the new life she and Luke had created.

Though Hattie had misunderstood her symptoms and overlooked the proper diagnosis, she could imagine Luke's excitement at the news. Wrapped in euphoria, she basked in thoughts of her new role as an expectant mother. She was determined to look her best for Luke when he arrived.

Pawing through her dusty trunk, Hattie unearthed a floral frock, pastel and filmy, smoothing its wrinkles with the steam of a teapot, aboil in her claustrophobic kitchen. Anticipating Luke's imminent return, she hurriedly dropped the dress on over her head. Adding a touch of color to her lips and cheeks had her grinning at her reflection in the mirror. She brushed her healthy, gleaming hair, finally corralling it with a rose-colored satin ribbon.

Hearing the creak of the poorly set front door, Hattie sashayed into the front room to greet him, gratified when his eyes widened in appreciation. With a groan, he snuggled her close, but said nothing. His despondency alarmed Hattie, and she decided to tell him their news later when his mood had improved.

Something had Luke depressed, so she moved quietly and fell into his mood. Setting supper before him without comment, Hattie wondered what had happened and patiently waited. Finally, he recounted his day. Her excitement over her own news grew more difficult to contain as he talked.

She listened to him complain about the changes to life on the base these past weeks. The Germans' big guns were so close that everyone on the base could almost feel the ground vibrating.

Fewer men were returning from the front lines each day. Hattie had seen many smiling wives become silent, now weeping in black mourning clothing. She showed compassion as best she could, and helped them pack their meager belongings. Some, though, simply disappeared, leaving no trace of their life on the base and without a word of goodbye.

"Things are desperate, *mon amour*," Luke continued. "The commandant is scraping the bottom of the barrel for soldiers and men to lead them. Many of our officers are either missing or dead. "

"Pierre and I *are* the bottom of that barrel, and we are being sent into battle. We have no choice about it. Chennault and I leave with our squads at dawn."

Hattie's hands flew to her mouth.

"What?" Her heart beat wildly with this new horror. This wasn't supposed to happen. She'd wished for, expected even, a marriage safe from the Germans. Having it torn from her had no part in her plan.

She could soon be set adrift, alone again. Hattie had always been cushioned from harshness somehow, just as when Luke had strolled down that Paris street to save her from a future alone in war-torn Paris. She began to realize the immaturity of her expectations. Now Luke, translator and physician, meant to be safe far behind the battle lines, Luke was to be thrust into combat where he could lose his life.

Hattie's hand dropped to her flat abdomen. That remote possibility she had put out of mind, unacknowledged. In her naiveté, she had thought they would stay safe.

"Don't go!" She clutched his hand. He gently disengaged her grip, shaking his head.

"This is a direct order. I don't have a choice, sweetheart. I *have* to go, but I hate to leave when you're not healthy."

This was an *ad nauseum* conversation that usually went in one of Hattie's ears and out the other. But that Luke might lose his life for this… this… foreign country. *To hell with the DeValcourt family connections.*

Luke had been more realistic, but neither of them was ready. Hattie stood up in a panic, aware he might not return and knowing she loved him to distraction. She pushed back her chair and ran around the table.

Luke stood to embrace her. Hattie pressed her cheek against his worsted tunic and rested her head against his warm chest. His rumbling voice in her ear eased her as his warm, steady hand stroked her hair.

She debated whether to keep their news to herself, before deciding it would be best to share it. "About my health…." She stepped back to see his face.

He tensed, knowing how ill she had been. "How can you be so sick? You look lovelier than ever, darling."

"My symptoms will soon be gone…," she managed to both blush and tease him at the same time, "except for the bigger breasts you hate. And they're going to get bigger."

"I'm not complaining." His fingers tickled down to caress those breasts.

Hattie grabbed his hands, laughing, and blurted, "You're going to be a daddy."

Luke cocked his head and blinked at Hattie, not immediately comprehending her words until his eyes finally registered a spark.

He sucked in a breath and whispered, "We're pregnant?" laying his hand on her flat stomach.

She nodded. "I don't know why it's called 'morning sickness.' It should be called 'all day sickness.'"

He yelled, "We're pregnant!" and swept Hattie into his arms for a long embrace. He ran to the front door, leaned out and yelled to the world, "We're pregnant!"

Coming to his senses, Luke returned to Hattie's side and said "Don't panic, honey," patting her back, his voice soft. "I have to obey my orders and fight.

I came to France for you, but I hardly expected we would find each other and you would love me, much less marry me. But here we are," he yodeled, "and best of all, I'm going to father a child with the woman I've loved all my life. Won't our parents be happy?"

He knelt in front of Hattie, his ear against her abdomen. "We've created a new life. I want you and Junior safe, so I'll fight as long and hard as it takes."

She laughed. "What makes you think it's a junior? As if!" She closed her eyes, wearing a confident smile despite her fearfulness. She wanted Luke to remember her as strong while he fought in this awful war.

In the glow of Hattie's news, they sat back at the table to force down their cold dinner, though neither was in much of in a mood to eat. Nourishment had gained a new importance for both husband and wife.

Luke shoveled in his food and lowered his fork, then pushed back from the table again. He complimented Hattie's pretty flowers, then used his napkin to wipe his lips, and grimaced.

"I have to get organized, sweetheart. We leave at dawn."

Hattie helped Luke with his gear by oiling the leathers to waterproof them and keep them pliant, specifically the chin strap of his helmet and his gun holster. She wiped away the excess oil with a cloth, and her silent tears with her knuckles.

Luke laid out his uniform and gear on their rickety table, ready for his dawn departure. *This is almost like getting ready for a funeral*, Hattie thought, *lacking only a crowd and a prayer.* She fought back her fear, determined to be encouraging and optimistic.

They crawled into bed when everything was ready. Exhausted, Hattie managed to straddle her husband and cover him with soft kisses, her hair falling in a fragrant, intimate curtain around their faces. They moved together in gentle and hauntingly sad lovemaking.

"I love you, Luke. I love you," Hattie breathed. "I'm so happy to be your wife. So happy to carry your baby. I'll be waiting for you." She shivered under his warm fingertips when he stroked her abdomen. They talked through the night, entwined and unwilling to waste these few hours by sleeping.

The night sky began to lighten. Dawn would arrive well before they were ready for the night to end, but they managed to tumble out of bed.

Luke dressed with Hattie's help, tugging his sleeves into place, buttoning his tunic, and guiding leather straps where they belonged. Reluctant, Luke stood before her, transformed into a warrior.

He gathered Hattie to him with a murmured goodbye into her tousled hair. She snuggled against his chest and inhaled his unique male warmth. She would know his scent anywhere.

"Tell our family I love them," he said.

His words held such finality she couldn't prevent a fearful sob. She stood at the threshold of the open door and watched her husband leave. He raised a hand in goodbye, then turned and didn't look back. She would've wailed if he had, her heart would've torn in two. Not knowing whether she would ever see Luke again, Hattie closed the door and bolted it, then ran to their abandoned bed and collapsed.

Luke's pillow held over her face, Hattie allowed herself to moan and cry, frightened for her husband and for the future of their new family.

Fear was tearing Hattie's heart to shreds.

Waiting with Marie for the return of their husbands that evening, she found herself nervously tugging at her hair. The last light of the day had disappeared, but Marie seemed unconcerned. Hattie marveled at her friend's composure, and said so. Marie made a face and gave the typical French *laissez-faire* shrug with Gallic aplomb.

Hattie left at midnight to go home, on edge now, and scared. Tears fell with each step, as she shuffled down the dirt street toward her one lit window. She fell across their bed, fully clothed and sobbing.

Now a second night of Luke's absence brought her awake in the middle of the night. Unable to fall back asleep, she stepped outside and sat on her front steps in the dark.

Her eye caught a movement down the street. Abruptly, she sat up and peered until she was sure someone was out there. Eyes narrowed, Hattie watched a dark shadow move to Marie's door, which suddenly cracked open. A dim light arrowed across the yard and into the street, interrupted as the shadow entered before the door quickly closed.

Hattie could hardly believe her eyes. Did Marie have a lover? She must, and that must be why Marie was showing so little concern over Pierre's absence.

The following morning at the base infirmary Hattie performed her volunteer duties like an automaton, exhausted from a lack of sleep. Fatigue also left her too emotional to deal with the pain of soldiers brought back badly wounded, given the infirmary's meager supplies.

One morning days later, Hattie didn't bother to dress and spent hours moping in bed. Late in the day, Marie knocked on Hattie's door and roused her from bed. Refusing a half-hearted invitation to enter, she insisted Hattie dress and share supper with her. They could wait together for their men to return.

During dinner Marie's behavior seemed oddly off. Her baby reflected his mother's mood by fretting and crying, and Marie was uncharacteristically impatient with him. She asked so many questions that Hattie finally told Marie she had a really bad headache.

"Stop whining." Marie disparaged her. "And do something with yourself. You look like a miserable cur." An hour later she did an about-face. "I'm sorry, chère. When I'm scared, I snap at everybody."

Short-tempered and irritable herself, Hattie said nothing. She had thought to share the news of her pregnancy with Marie, but changed her mind. She didn't fully understand her reasons, but for now wanted her news shared only with Luke.

When her glance dragged across Marie's living area and realized the woman had begun to pack up her belongings, Hattie emerged from self-absorption and stared at her friend. The woman practically vibrated with urgent energy and agitation.

"What're you doing, Marie? Have you given up on Pierre?"

Marie snapped, sounding waspish. "I'm being realistic. They've been gone a week already. How long am I supposed to wait? Tell me—how long?"

Hattie stared at her friend. After a few more polite minutes, she thanked Marie for the meal they had ignored, and returned to her own strangely large and empty cabin to sulk.

Curious and somewhat reluctant to abandon her relationship with Marie, she kept an eye out and became aware that Marie and her baby left the base every morning, sometimes to be gone for several hours.

Occasional visits revealed Marie's spotless home suffering from neglect. Her vibrant living room smelled dusty and looked unused and dingy. Marie seemed tense and somber, and her energy level had dropped along with her mood. The cabin's gay colors no longer reflected the personality of her friend.

Their visits became sporadic. It was impossible to guess what Marie was thinking. At times she seemed happy that Pierre was gone, cheerful even, which left Hattie confused. Then, a moment later, her mood would undergo a dramatic change, and she would become withdrawn and touchy.

When days passed and the men didn't come home, Marie refused to go to headquarters unless Hattie wheedled and begged. Hattie would occasionally prevail and they would stroll to headquarters for the daily report of the missing. Lost in the large group, they were simply two more women added to other wives wearing men's trousers. Many of the anxious women whined or wept, but that didn't suit Marie. She brushed away any emotional display with a wave of her hand, saying her troubles were private. Her harsh attitude left Hattie aghast.

Today, the rumpled commandant had a deeply lined and sallow complexion. When he at last emerged and stepped up on a chair so everyone could see him, his hair was mussed as though he'd been trying to tug it out by the roots. Unsteady on a spindly chair, he looked years older than the day Hattie had first met him, only a few months before. His reddened eyes swept across the upturned faces. The wives weren't technically his responsibility. He could have disregarded them, had he been that kind of man, but he had a family, too, with a wife and children. Of course, he'd made sure they were safe in neutral Switzerland well before Hitler's insane invasion encroached on France.

The women's riveted attention forced the commandant to come to attention. He pulled back his slumped shoulders and straightened his spine. The women assessed the man. His expression was stressed and defeated, a reflection of their own fears. A tremor in the commandant's voice reflected his emotion.

"The war is not going well for France," he began. A profound understatement.

The women glanced quizzically at one another, snorting and raising their eyebrows. Who knew the war better than these women? Women whose men were laying their lives on the line. These women knew exactly how the war was going.

He pushed his hands nervously through his tousled hair and started again. "The Germans changed their communication codes and we lost our advantage. We haven't broken the new codes yet, but we will. It'll take time, given that we're shorthanded.

"Our men continue the fight, but we've suffered severe setbacks…." He focused on the floorboards, his eyes fixed on their dirty grooves as though they were one last reminder of stability. Summarizing the most recent reports in a somber voice, his mouth turned down at the corners and his chin began quivering to hold back his emotion. The longer he spoke, the more his shoulders slumped, seemingly caved in to protect his aching heart.

"We received an urgent message from the front asking when our reinforcements are due to arrive. It appears the reinforcements we sent, our two squads, were ambushed still far from the front just hours after they left our base."

The horrified women watched exhaustion etch ever deeper grooves in the commandant's cheeks. The longer he spoke the lower his voice dropped, until it became no more than a sibilant whisper.

Hattie saw perspiration appear on his upper lip, and she felt a twinge of sympathy for the poor man carrying such a heavy burden of responsibility.

"The Nazis penetrated our lines without being seen. We found our squads' vehicles this morning in a large area of flattened grass churned into mud. They apparently hid along the path they knew our soldiers would take, waited for them to pass, then surrounded them. Nearly all our men are unaccounted for. Two escaped, one making it back to base. The other is still missing. He is Lt. Pierre Chennault, the leader of the second squad. We hope he will make it back here soon."

The women moaned in disbelief. Hattie turned to Marie for shared emotional support, but the petite woman was stoic, staring ahead, her face blank as she jiggled her baby boy against her chest. Was she unconcerned, in shock, or hiding a deep emotion by pretending to look at the soiled floor? Her reaction was so puzzling, Hattie felt a flare of anger.

The commandant's description of the ambush reinforced the women's impression that Germans' ingenuity was as overpowering as their weaponry.

Growing up in the extroverted, semitropical New Orleans Hattie was used to people being open and sharing their emotions. In the more reserved university environment of the Sorbonne, she'd learned that not everyone was an extrovert. And so she granted Marie's behavior some latitude, but found it appalling that Marie was apparently wasting no time engaging life as a single mother.

The commandant continued to speak, and while he did, Hattie's thoughts swirled. Whenever she glanced up, his kindly face reflected real pain.

"It's useless to speculate whether we'll see our soldiers again or not, much less how many may have survived. I can say for certain that we have found no bodies, no spent cartridges, and no blood traces. My superior officers suspect the men have become German prisoners, and if so they'll likely be sent to work details in Germany."

His hoarse voice roughened. "The battlefront collapses more toward Nantes every day, and the enemy will soon be here. Staying here is becoming more dangerous every day, and I encourage you to leave immediately. There's no one left to protect you—we cannot ensure your safety. When the last one of you leaves, I'll shutter the camp and evacuate right on your heels."

The women hurled questions at him in increasingly shrill voices, their shouts desperate. The exhausted commandant, his face sickly gray, raised his hands, palms out, to deflect the onslaught. He shook his head, his uniform shirt by now soaked through with sweat.

"We *don't* know where they are. I wish we did! Stop asking me that. I don't know—not *where* they are or *what* their condition might be. God bless them."

Hattie leaned closer to Marie and nearly lost her balance. She was gone, but Hattie hadn't noticed her leave. If Marie had bid her goodbye, Hattie hadn't heard it.

Those women beseeched the commandant to send someone to rescue the captured soldiers. He shrugged. He had few battle-hardened soldiers left to him, far too few to attack the Nazi war machine. The women begged to know where they should go.

Unable to offer encouragement, the commandant grasped the chair back for support and stepped down. The walls of the room barely contained the wails of heartbroken wives and lovers.

Hattie left headquarters, unsure why Marie left early. She spied her striding far down the street, holding her baby. Had Marie ever truly loved Pierre? She certainly gave every indication of being unconcerned about his fate. Having had enough, she took the long way home to avoid walking past Marie's cabin.

At dusk that evening, she forced herself to eat more of the leftovers that Luke had called delicious, but she couldn't swallow. It tasted like cardboard, even though she knew she should be eating for two. The irony of it was that she hadn't experienced any nausea at all that day. In better circumstances, the rosemary chicken and spinach sautéed with garlic and bacon would probably have been very tasty.

Hattie bathed, then dabbed cologne behind her ears, determined to be optimistic that Luke would burst in during the night. She crawled into bed and tried to read a book, but the words blurred until she gave up and doused the light. She curled in a tight ball, feeling alone under the covers.

Holding Luke's pillow to her face, she burrowed into its softness, inhaling the man-scent of her husband. She lay staring up at the ceiling for what felt like an eternity, then eventually rolled onto a still-flat stomach. A nebulous idea began to bother her.

As a child, Hattie had exhibited uncanny intuition, based on unconscious reasoning that accepted the simplest explanation as the most likely. That had always been the way her mind worked. That trait was further enhanced by the diagnostic training she received at the Sorbonne. There her intuition began with a set of observations leading to many possible diagnoses, finally yielding to the most likely consistent with the incomplete information at hand.

Something had been niggling Hattie's subconscious all day, but she couldn't bring it to consciousness before sleep claimed her.

Not long after dawn, a messenger's heavy fist rattled the front door on its hinges and woke Hattie. Bleary-eyed, she answered the door and learned that everyone had been summoned once again to headquarters.

The cool early morning unfurling with a cloudless blue sky worthy of songs and poetry went unnoticed. She squinted in the morning glare as she approached Marie's cabin and mounted the two front steps.

The door creaked ajar with Hattie's knock. Startled, she grabbed the door-knob and leaned in, wondering what to expect, and called, "Marie?"

Thinking she'd heard a faint response, she stepped inside and gaped at sealed boxes strewn around the room.

"Coming," her friend called, sounding irritable. The click of heels grew louder, until Marie stopped at the sight of Hattie standing there in the gloom.

"Hattie! What are you doing in my house? How'd you get in here?"

"It… the door… was open."

Marie approached, her anger apparent, the baby slung on her hip. Instead of her usual garb of a man's trousers and shirt, Marie had dressed in a stylish navy-blue nubby silk dress, revealing a figure slightly lusher than Hattie's. Nothing Marie wore ever disguised that her body was worthy of attention. She and Hattie could both cover themselves with cardboard, and somehow men would intuit what lay beneath the corrugated paper.

Marie's hair gleamed, sleeked back and twisted low into a dark, shiny *chignon* on the back of her neck.

Hattie said, "You're leaving already?" Surprised not to have been told, Marie's thoughtlessness arrowed into Hattie's chest, though the hurt wasn't nearly as awful as the pain of Luke's absence. Still, the woman she'd known as a friend could've mentioned her intentions. *Though maybe I should have guessed*, Hattie thought. *And maybe I should be packing up too, instead of moping around.*

Marie refused to meet Hattie's eyes, a deception that left Hattie further confused.

"Why shouldn't I go? You want me to defy the army and stay? That what you think?"

Hattie brushed off Marie's rude questions. Instead, she told Marie of the call for them all to go to headquarters, and urged her to come along. Marie declined, saying the men were no doubt idling their days away down on the coast, glad to be safely out of the war. Hattie left. Lost in thought, she hesitated in the warm sunlight after a few steps, trying to make sense of Marie's dramatic change in behavior.

Could it be? No… She resumed the walk to headquarters in steps so rapid that chugging dust puffs followed her down the street.

And now, as she had done since early childhood, her unconscious began combining observations and snippets of conversation, the way a chef mixes raw ingredients, to end up with an entirely reasonable result.

Hattie's unusual intuition first occurred at the DuMonds' summer beachfront home on the Gulf of Mexico when Maman's maid vanished…

The annual migration to "the Coast" was a tradition more than anything else. Nearly all of Uptown New Orleans, like a hive of bees with a new queen, buzzed off *en masse* at the start of summer for breezes off the Gulf that made the summer's heat and humidity tolerable.

The beach was idyllic compared to the sweaty city. The men commuted by rail to New Orleans on Mondays and returned at the weekend. Women and children stayed at the beach.

The DuMond family's servants traveled with them. Nadine and Avril polished the cool hardwood and dusted airy rattan furniture as part of their summer chores. The help had their own private level below the main floor, with accommodations similar to the family's rooms.

Hattie and her brother swam and filled their bellies with fresh seafood. Friends visited and bunked on a screened sleeping porch open to cooler Gulf breezes. Ceiling fans added soft hums to dreams, and by morning sheets were damp with humidity and gritty with windblown sand.

Avril, the young housemaid, often chatted with Hattie. On that particular day, Hattie was sprawled on the cool hardwood floor watching Avril brandish a feather duster.

Little Hattie noticed with alarm the fading bruises on Avril's smooth neck and wrists. She didn't like what she saw. Young though she was, she knew not to ask a direct question, instead asking one more oblique.

"You have a beau, Avril?"

The feather duster wavered and Avril's sunny smile disappeared, replaced by a fearful expression.

"Please don't tell *Madame*. I'm married, miss. He's a mean old man—very mean and very old." Under her breath, she muttered *and I hope he stays far away.* Avril underestimated Hattie's hearing, unaware she'd been heard.

Hattie frowned. "Hunh?" Avril hesitated, then swore Hattie to secrecy before she would answer. The little girl wouldn't mention it again—unless it became necessary.

The Schmitzers arrived a week later and also brought some help, including a butler who organized the other servants, along with his other duties. The two families knew each other socially, and the children happily played together on the sandy beaches.

Hattie brushed off sand that was sticking to her feet and legs. She could hear Cook banging pots around, talking to herself. She was angry, and taking it out on the cookware.

"That damn Avril," Cook muttered. Behind Cook, Hattie cleared her throat and made the heavyset woman yelp.

Pressing a pudgy hand to a truly extraordinary bosom, Cook growled, "Girl, you gonna get me a heart attack. Thought you was yo' mama."

Undeterred, Hattie asked, "What about 'that damn Avril,' Cook?"

"Nothin', little girl, nothin'. I talks to myself. Don't you cuss."

Not convinced, Hattie grabbed Cook by the apron strings and lightly tugged. The gentle, affectionate cook was the source of excellent treats and practical wisdom for Hattie, who loved and trusted her. The relationship was more one of mother and daughter than employer to employee.

"Something's wrong, isn't it? You know I won't tell." Cook swatted away Hattie's hands, but worry had gnawed its way through her good sense, and she couldn't keep it to herself.

"Cross your heart?" Like that would stop a child from speaking out.

Hattie pantomimed a promise across her chest and the dam of secrets burst from Cook, who poured out a flood of everything she'd seen and all the things she suspected.

"That fancy-assed butler next door banged our window looking for Avril last night, saying she his wife. I 'bout passed out from shock *and* his stinky cologne."

"Is he old? Avril told me her daddy made her marry an old man." Nearly everyone was old to the little girl.

Cook snorted, alarmed.

"Married? She done tol' you she married? Hunh! Help ain't s'posed to be married an' come to the beach. He ain't *that* old, but that ain't the worst. It don't matter nohow, 'cause she gone. She lef' and she ain't never come back."

Hattie frowned. Avril loved it here, and she didn't even like that old man. Did pretty Avril run away? Did she leave *with* him? Or run *from* him? She turned on her gritty heel.

"I'll take care of this…" Cook grabbed her by the swimsuit strap and pulled her off balance, stopping Hattie in midsentence.

"You stay out of this, missy. You ain't supposed to know nothin'. I shoulda kept my mouth shut, and you…" She jabbed Hattie's breastbone. "…you promised not to tell. This here's a grownup problem."

Hattie remained silently fidgeting all day. Avril wouldn't just leave, and that was making Hattie anxious. By late that afternoon, she told Cook she had to tell her mother. Her concern was palpable, and she followed her mother around the house.

"Maman, please. Please? Call the police. Something's wrong with Avril. She wouldn't leave us."

Maman gently detached Hattie's fingers from her skirt and looked in her eyes.

"Avril's gone. She's a grown-up and she didn't want to be here. We cannot chase her."

Hattie stomped on the cool floor.

"That's not true, Maman. We're her family. She can't help it that her father lost her in a poker game to that Lattimore man."

Horrified, Maman grasped her little daughter's shoulder.

"Avril told you that? What was she thinking, saying that?"

"Because we're friends, Maman. That mean man *did* something to her."

The Biloxi police could now name the badly beaten, still unconscious young woman found lying in foamy Gulf surf. They had taken her to a charity clinic that was tucked under ancient mossy oaks just blocks off the beach. She was lying in damp nightclothes on a thin pallet, moaning, when *Madame* DuMond and Nadine arrived.

At home, Hattie and Cook hugged each other as they waited. Maman bustled inside, pulling off her gloves, and hugged her daughter tight. Cook rolled her eyes behind Maman's back, but said nothing.

"Thank you, my little love. We only found Avril because you insisted. You're quite a detective."

Those few words gave Hattie the validation and assurance to trust her intuition, which so often paid off even as circumstances differed.

The police told the Schmitzers that Lattimore was a risk to children and put the violent butler in jail.

Hattie shook off her reflections of Avril to hear the commandant announce that the base would close in forty-eight hours. The French front lines had been overrun and the Germans were marching on Nantes. France had suffered a devastating defeat.

The commandant's tone was urgent, underlain with a thread of fright. "Our enemy is climbing into our laps and it's too dangerous for any of us to stay here.

Do not wait. This is my last warning—pack up and go now. Now, because if you don't, I'll be gone and you'll be here all alone, in danger and in the dark."

Lost in thought, Hattie barely heard the commandant. Suppositions, half-remembered facts, and odd behavior churned in her unconscious, and things barely fathomed clicked into place. Hattie was heartsick, though she doubted she was wrong. To verify the facts while she was still at headquarters, she approached the commandant's secretary to check a few things. By the time she walked away, her decision was made. She went directly to Marie's cabin, hoping she wasn't too late.

Marie Chennault sat on her steps in her silk dress, surrounded by boxes and bags. She pushed her baby's stroller back and forth in the unseasonably warm October air with one hand, and fanned her face with the other, graceful and unconcerned. Hattie was an emotional wreck, on the verge of tears as she approached.

"You're leaving?" Hattie had hurried and was out of breath. Marie nodded.

"Yes, I hope the truck gets here soon. He's late." Unsmiling, she hardly acknowledged her loyal friend's presence, which to Hattie felt like a physical slap.

Hattie decided to ignore Marie's insulting behavior, and hoping to learn more, followed her instincts and began to ask questions.

"Where will you go?"

Hattie had finally intuited the reason for Marie's odd behavior. She had recalled Pierre's probing questions to Luke. Marie's trips into Nantes usually followed some unusual activity on the base. Hattie considered Marie's apparent lack of concern about her husband's capture.

Hattie remembered Marie's midnight visitor, followed by this rush to pack up and leave the base. She thought of all these things while she stood in front of Marie, as well as the new details uncovered at the commandant's office.

To Hattie's surprise, Marie answered her question.

"Pierre's family expects us. The baby and I will stay there until the war is over. The village is very isolated and we'll be safe." She shrugged. "I'm leaving many things behind, but it's worth it to be safe. You're welcome to it."

"I don't think so, but thank you," said Hattie, angry with herself for being polite.

"Come with me, Hattie. *Please* come. We have plenty of room and Pierre's family is hospitable." Marie's words were spoken insincerely and in a way that made Hattie's skin crawl. The woman couldn't manage a direct look at Hattie.

Years later, Hattie would discover Marie's hopes for Pierre's village were in vain, that most of Chennault village was destroyed and nearly everyone there killed.

Hattie contemplated the woman sitting on the steps in her fine clothes and shook her head, thinking how different she seemed from the gracious woman who'd welcomed her to the base. That woman had offered much needed reassurance and comfort to a new bride.

How could Marie have changed so quickly?

"I have other plans," Hattie answered flatly without bothering to add a thank you. She would miss the old Marie, but not this... this changed woman. Someone Hattie would never be foolish enough to follow now. And, it was obvious, a woman who didn't want Hattie around either.

What Marie didn't know was that the two of them were about to have a difficult conversation.

Hattie was glad she hadn't told Marie about her pregnancy. Her hands curled into tight fists as she stepped closer and deliberately crowded the seated Marie. It looked like, and was, meant as a threat.

"I stayed after the meeting this morning and asked the commandant a few questions." Abruptly she demanded, "Where is Pierre?"

Marie blinked rapidly and frowned. She licked her lips, swallowed, and clutched her purse to her chest. A myriad of expressions from confusion to fear to anger played across her face. Finally, she stuttered a response.

"What? What do you mean? Surely he's with Luke. You *know* that."

"I *don't* know that. I don't even *think* that."

"But how... I mean," Marie tried to rephrase her question. "How... What makes you say something terrible like that?" Her words, as hard and opaque as rocks, tumbled from a rigid mouth Hattie had once thought soft and pretty.

Marie dropped her purse into her lap and flexed her fingers, as if getting ready for a fight.

Signaling her own readiness for battle, Hattie drew up to her full height, looming over the seated Marie. Until confronting her anger this morning, she'd thought of herself as a nice girl, always considerate of others' feelings. What she was doing today ran counter to her former self-image. She might suffer a rotten twinge later, but she was sure this confrontation was the only way forward in the search for her husband.

Hattie crowded Marie, intimidating her but nauseated by the woman's cloying perfume. In deliberate, aggressive tones, Hattie continued to speak. Marie looked like a supplicant in Hattie's dominating presence.

"And how *is* Pierre? You saw him last night." Hattie's words threw Marie into a tailspin.

Marie jerked and shook her head, able only to remain silent. Her complexion betrayed her. Blood drained from a face ashen and shocked. Hattie bent and gave the woman's shoulder an unfriendly squeeze.

"This wouldn't be a good time to lie, Marie. You owe me the truth, so spit it out. And maybe I'll wait till you're gone to report you to headquarters."

She paused, then continued, "Your husband is a spy. He told the Germans Luke had broken their codes, and that's why they changed their system. And Pierre told the Nazis when and by what route he and Luke were taking their squads to the front lines."

Marie hesitated, trying to regroup. "What makes you think Pierre would do such a horrible thing?"

"Because you're a terrible liar, that's why. You can't look me in the eye, and you act guilty as hell. And you're jumpy as a cat. You've been ready to leave for days; you packed up way before anyone else considered it. Before the commandant told us the base had to close."

Her words angry, Hattie pressed on. "According to the commandant, the day the Krauts changed their transmission codes was the morning right after our dinner at your house." Marie shrank back, her eyelids fluttering, at the crude word "Krauts." That was only a few hours after Luke told Pierre how busy he was, when Pierre was quizzing him about his work. Luke trusted him as a friend and because he was the commandant's assistant. So Luke told Pierre how he was translating Germans transmissions coded in English into French, to make them understandable by French intelligence.

"Those soldiers Luke and Pierre took to the front? Odd, don't you think, for two entire squads traveling separately to disappear at the same time? Poof," Hattie threw up both hands, "like everyone evaporated, except for two men. The squads were ambushed—within two miles of base.

"Your husband somehow managed to be one of two men to escape. One man slipped back to base, but not the other. Your husband? What happened to him? Pierre was not to be found. But you, Marie. *You* knew he was close by. It was a bad mistake when he sneaked back on base to see you and the baby, because I *saw him*!

"It was in the middle of the night and I was sitting outside on the steps. Ironic, isn't it, that just as I was squinting over at your house, concerned about you and your baby, a light flared in your front room. Then your door opened and light flooded across the yard into the street. A dark shadow crossed your threshold and the light blinked out when you shut the door behind him.

"And what did I think?"

Indignant, but unbearably sad at the same time, Hattie watched Marie's eyes evade hers. She wondered how this dainty, petite woman could stay with a traitor.

Her supposed friend's face had paled from Hattie's accusations. Marie's lashes beat crazily and she pinched her licked lips into a tight line, holding back any reply. Marie sat trapped, flinching against the splintered wooden steps as Hattie accused Pierre.

Hattie continued, shrugging, "At the time, I ignored what I'd seen. I thought the shadow might be a lover, and that was none of my business.

"Next thing I know, you're packing up—only dust bunnies and debris left scattered in your house." She laughed. "Your meticulous housekeeping, too. Another lie.

"You showed no anxiety, no concern, at the commandant's first meeting. Then you refused to go to the meeting today because you already knew what the poor man had to say."

Hattie's onslaught wilted Marie like a roadside weed under the summer sun. Sagging, she hid her face in both hands, her elbows balanced on her thighs. When the stroller stopped moving, her infant whimpered for the soothing push-pull, while Marie struggled to respond.

"You have to understand…"

Hattie shook her head, disgusted, and forced herself not to laugh. Marie's pursed mouth looked anal. *Tres à propos*, she thought, very appropriate.

She interrupted. "I really don't care *to understand* why Pierre's a spy. Luke is all I care about. I *will* report your husband, and you too, it's just a question of when. And if you tell me where Luke is. Do I have you arrested now? Or do you get a head start, and I tell the commandant what I know after you've gone?"

Towering over Marie like an angel of vengeance, Hattie was determined to outwait her.

"All right," Marie sighed. "It's true. Pierre was as stupid as ever."

That she insulted her husband appalled Hattie.

"He sneaked back to base and rapped on my windowpane. I had to let him in before the guards saw him, but I only let him stay long enough to give me an update.

"The Germans have overrun central and northern France. Victory is inevitable. He and his parents have been German sympathizers for years, and as Pierre's reward for supplying them with information, the Germans have promised him an officer's commission in the *Wehrmacht*.

When we leave this dusty place, the baby and I will join him in his parents' village. We'll be safe there."

Hattie could only think how foolish Pierre was—to betray his country, not for money, but for some nebulous promise. She stamped her foot with an uncharacteristic vehemence that startled Marie.

"Just stop it! I don't care about the war! What about Luke? Is he alive? Where are his men?"

Marie shrank back. Her self-assurance began to evaporate, but then she lashed out with fire of her own.

"I don't know where they are," she spat. Her eyes had a malicious glint. "I have no idea. Pierre said something about a stockade in the woods that would hold the prisoners until a train takes them to Germany for manual labor. Good luck finding *that*."

"Woods? What woods, Marie?" Hattie swept her arms wide. "Which woods? Where?" Everywhere you turned in France, there were woods.

Marie made a rude sound and Hattie raised her voice, frustrated. She pushed Marie's shoulder.

"Tell me. Far? Near? Where?" Hattie had an urge to hit this woman as hard as she could. She looked around her for a weapon, wanting to smack her silly.

Marie held up her hands, a supplicant asking for one last miracle. "All I know is it's not too far from the coast. That's all Pierre told me."

Hattie spun on her heel and stalked away from her "friend". As a crow in the street flapped its wings and flew off, cawing protests, Hattie flung parting words over her shoulder, dismay in every syllable:

"I'm reporting Pierre right now."

Marie, brave now that Hattie was leaving, shouted back. "You're wrong. Typical. An important *docteur,* with your smart education, but you underestimate what a woman can do. He *is* a spy, but only because I insisted he join *me*." Marie thumped her chest while her baby mewled, forgotten beside her in his stroller.

"I'm the spy. Me! For months I've been talking to people and gathering information. I've been delivering documents Pierre stole from right under your nose, *Madame* the smart *docteur*, and everyone else's nose, too. You fools don't see that this pitiful country will soon be under German control. Me and Pierre, we helped do that."

Thoroughly shocked and scarlet with anger, Hattie spun, her mouth thinned to a white line, for another look at the stranger she thought she had known. The more Marie spoke, the smaller and uglier she became. Right before Hattie's eyes, the woman turned loathsome, nowhere close to a fashionable or petite woman. No, she was visibly smaller. And as nasty as the most virulent virus there had ever been.

Hattie felt sorry for Marie's child, an infant who would become an adult knowing his parents were traitors.

Furious at Marie's duplicity, Hattie sneered "traitor" at her and stalked away, Marie's reply an obscene gesture sent after her.

Hattie swung into action. Marie's final revelations had so sickened her she went straight to headquarters. She had decided to report the Chennaults without delay.

Hattie reported the Chennault couple's treason to the man who had replaced Pierre as the commandant's aide. She included that the traitor Marie said the missing men were prisoners in a forest near the coast. She also suggested they let Marie leave the base believing herself safe, then follow her. She would lead them to Pierre and the nest of German sympathizers.

Fear fell on Hattie like a dense shroud, prickling like the itch of a cheap woolen sweater on skin. She wasn't sorry for herself—though she could have been: She was newly pregnant with a husband she hoped was only captured rather than dead. Her life was in more danger now than it had been in Paris.

Using memories of childhood adventures as inspiration, Hattie concocted a plan to find her husband. Unrealistic? Yes. Insane? Perhaps—but at least she could say she tried her hardest.

"Please, *M'sieur le commandant*," Hattie pleaded. She stood in front of his desk. The poor man was suffering, overwhelmed and out of his depth, and struggling with the details of a pell-mell departure.

She needed his help so badly she thought her anxiety had a sharp smell. She begged the commandant, "I need to get to Vierville-sur-Mer."

The man, dwarfed by his desk and shorter than Hattie by several inches, was seated and had to angle his view up to the attractive woman who claimed that spies had been living and working among his soldiers.

Now, this… this… foreigner, this American, wanted to pile another problem on his already teetering stack. He scowled at Hattie.

"You think I have nothing better to do than find you transportation?"

She rocked her head toward her shoulder and spread her hands in mock surprise. If she could make the commandant feel guilty, she might get what she needed.

"Has your aide not given you important information that I provided, *m'sieur*, about the traitors? How can you refuse to help me in return? And to help yourself. There are thick forests around Vierville and it's near the coast, so it's probably a good place to search for *your* men. You can't spare anyone, *m'sieur*, and I'm willing to go look for them."

More miserable than he had ever dreamed he could be, the commandant pinched the bridge of his hooked nose and smoothed his pencil-thin moustache, searching in vain for relief from an unremitting headache.

It occurred to him that getting rid of Hattie might help. Complaining and grousing, the commandant ordered up a dilapidated wagon, a swaybacked mule, and an irascible driver to transport her and a gargantuan trunk westward to the shore of the English Channel. A warehouse located just outside the tiny obscure seaport of Vierville-sur-Mer was her destination.

PART TWO

HATTIE BREATHED DEEPLY and creaked erect. She'd packed for hours, finally fitting their most important belongings into her trunk. The shabby, enormous receptacle was the chrysalis of her journey from student to married woman. Along with tangible items, it was full of her life stories.

She had dragged it to the center of the living room, first packing their most valuable possession: their marriage certificate, carefully cushioned in fancy dresses at the bottom of the trunk. Keepsakes once considered indispensable lay abandoned in a growing heap outside the cabin. Hattie disposed of those things with little regret, knowing they had no place in her murky future. Based on the Nazis' rapid advance, she wasn't that likely to live very long, in any case.

It seemed to Hattie that her life had hiccupped in the middle of its story, a thought reinforced by the hard metallic click of the trunk latch.

In less than three whirlwind months, Hattie had married a man who'd loved her most of his life, who was then lost to the Germans, leaving her stranded with her life in danger.

Luke thought he had brought his bride to safety from the danger of facing the German army alone in Paris, but it was to a life alien to anything she'd known. And now it was no more safe than Paris. He was gone, and emptiness filled Mrs. Luke DeValcourt.

Her husband's likely abduction (they hadn't found bodies) combined with the nausea of pregnancy left Hattie shattered. The two events, both of such vast importance, overwhelmed her. How could Hattie draw upon strength from such an indulgent self-absorbed childhood? How could she push herself to take full command of her life?

She shook her head. This was not the time to think about how she'd ended up on a dusty military base. Hattie padded barefoot across the cool floor to her small kitchen for a sip of water, resting against the counter as she drank. The manual labor of packing the trunk, then dragging it to the door had tired her, but not overly. She listened to the cabin echo, desolate and already feeling empty. Hattie rubbed at the goose bumps on her arms. She could hear herself breathe off the hollow walls. She felt miles away.

Hattie slipped sockless into untied shoes, grabbed a houseplant off a window-sill, and took it outside along with a discarded spoon. She crunched across the weedy yard to a spot with purple clovers and yellow dandelions. There she dug a shallow cavity and planted it, hoping the pretty plant would survive the war.

The sun had inched invisibly to the horizon's edge when Hattie, dulled by exhaustion, arrived at her destination just outside the port village. She stared up at an off-kilter, bare wood structure that seemed on the verge of collapse. A faint haze hung in the air like fine gauze, tinted in the sherbet colors of the setting sun.

A beefy warehouseman, rough-dressed in streaked canvas pants and a sagging hand-knit sweater, emerged. Shabby though it was, the barn was attractive in its own way, sepia-toned and picturesque, set between a large field of freshly turned soil on one side and on the other a paddock of rich green grasses that served three sleek horses. The warehouseman remained jovial as he and Hattie's driver manhandled the enormous trunk down from the wagon and into the weathered building. Taking a modest precaution against the growing number of thieves and profiteers roaming the countryside, they threw a mound of loose, dusty hay over the trunk to hide it.

It was fitting, Hattie thought, that she arrived at the base in a truck and left in a mule-drawn wagon, somehow a reflection on the fate of the base itself.

She shook herself alert again with a deep gulp of air. Taking her patient driver's callused hand, she paid him and added a bonus.

"Thank you, *m'sieur*. You've been a great help." Wishing him *bonne chance,* she silently prayed he would survive the war.

Turning to the owner of the barn, Claude Rousseau, Hattie paid him in advance to store her trunk, labeled with her name and address in New Orleans. And in case no one came would he please send it to New Orleans after the war? Rousseau tugged his cap and took her money, but he shrugged. He'd lost any optimism he'd once had.

"I'm honest, *Madame*, but I don't talk for no Nazis. We can hope that trunk stays hid from those *merde* thugs 'til you come back—*if* you come back at all."

"That's what I hope for, *m'sieur*, that my husband and I will be back. I hope you meet my husband, Luke. You'd…you will like him." She could've told *Monsieur* Rousseau that her husband would greatly disapprove of her unlikely to succeed and very dangerous plan to find him.

Rousseau snorted, pessimistic that he'd see either of them again. When Hattie asked about places to stay in the village, his response was gruff. He was starting to like the pale young lady.

Madame Annette Rousseau happened to be the sister of Claude, the owner of the warehouse that housed Hattie's trunk. That was sufficient for a good recommendation, but an honest one, as well. The efficient, no-nonsense *Mme.* Rousseau ran her home as an *auberge,* or guest house, in the harbor village of Vierville-sur-Mer.

Her sturdy stone building had been built as a large private home two centuries before, using boulders from the surrounding fields in its construction. Mortared stones were covered inside and out with a slathering of creamy stucco to keep out wind and rain. Its exterior had become mossy with age. Most of the neighboring houses used similar construction methods and materials, every house so like the others that all seemed built by the same hand. On rainy days, of which there were many, the stone houses glistened wetly as they darkened, while their interior rooms remained snug and dry.

Though modestly successful in the past, *Mme.* Rousseau's business these last months had trickled to a stop. She wasn't the only villager affected by the war. Although everyone in Vierville-sur-Mer suffered to some extent when summer business declined in the fall, they adjusted by storing crops and raising chickens. The effects of the war, though, went far beyond any seasonal variation. Her business had dried up completely as the Nazi marauders moved closer. She had been used to sea-loving vacationers arriving with their wallets open. They were her sole source of income and the lifeblood of the village. All the happy visitors were gone now, deserting not only the village of Vierville but it seemed the entire country…and perhaps the entire European continent altogether.

Hattie set off on a long, sweaty hike to the village, planning to check on Claude's recommendation. If not for fatigue brought on by the bone-jarring journey, Hattie would have noticed and been charmed by the abundant green-ery, the wildlife, and the sweet warbling of songbirds along the way. Nowhere did she see French military uniforms, which left her flushed and unbalanced with foreboding.

As she approached, a clean, orderly village sparkled in the twilight. Its storybook appearance delighted Hattie, who craned her neck as she walked along. Situated so close to the Channel one could hear the lapping of waves. Vierville-sur-Mer was intimate in scope and far more attractive than the *arrondissments* of Paris.

Along the rough, uneven cobblestones of a quiet street she scuffed past an ancient covered well surrounded by worn benches. Hattie longed to pause there for a rest, but knew she should continue.

Judging by the frayed rope she saw wound around its shaft and the array of neatly stacked buckets beside it, the well was a village gathering spot and very much in use.

A few steps further on, Hattie reached a hoary stone church. Its steep-slanted slate roof was capped by an openwork metal cross, large and graceful. Its stone threshold had been worn down by thousands of footsteps, and its twin doors were held together by a rope, tied in a bow.

Homes and shops constructed of greystone crowded the edge of the street, their stoops meticulously maintained. Pots of blooming bright red geraniums provided spots of color. These structures were so unlike the flimsy cabins and dirt streets of the army base that Hattie had left behind. Several of the village buildings displayed new, fresh-smelling thatched roofs.

The exquisite village was dramatically different from any other place Hattie had ever been, perhaps most dramatically Paris. This was another world, where it was easy to imagine one was stepping back in time to a gentler age.

Dusk had nearly faded to darkness by the time Hattie urged herself up the *auberge* steps to the door. Exhausted and famished, she was low on nourishment and energy. Her footsteps had delivered her to a heavy wooden doorway, freshly painted brick red and scrubbed.

The modest building nestled inconspicuously and quite at home among the surrounding structures. There was no obvious sign to advertise that the place rented beds and meals to travelers. Hattie DeValcourt hesitated, wondering if she had the right place.

Her dusty valise dropped onto the spotless doorstep almost of its own volition, but the reduction in weight barely buoyed her. Hattie had been awake since before sunrise that morning, and the day had been difficult. Her empty stomach gurgled, embarrassingly loud. Dusty clothes covered grimy skin, and her thirst was ferocious. She crossed her fingers like a child, hoping the place had an available room.

Hattie staggered against the wall with fatigue, finding it difficult to raise her heavy hand to the bell pull beside the door. She willed her fingers to close around the cord, and pulled. A bell tinkled deep within the house, and her lips curved appreciatively. These days, when things worked properly, it seemed a bit miraculous. She waited at the door, wilting into an exhausted puddle.

With a deep sigh, she lifted her hand to try the bell a second time just as a petite, exasperated woman flung the door open wide to crash against an interior wall. Startled, an adrenaline surge forced Hattie back a step, making her heart thump and leaving her speechless. Air fragrant with the homey smell of rich stew rushed into her face and she inhaled. Saliva filled Hattie's mouth so that she had to swallow. Her eyes glistened, suspiciously moist.

A thought of Cook's kitchen at home on Octavia Street overcame her mind.

Birdlike, the woman at the door tilted her head. She spoke sharply. "Well?"

Her abrupt aspect was tempered by the pair of shabby men's work boots that peeked from beneath a capacious apron that enveloped her. She had a smallish foot that tapped its irritation. A scowl of vertical frown lines marred her face. If not too cowed to look closely, one could have seen a kindly gleam in a pair of compassionate gray eyes. The birdlike woman pursed her lips.

"What? What is it?" A guarded expression told of dangerous times. "Speak up, girl. What's so important that I left my supper to get cold?"

The woman's body was completely concealed by a voluminous apron except for two thin arms (covered in saturated blue worsted, the same shade as Hattie's maman's plumbago in New Orleans) that were crossed firmly over her chest. The homespun apron hung long enough to graze the tops of the woman's scuffed boots.

Although unsteady from raging thirst and debilitating fatigue, Hattie yet noted how chic the Frenchwoman managed to look in her boots and apron. Hattie sighed, fearing she was off to a bad start, then straightened her spine. Her parched throat forced her to swallow. She licked her lips.

Seeing Hattie's wavering stance, *Madame* Rousseau's irritation became more a worried compassion, and she stepped across the threshold to gather Hattie's arm in a firm grip.

"You're sick, *madame*?" Her words were emphatic, "If you are sick, you cannot stay. Water, yes. I'll give you water, then you have to go." Her severe tone suggested familiarity with such matters, and it brooked no compromise.

Dismayed, Hattie shook her head and protested, "No, *madame*. Not sick, simply exhausted." *Mme.* Rousseau remained suspicious, but half carried Hattie into her spotless foyer and settled her on the woven cane seat of an old, slightly the-worse-for-wear, straight-backed bench.

Through a wide doorway, Hattie glimpsed a cozy room with a settee upholstered in soft gold fabric that held scattered faded red pillows. Throw rugs in rose and beige warmed a bluestone floor. Starched white lace curtains over small windows softened the rough stuccoed stone walls. A fireplace with a raised hearth held the embers of a banked fire at the far end of the chamber. Hattie blinked. The place was not at all like Hattie's family home, but its ambiance in some way reminded her of it, like a comfortable watercolor of the life she'd once had.

She prepared to discuss business with *Madame*.

"Claude Rousseau sent me." That surprised the *auberge chatelaine*, who stood stock-still and cocked her head, once again looking birdlike.

"Claude? That rascal sent you?" Her colloquial French rattled out faster than the shots from enemy tommy guns. Her questioning chin thrust up and out. "And you know Claude how?"

"*M'sieur* Rousseau is storing my belongings, now that the army base at Nantes has shut down. I asked where I might find a room and he suggested this place. I'm looking for Annette Rousseau."

"The base shut down? Closed? They are such cowards, turning their tails to the Nazis. *Merde.*" Contemptuous words from the fiery woman.

Abruptly, she shifted from adversarial compassion to that of an efficient businesswoman, leaving Hattie confused by the rapid change.

"Claude, *c'est mon frère,* my brother." She thumped her chest with a flourish. "*I* am Annette. Annette Rousseau. But we wait to talk business." Her expressive hands fluttered without pause, to emphasize her words.

"We'll discuss everything over *les viands, non?*" Interrupted by one of Hattie's small sounds, she said, "Yes, yes. You, too.

"Dinner's waiting, getting colder every minute. Come. Wash in the kitchen, at the pump. Eat my veal stew. Do you like veal?"

Not waiting for an answer, she said, "We'll talk at the table."

Annette and Hattie agreed to a rental fee over hearty, aromatic veal stew and long refreshing swallows of home-pressed, ruby-red table wine. The *chatelaine* apologized for what she considered a meager meal.

Except for Hattie, she had no other boarders and no prospects for any in the near future. She used liberal epithets for both the French government as well as the Nazis.

Warm kitchens had always nourished Hattie with more than good food and mouthwatering smells. In New Orleans, and at the summer house on the Gulf Coast, Maman's cook had coddled the little girl through adolescence, giving

Hattie wise homespun advice and delicious cookies. Annette's cozy kitchen in Vierville-sur-Mer gave Hattie an odd sense of coming home.

Rejuvenated by the good cooking, Hattie refused to accept Annette's description of her meal as "meager."

"How can you say that? The food was delicious, Annette, and there was plenty of it." She patted her tummy. "That was the best fresh-baked bread I've ever eaten. You want what—a bigger compliment?"

"*Peut-être.* Maybe so, Hattie. A compliment never hurts, I always say." A smile revealed how sweet Annette's face could be when she was in a better mood.

"Not bigger compliments, though—more of them." She looked around the room as though other appreciative souls should be there with them. She and Hattie shared a smile, on a first-name basis before supper ended.

Annette retrieved her new guest's valise, having thought it light rather than as heavy as it was, saying as she headed up the stairs, "What is *in* here—rocks? Come on, *Ha-tee.*"

Hearing her name pronounced the way her fellow Sorbonne friends had, brought on waves of nostalgia like physical blows.

Annette spoke over her shoulder as she mounted the stairs.

"You're alone up here, so for now you have the bathroom down the hall to yourself. I expect you won't object."

Hattie stopped in the doorway of the room, admiring the serenity that was to be hers. Annette lit a lamp. The room's ochre walls glowed warm and cheerful. A plump blue and white toile duvet decorated a generous bed grounded by a white eyelet bed skirt. The duvet and the matching shade on the bedside lamp contrasted nicely with the ochre walls.

A strange emotion, of being *home* with all its attendant comfort, settled on Hattie as she looked around the room. The tiny hairs at the back of her neck no longer stood on end, and she could relax for the first time in days. The feeling of home was pleasurable, though she believed it quite temporary. There was one window that overlooked the area in front of the house. It was quite large and gave a wide view of the picturesque brick street, and beyond of tranquil waters in a minuscule harbor.

Annette offered her guest *bonne nuit* and left Hattie alone and exhausted. Hattie headed for the bathroom, hair pinned up in a messy bun high on her head, and carrying Luke's soft white nightshirt draped over her arm. Though tired, she looked forward to a long soak in Annette's deep cast-iron tub.

Pumping well water up to the tub by hand proved to be more of an ordeal than Hattie thought, one that forced her to groan. But in the end, even cold bathwater was worth the effort. She emerged refreshed and ready to fall into bed, detouring a moment to open her window to the autumnal night air.

A beautiful, gibbous moon, half-risen , appeared close enough to touch. It paved a glittering path across the harbor's gentle lapping waves straight to her. Her lips curved. Surely, it was a harbinger of good things to come.

Lying between smooth, clean sheets under a warm, fluffy duvet, Hattie thought of her husband, missing him more than seemed possible. Wishing he was by her side, she recalled a favorite benefit of their time together—snuggling next to his warm body. Sleep would be impossible tonight.

When she opened her eyes, bright light filled the room and mild guilt washed over Hattie. She'd overslept, but blamed it on her pregnancy.

Hattie skipped down the stairs to a silent house. A large cup of *café au lait* sat cooling on the kitchen sideboard with a plate of mouthwatering *brioche*, a pat of butter, and a generous pot of grape jam sitting beside it. Taking breakfast to the kitchen table, Hattie hummed tunelessly while savoring the *brioche* and draining her cup. She left her washed dishes by the sink to dry, thinking her search was off to an excellent start.

Hattie settled beside her bedroom window in a rocker, wrapped in silence while she strategized her next steps. Sunny warmth filled the room. A soft breeze wafted in. Outside, bread crumbs left to feed wild birds attracted sleek pigeons that waddled and pecked among the weeds of the roadway. Doves perched on low tree limbs and preened, burbling satisfaction with the world.

She mused on the difference between a wartime French breakfast of just *café au lait*, a small *brioche*, pat of butter and teaspoon of homemade jam compared with Cook's expansive, and really too large, breakfasts of bacon, sausage, eggs cooked to order, baskets of fluffy biscuits, large shaped mounds of fresh butter and jars of fig preserves. Hattie suffered a moment of irrational embarrassment that she had so heedlessly indulged herself there when others in the world were deprived of breakfast altogether. Introspection was new to her, and left her feeling uncomfortable.

Claude Rousseau's recommendation had steered Hattie to a place that was more advantageous than she could have imagined. She had limited funds, but there was enough to afford Annette's fee for a lovely room and a comfortable bed, with meals included, especially compared to prices in Paris.

If she had to be somewhere without Luke, this *auberge* was the perfect place to gather her thoughts and make plans. She hoped her money would last long enough to find Luke and pay for a way home. A hopeful wish, she realized, for a naïve young woman with very little real-world experience.

The existence of an old rhyme about beggars and horses came to mind, but she couldn't recall the words…

Sea waves lapped to within a few dozen cobblestones of the *auberge*. Secured fishing boats jostled in a gentle rhythmic motion, their mooring chains clanking in discordant music against the massive wooden posts covered in barnacles that underpinned the wharf.

Hattie's head drooped as she rocked and daydreamed to the sounds of the sea. Sunlight streamed in broad stripes across the faded blue rag rug. If Annette Rousseau padded past her room, Hattie didn't hear the footsteps.

Her mind detached from unimportant thoughts and she concentrated on how best to search for Luke and the soldiers under his command—if Marie had told her the truth, that the men were secretly imprisoned in a forest somewhere near the sea.

Hattie thought she'd chosen Vierville-sur-Mer well; this isolated village was surrounded by woods on three sides with the sea on the fourth and it was well centered as a hub for her to seek the prison and Luke. She needed help, and cast about for ideas on where she might find it.

Absorbed in thought, Hattie wasn't aware Annette stood in her doorway until the landlady spoke.

"Lost in another world, *chère?*"

Hattie jumped, and her heart fluttered. She had better toughen up. Jostled from her thoughts, she invited Annette to join her. Exploring the landlady's features, Hattie decided the woman was quite handsome, especially in the clear light of day.

"*Bonjour,* Annette. Thank you for the coffee and *brioche.* Everything tasted delicious."

"It's already lunchtime, sleepyhead."

"Blame it on your bed. It's too comfortable."

Annette chuckled, and teased Hattie. "Too comfortable! Maybe I should give you a board instead.

"I'm glad you slept, *chère.* You needed it, I think. Today you're a different person—clear-eyed, not washed-out like yesterday." Not waiting for a response, she kept talking.

"I have a serious question."

"What is it?"

Annette swept her arm wide with her shoulders shrugged close to her ears, because these days no one could be too careful. A group Annette had just come from had sent her to get answers from the new guest.

"Why did you come to our little village—to Vierville-sur-Mer? How long are you staying here? Your French has a different accent. Perhaps you are a foreigner. I'm asking because I'm nosy, *comprends?*"

Hattie said, "No, your questions are fair. You allowed me to stay last night, not knowing why I was at your door or anything about me. I *am* here to do something important. You deserve to know what I'm doing, and why."

Annette frowned. Strangers were suspect these days, dangerous and unwelcome visitors in the small villages.

"You don't have to answer. Why don't you just leave?"

Hattie decided to make a joke of the situation, not aware that Annette wasn't kidding.

"I'm sure you're not a Nazi sympathizer. If you are, I can't do anything about it, anyway."

Annette's fist slammed on the bedside table and Hattie's eyes widened. She recoiled, not sure how she'd provoked such a strong reaction.

Her color heightened, Annette's smooth olive complexion flushed and she spat, "You insult me, madam. Me, a Nazi sympathizer? I should throw you out!"

The color drained from Hattie's face and she raised her hands.

"Don't be angry, Annette. I was trying to make a joke, but I didn't do it very well. What I was trying to joke about is you are very sympathetic. I didn't mean to imply you're sympathetic to them. Here—let me tell you the whole story."

Dripping tears, Hattie told Annette of Luke's capture and of the betrayal of the two squads by Marie and Pierre Chennault, and that all she had left were memories now of her first married home.

Her only desire now, she said, was to find Luke, so they could resume a life together, a normal life, though she suspected their lives would never be the same again.

Annette calmed down, but her fury at the Nazis only grew. Though her lips clamped down into a thin, angry line, for Hattie she clucked only her sympathy and offered a clean handkerchief from her waistband.

"What do you think *you* can do, Hattie? This is a job for… I don't know… for strong men who know their way around the woods."

Hattie said, "Maybe I can *find* somebody to help, maybe not. Either way, I have to try somehow."

Though the French Army wasn't willing to look for Luke and his soldiers, that just meant Hattie would have to do more than anyone could imagine. She had once been a little girl who accepted no boundaries, who would take on any challenge. That girl was still a big part of Hattie.

Hattie talked on. Her goal was to rescue Luke and return with him to Louisiana, but she knew that was impossible by herself. Hattie needed the help of the French Resistance—but she had no way to find them. So she would have to rely on luck and persistence.

Annette became increasingly more thoughtful the longer Hattie talked, until at last she interrupted, lifting a capable hand.

"*Arête*. Stop dreaming, Hattie. Why should the Resistance help you? What you're saying, to say these things aloud is dangerous. And not smart. It's one thing for the Resistance to ambush one or two soldiers who walk down the road. It's a whole other thing to break into a fortified stockade—supposing you find it."

She held out her hand to help Hattie as she rose from her seat.

"We meet every day. You can come with me and ask for help. We're already late."

"Are you saying what I think you are?" The last vestige of fatigue dropped away, and Hattie's heart soared with new enthusiasm.

Annette's nod seemed to signal the change in fortune that Hattie had been hoping for. It filled her with relief and renewed purpose. Her landlady's presence brought to mind the small, weather-beaten boats bobbing in the harbor—rather typical, but capable of getting a passenger where she needed to go. Without realizing it, Hattie had found the very person she needed—a member of the French Resistance—in the unlikely sturdy body of competent, middle-aged Annette Rousseau.

A drop of perspiration slid down Hattie's back. The crowded, smoke-filled room vibrated with testosterone despite the presence of a few women. Even the noise was intimidating. Would this motley cluster of well-dressed merchants, rough farmers, and a few giggling housewives give her their help? They just looked like ordinary people, not capable of rebellion. Or were they? Of violence? Stealthy attack? No, it didn't seem so at all. It was a mistake to have come here with Annette.

Could they be suspicious? Of Hattie, yes, of course. All they could see was an attractive woman, sleek and tall, her hands smooth and soft, not roughened with work or chores. On the other hand, Annette *was* here with her.

The others were perturbed that Annette had brought *un étranger* into their gathering, but they quieted down to hear Hattie's story. They knew betrayal all too well.

From the beginning of the war, anyone with brains knew the French army was hopelessly overmatched. Their soldiers had been schooled in methods used in the previous century that were not effective any longer. This new war used powerful new machines.

The newly mechanized German fighting force was far too fierce for complacent countries, overwhelming lesser defenders. And so General Charles de Gaulle, unable to get support from his own government, had appealed to the populace, private citizens, to resist the Nazis by any means possible. In response, French citizens mounted coordinated underground guerrilla offensives that coalesced into an organized movement. Their purpose was to delay and disrupt the Nazi onslaught.

Few *résistants* had had any formal military instruction after the Great War of 1914, later known as World War I. As a result, these earnest patriots instead had to invent the art of sabotage, employing dangerous and sometimes ineffective trial and error attacks.

They did have one major advantage, however. The *résistants* knew the countryside, its hiding places and escape routes, far better than the Germans.

Like clandestine wasps, they would sting, then fly into hiding. With enough wasps and enough targeted stings, they hoped to defeat the enemy, at least to delay him. The end goal of the Resistance was to regain full French autonomy.

The members of Annette's small cell listened grudgingly to Hattie's appeal for help. She imagined their objections: she was a foreigner, and asking the impossible, at that—to find a Nazi stockade that might or might not exist, and about which she knew nothing, not even its location. She wanted them to find the place, then rescue the prisoners, if in fact any were still alive. Why would it be anywhere near their village? And wouldn't they already know about it, if it was close by?

Hattie put her finger on the map and told the group the search would begin in the Vierville area. She could see from the expressions staring up at her that they were thinking "what the hell?"

Her audience of *résistants* threw up their hands. Luke's soldiers might already be dead. Why were they asked to do this thing? Just because *one wife* loved her husband and feared for his life? Lots of people were dying. Hattie DeValcourt again urged them to help her find the love of her life.

They had to admit that she was plucking a few heartstrings. Her story supported their romantic inclinations and had a certain appeal. In the end, the group agreed to help—promising to search, but for one day only…in their free time…maybe do more if…(whispering behind their hands, saying "not likely")…they found the location.

After all, resistance fighters could do only so much before other responsibilities claimed their time. But they could use *her* help, too, in between times when she wasn't busy searching on her own for her husband's prison.

Hattie felt mostly at home with the *résistants* in Vierville-sur-Mer from the start. They understood and sympathized with her predicament. Many of her new acquaintances were the parents or wives of men whose whereabouts were also unknown. The new widows wanted their own revenge, and in time they offered Hattie their trust and their friendship, often combined with tough love and a great deal of advice.

Needing all the help they could get, they decided to ask Hattie to join their resistance cell, so she did.

Her first foray with the French Resistance nearly ended before it began. Their small group approached a warehouse in a secluded, heavily wooded area. They'd been tipped off that the warehouse was full of stored ammunition. As they moved closer, Hattie's head jerked back and she found herself crashing to the ground, flat on her back, with her neck stretched upward at an angle. Low branches had snagged her hair, pulling at the long strands and holding her firmly hostage. Unable to rise, she struggled.

"*Mon Dieu*, Hattie," hissed the man at her shoulder. "Shut up. You'll get us all killed."

His knife snicked from its leather case and he jerked her against him, a hand over her mouth, then sawed at her hair with rapid downward movements. That forced muted yelps from her and left long hanks of wavy chestnut hair dangling from the branches. His fast action averted real disaster when he pulled Hattie into hiding bare seconds before the Nazi guard walked past on his rounds.

Mortified that her vanity over her long, useless hair had endangered companions, Hattie pulled her own sharp knife the instant the guard was out of sight and sawed off the remainder. A crude inch of hair now rebounded into uneven curls. The *résistants* cell approved, smiling at two bouncy wisps that she'd missed at the crown. This pretty woman now looked even more adorable, like a *gamine* now serious about her soldiering.

From that point forward, Hattie worked hard at Resistance exploits, unaware that her enthusiasm was in revenge for a missing husband. Yet her focus in every mission was to find out what happened to Luke.

In the village, she purchased a pair of barely worn, sturdy boots that protected her feet and kept them dry. The *résistants* sabotaged their targets often on cold, damp nights, and the warm boots lent Hattie a swagger and a tough new personality.

After the first frightening foray, Hattie began wearing the rough woven trousers Annette had found for her. Pants were smarter and far more comfortable in the forest undergrowth than were troublesome skirts. She could move much more freely, and rough attire had become customary, at least acceptable, wear for the village women. Salt water abounded, but there was less access to sources of clean water and even soap as days turned into weeks and the Germans took such luxuries for themselves.

Hattie gradually gained gravitas in the smoky, low-ceilinged Resistance meetings. To earn acceptance, Hattie took on the thoroughly disliked job of converting verbal reports from the small teams into a written record. She patiently wrote everything down, then removed a stone in the wall at floor level and added each report to the cache of information already there.

In a concession to their new recruit, one who was unfamiliar with the area, the *résistants* tacked a large map to the wall which they used to track their search for the elusive prison, a search that, while sporadic, now extended much longer than the one day they'd promised. Slowly, color spread across the map. Each small exploration eliminated a swath of the woods, until only a few unexplored areas remained.

France's dense population of some forty-two million souls lived mostly in cities. There were, however, a large number of wooded areas in the countryside. Accustomed as they were to the many forests of Germany, the Nazis found French forests useful for military purposes, one of which was for hidden prison stockades, using prisoner labor and forest timber to build them.

Exhausted and poorly fed prisoners cut down trees and dressed them, then wrestled them upright into deep, regularly spaced holes they'd dug earlier. When a stockade prison was complete, the Germans pushed their "lucky" prisoners (because they'd survived the battlefield) into the finished enclosures at bayonet point.

Captive soldiers strong enough to work were packed off to Germany to replace German workers who'd been conscripted into Hitler's *Wehrmacht*. Many French prisoners died of disease, starvation, or beatings in the temporary prisons, either waiting for transport to Germany or simply too old or injured to bother with. When circumstances dictated, prisoners were simply lined up and shot.

It seemed to Hattie that her search was a race against death. She questioned whether Luke still lived or was even now in France. Nevertheless, her quest consumed her thoughts and most of her waking hours, and she vowed to continue exploring the area until no hope remained.

And that was how Hattie found herself sitting hidden in a small depression on a wooded hillside above the town of Vierville-sur-Mer, a spot that gave her a clear view of the daily activities of the Germans.

The small basket of wild *champignons* sitting beside her in the grass was her excuse for being on the hillside. By chance, Hattie had seen the fairy circle of mushrooms close to her observation post and taken advantage of it. The spot afforded an excellent view of paths crisscrossing into and out of the village, and if discovered, she could point to the basket of fungi as her reason for being there.

Vierville-sur-Mer was one of many small villages dotting the eastern shore of the English Channel that were chosen by the Nazis as forward bases. From them, the Germans could man batteries of cannons aimed westward. As done in the takeover of other hamlets, villagers were forced to share their homes with Germans, or even vacate them. Though the troops thought they'd traipsed through every foot of the village and every room in every house, the locals had kept many secrets from their occupiers.

Hattie had observed the Germans from the hillside for several days now, and she suspected there were things of more interest than their change of shifts at the cannon batteries; she'd learned to distinguish between usual and unusual Nazi movements along the paths. The Germans believed the villagers to be completely cowed, and the soldiers soon became complacent, conducting most of their activities without resorting to subterfuge.

Hattie sucked the last of the juice from her lunch of a fresh-picked apple, tossing away the core as she chewed. She wiped a sticky hand on her long black pleated skirt, then stood, picking up the basket of mushrooms. She'd seen enough, and could implement an important plan for the following day. She wouldn't wear a skirt tomorrow. No, tomorrow it would be a pair of Luke's trousers and she would follow along the Germans' most often used path.

Hattie was confident she'd find the hidden prison she had been seeking—and hopefully, her husband.

Hattie coughed to a hazy consciousness, wondering where she was. Tormented by ferocious thirst, she opened her eyes and blinked. Everything looked blurry. Her face and hair, even her teeth, were gritty with debris. She was surrounded by silence except for the soft rustling of crispy fallen leaves pushed around by a breeze. The familiar sound reminded her of childhood hikes in the woods of Louisiana. Persistent pain brought Hattie's focus to her present situation.

She tentatively explored her body for injuries while staring up through a leafy canopy. Despite her wounds, she grinned, pretty sure she'd discovered the Nazi's prison stockade.

Hattie's every breath hurt, and from changes in the light it seemed she was fading in and out of consciousness. As twilight dimmed the day, her thoughts skittered from the danger she'd escaped to recollections from her past.

Deep in the ravine the burnt sienna autumn heat began dissipating. Chilled and needing the heat from her own core, she curled her bruised body into a tight ball and fell into reverie.

Nestled there, she thought back to the first dare she'd accepted as a child.

Crouched outside beneath an open kitchen window, her small nine-year-old hands spread wide, she balanced in the loose dirt. A tantalizing aroma from her target spiraled down and her mouth watered. She peered up between an azalea's dark green leaves and its fuchsia blooms. She was well aware of her co-conspirators, but stayed focused on her task, determined not to fail the two boys, both older than her.

As they watched from behind a tree across the yard, Hattie grabbed the hot dish of cobbler and scampered away, her braids flapping wildly and her skinny, white-stockinged legs pumping like flashing pistons. Her confederates grinned as she collapsed into the grass, her prize nestled in the folds of her short, blue-flounced skirt.

She hissed, "Ow…hot," then turned to her brother, Jack. "You better have the spoons."

He raised insulted eyebrows and sneered, "Of course I do," pulling three filched silver spoons from his knickers.

Hattie looked a mess. There was a dirt smudge on her forehead where she'd pushed back unruly hair, and her ruffled frock was grimy where it had swept the ground below the window.

The second boy, Luke DeValcourt, was a year older than Jack DuMond and three years older than Hattie. That morning he had left home in his favorite trousers that he'd snagged from his mother's dirty clothes hamper.

Luke's presence thrilled Jack, but disgusted Hattie. She thought Luke was *always* at their house, pulling her brother away from playing games with her. Luke annoyed her, and today he'd been the one to challenge her with his taunts.

"There's no way you could steal that blackberry cobbler, Hattie. You're too little, and you're not fast enough to get away with stealing anything. Or brave enough, either."

That had made her furious. She was suspicious that Luke was bothering to talk to her at all, but maybe gratified, too. The two of them ignored each other most of the time.

Jack chimed in. "Come on, Luke. She's too little. Cook'll catch her. Anyway, *I* want to do it."

Luke answered, using a patient and reasonable grownup-sounding voice, looking from Hattie to Jack.

"Listen up, people. If a *girl* gets caught, Cook probably won't raise Cain, but if it's you or me, Jack, there'll be hell to pay." Hattie jumped, startled to hear "hell," one of her maman's forbidden words.

Hell!

The recalled word pierced Hattie's dream. It was sharp enough, hard enough, to bring her to consciousness. She was trembling and chilled, and briefly confused again about where she was and how she'd gotten there.

Why *was* she on the ground? Hattie lay motionless on the ravine's leaf-covered bottom, concussed and barely conscious.

Day faded to twilight, and still Hattie lay there, her eyes closed.

The temperate forests of France differed from the dense subtropical, swampy Louisiana cypress and oak woods. Without Louisiana's poisonous snakes and spiders, French forests weren't nearly as frightening, though Hattie was explored, and then ignored, by several curious insects.

One solitary bug, in the unfortunate last act of its life, chomped a nerve ending on Hattie's neck. The sting brought Hattie to full consciousness. Her fingertips found the insect offender and rubbed it out.

Her aching, bruised body brought forth whimpers. Her throat was parched. Still on her back on the cold moldy earth, Hattie struggled through mental confusion to recall how she'd ended up in a deep trench. She explored her extensive aches and pains with tentative touches and squinted at a stickered vine inches away from her scratched nose. *An edible berry? Non.*

Hattie winced at a painful lump when she inventoried her head, then explored her body, finding scrapes and scratches but no broken bones. She had escaped without being shot to death or raped, and before her brains were beat out. She ventured a glance up through the forest canopy, her eyes half-closed. That brought a wave of nausea, and she blinked at double images.

She expected but found no bullet wound. *How could I have dodged that bullet?*

Twigs and dirty grass festooned her torn clothes and she slowly brushed them away. The bright sunlight had gone, leaving everything more difficult to see in the twilight haze. Had she been unconscious all afternoon? At least she was alive.

She couldn't stay there, no matter how injured she was or how bad she felt. Hattie knew she had to sneak back into the village, though it hurt to stand.

Gritting her teeth against the pain, she managed to groan to a sitting position. Her muscles spasmed, making it difficult to catch her breath. After a few minutes, Hattie willed her body to release its tension. The dizziness and nausea subsided and the double images merged back into one. She staggered upright, the crickets in her brain clamoring louder than ever. A steady cramping squeezed her abdomen. Being alive and not a prisoner, though, felt like a miracle.

The distance back to the village seemed insurmountable, but she'd be damned to not give it a try. Unbuttoning the pocket of her drab canvas shirt, she pulled out her compass, relieved to discover it undamaged, and found due north. She knew the direction she'd traveled from her observation point, and the direction from the observation point to the village, and the approximate distances involved, so she knew she could find her way to the village. The question was whether she could do it without stumbling into more Nazis.

Hattie licked her parched, bruised lips. *Water. If only I had water.* Her pack had been light to start with, empty except for bandages and her canteen, but she had jettisoned it for more speed when the sentry spotted her. That she'd been discovered was entirely her own fault, a lapse of concentration. She hadn't heard the rustling leaves and twigs under the soldier's boots. But pointless to mull over the mistake. That was then.

Now, she gauged the ravine's steep incline, hard to do through the lengthening shadows. Hattie concluded she wouldn't be able to climb up, not the way her ankles hurt. But maybe she could follow the meandering ravine toward the village, the direction seemed about right. The ravine's narrow walls might funnel her like a steer to the slaughterhouse, but an easier way out of it might turn up somewhere down the line.

Hattie itched with anxiety, knowing each step could make her a target for anyone standing on the edge of the ravine and looking down. But waiting wouldn't help. Plus Annette and the other *résistants* needed to know that a prison stockade was in their own back yard.

Hattie mused about the time not so long ago when she could move around nearly as fast as the gossip. Though not fast at the moment, her progress was steady, her rests were brief, and fear was keeping her motivated. She pressed on even as the pain in her ankles worsened. The forest became quieter as evening descended, and a light evening breeze kept her company. An occasional dove cooed, and an owl would hoot. Her pain was constant now, and both swollen ankles tightened the laces of her boots.

The ravine narrowed as though nature begrudged her presence, until its sides grazed her shoulders, so close Hattie glimpsed small-veined plants growing on its sides and remembered as a child watching ants carrying leaves many times their size.

The lush fertility of the forest kicked up underfoot. The long dusk of summer allowed the remaining light to sift lightly through the forest canopy. Night unobtrusively fell.

To distract herself from pain, Hattie dwelled on earlier, simpler days. But like a finger drawn to a sore, her thoughts lingered on the twist life had taken from one of her impetuous decisions. Years ago—how many years had it been? —her family had begged her not to go to the Sorbonne because European politics were so unsettled. But she knew better than her parents, because she had a college degree. Sure their fears were overblown and determined to become a physician, she'd chosen France as her best option. Probably her only option, with medical school admission policies so antediluvian in the U.S.

Now she knew that her parents had been right. An American woman had no business being by herself in a remote French forest during a godforsaken war. How she wished she'd listened to her parents and stayed in New Orleans, though who could have guessed she would end up in such a mess.

And to think of all those years wasted by not being with Luke. She missed her husband, had to know where he was and if he was alive. Such intense love for a man in such a short time. Yes, their sexual life was a big part of it, but he was such a good man, a man who shared her values, and…well, there just weren't words for the rest of her yearning. And the father of her child. And Hattie wasn't sure she could live without him.

In the dark, a silhouette limped past the flowers planted at the entrance to Vierville-sur-Mer. The figure, indeterminate of sex and age, went unnoticed in the dark, its injuries undisclosed.

A crescent moon snagged in the sparkling fabric of the sky above a silent shadow, a woman moving past the stone houses of the village, a wraith like many the war had created to wander through the French countryside.

Hattie's concussion created intermittent double images of the clouds that scudded across the face of the crescent moon. Her depth perception was still compromised, and she saw the world in two dimensions, like a pencil drawing on paper. Cloud shadows flitting across the Channel waves seemed ghostlike.

She shivered, doubled over as she walked. She wondered if she would make it home to Annette's *auberge*.

The briny smell of the sea tickled her nose, and even on a pitch black night she would have known she was almost home. Shoulders that had been tensed up to her ears now relaxed. She managed a faint smile at the glowing semaphores of fireflies flashing amongst the flowers. Her hearing became attuned to the sawing cicadas and the unmistakable hoots from the peak of a thatched roof, an owl's warning of danger. *How odd*, Hattie thought, *that anything would believe she posed a danger.*

She fought to hold herself together until she reached home.

The smooth, whitewashed façades of the stone cottages didn't fool Hattie. Serene though they appeared, many held the defiant hearts of strong, patriotic French men and women. She had counted on, and would still count on, that spirit of rebellion to help her rescue Luke.

Hattie saw flickering candles through gapped curtains and wished they could cast their light down on the street as she felt her way home to Annette.

A Nazi patrol marched by in search of curfew violators. Hearing their approach, she sank into the dark shadows and held her breath until their steps receded.

Finally, an exhausted Hattie reached the *auberge* and entered Annette's cozy, warm kitchen. Its appearance was so normal after her afternoon trauma, it was a surprise. The small kitchen table still sat against the wall, covered with a brick-red cloth to match the scalloped curtain drawn tightly closed at the window. She had missed this simple homeyness and Hattie was happy to be there.

Standing at the stove, Annette didn't turn to greet her when Hattie walked in. A creamy canvas apron shrouded Annette's oft-washed blue dress, sprigged with delicate faded flowers. Steam rose from the bubbling contents of a large, dented pot, and haze circled her head. The fragrances of Annette's excellent cooking unfailingly reminded Hattie of Maman's kitchen, and Cook, and New Orleans.

She relaxed at last in the comfort of being home.

Annette frowned, but still didn't turn. Had she done so, her tenant's battered, filthy appearance would've appalled her. Instead, she spoke, staring into the pot while she stirred.

"Finally you are here, *ma petite*? You are the only one with problems, *eh?*"

Hattie managed a wan smile at Annette's back, lately a more diminished silhouette. Annette had dropped considerable weight. Though wrapped in a voluminous apron, her once sturdy frame was more slender now, no more than perhaps fifty-six kilograms.

The two women had developed a strong friendship over the past six cool weeks, as summer rounded into autumn's flaming vanity. It was then that Hattie watched her landlady's face as she announced she was *enceinte*. Her pregnancy was beginning to show, and while still hesitant to share such personal information, she wanted to know Annette's reaction.

Annette heard Hattie's news with concern, knowing how difficult childbirth could be with the deprivations of war. Her breath gusted out short and sharp, but she responded with a loving expression. How wonderful it would be to hear a child's cries in the place. From then on, the women tiptoed around the pregnancy, though each delighted in the changes to Hattie's body.

Hattie's breath hitched now and she shivered with each pulse of pain. Her baby's life was at risk from her violent fall. She grasped the table's edge and sank to the hard, slatted chair.

Hearing no response to her question, Annette shrugged and returned to her cooking. Hattie's routine was beginning to frustrate her. Every evening Hattie came home later and seemed increasingly agitated and frantic to find her husband.

But what else could Annette expect after so many fruitless weeks? This was Hattie's focus. It was not Annette's business to get involved in, so she hesitated to express her opinion. She had already told Hattie bluntly that she thought it was too late to rescue Luke. Yet every night, she would have to listen to Hattie's lamentations, the same sad old tale. Annette had run out of encouraging words and was powerless to help.

The pervasiveness of the German presence stifled the citizens of Vierville-sur-Mer. The presence of the soldiers kept the countryside paralyzed and off-balance. People never knew where the Nazi locusts would descend or what they would do next, from looting a family's food store meant to get them through lean winter months to appropriating household items for use or amusement. In particular, the Nazis confiscated all the protein they could find—beef, chicken, sheep, ham, eggs, cheese—to feed their troops, leaving little to appease growling French stomachs.

The soldiers also enjoyed the town's bread and butter—and women of all ages.

Coffee, for everyone, was a lost cause. The Germans and French alike choked down a watery ersatz of roasted chicory, malt, barley, rye, or acorns. The hot liquid contained no caffeine, tasted awful, and had only warmth to recommend it.

With the approach of winter, hungry French children cried themselves to sleep. Annette's voluminous apron sagged around her reduced bulk like a collapsed parachute.

Determined to keep herself and Hattie fed, Annette took every dangerous opportunity to slip away from the village to visit the communal farm hidden deep in the woods. She worked hard while she was there, tossing hay to the cows and cleaning the chicken coop, before harvesting a few late summer vegetables and collecting shallots, eggs, and milk.

Annette prepared large meals that she parceled out among their neighbors, but she kept the largest and best meat portions for Hattie. She never mentioned her own hunger though her sacrifice was clear, and she refused to waste her valuable energy on anger when Germans grabbed bread still hot from her oven.

Though she'd been staying out later each night, Hattie had never suffered as she did now after stumbling home to Annette's kitchen. Just getting there was a minor miracle with all her injuries. Her ankles and feet were swollen twice their normal size, and just standing drove excruciating bolts of pain up her legs. She moaned, then cried with pain, each time she loosened the bindings that supported her sprained ankles. The deep indentations in her red, swollen feet were a grotesque parody of what might come from an ordinary wearing of shoes.

A quiet groan made Annette glance over her shoulder. Hattie's head rested on the tabletop and her arms cradled her abdomen. In the kitchen's warmth, she still shivered.

Annette dropped the wooden spoon on the counter and hurried over to Hattie, wiping her hands on her apron and clucking her distress at the bits of twigs and debris in her friend's dusty, disheveled hair. She removed what she could and smoothed Hattie's hair back from her forehead.

Annette set a cup of cool, earthy water on the table, and when Hattie began to sob she grabbed Hattie's nicked, scraped, sore hands.

She demanded, "What happened? Who hurt you?" But she already knew, saying, "I can answer that myself, but what were you doing out so late?" She lifted Hattie's chin from the table and saw the scratches and bruises on that lovely face. Annette gasped.

"*Mon coeur!* What happened, my heart?"

Hattie reached for the cup and thirstily drained it, then held it out, trembling, mutely asking for more water. Each swallow hydrated her depleted cells. The restorative value of water.

Her tears subsided and Hattie, ignoring the ongoing contractions low in her abdomen, whispered, "Write down these coordinates, Annette. I found the prison…"

Annette exclaimed, "*Merde!*" and forced another groan from her friend when she tapped Hattie's shoulder. "*Désolé, mais c'est un miracle!* I'm sorry, but that's a miracle. You found it? Exactly where?"

She burrowed in kitchen drawers and found a wrinkled paper and the nub of a pencil, then sat in a paint-chipped chair beside Hattie. Annette licked the thick lead tip of the pencil, "Exactly where?"

Hattie recited the coordinates she'd memorized and Annette wrote them down, reading them back to check their accuracy.

"That has to get to the *résistants* right away… but I'm so tired," Hattie said. "Will you take it to them for me?"

Annette immediately stood, clutching the paper. "Of course. Eat. Your supper is on the stove." Still wearing her apron, she pushed her feet into clogs and rushed out of the house and down the street, keeping to the shadows.

Hattie groaned to her feet and whispered a prayer, "God, I pray Luke is there." Her thirst was slaked, but she had no appetite.

Limping to the stairs, Hattie wondered if the treads might be insurmountable. As she dragged herself slowly up her pelvic pain worsened.

At the landing, she collapsed to her knees in agonizing pain, thinking to stay there on the polished wood until she gained some strength. Without warning, her dirty gray trousers darkened with new wetness and Hattie whimpered, fainting where she lay.

"I'm back, *chère,*" Annette called out.

Tired and cheerful, she stepped from her dusty clogs at the kitchen door, still talking.

"The men were all in the hall, cleaning their weapons. I told them about the prison and gave them your coordinates, so they picked up their guns, piled into that rusty old truck, and drove off. It won't take them long to get to the right place. What took hours to walk will take them only minutes to drive."

Hearing no response, she called, "Hattie?" and mounted the stairs, expecting Hattie to be in the bath. Instead, she found an unconscious Hattie sprawled in a pool of blood, still in her filthy clothing.

Annette whispered, "*Mon Dieu! Mon petit poussin!* My little chick…"

PART THREE

THE MEN OF the village Resistance cell jumped down from the back of the truck, careful with their weapons, quiet in the night's silence. Their leader followed Hattie's coordinates until he glimpsed a faint glow through the trees. The men crept closer, concealed more by darkness than by undergrowth, and then knelt, their knees and hands in the familiar earth of the forest. From youthful excursions to observe forest creatures, the *résistants* knew how to remain undetected.

A sensitivity to the unusual was a key to ensuring a safe reconnaissance. On this particular night, the smoky scent of pipe tobacco wafted in the air.

A sleepy sentry sucked noisily on his pipe stem. Thinking himself safe in the forest darkness, he held his weapon carelessly and made no attempt at stealth as he shuffled through underbrush near a wall of hewn tree trunks. The *résistants* were only a few feet away.

Sure their prison was safely hidden, the complacent Germans couldn't imagine that a careless sentry and tobacco smoke would threaten their security. And this lazy sentry had left behind the dog that was supposed to accompany him.

Their luck held, and Raoul, the leader of the *résistants*, grinned. Hattie's coordinates were correct. The *résistants* had scoured the woods for weeks looking for the prison. They'd started far from the village, reasoning that the prison stockade would already have been noticed had it been close.

But this Nazi encampment was within easy reach of Vierville-sur-Mer. And it must be the prison stockade, for why else would a soldier be assigned to patrol in such an isolated spot at this hour? The Germans wouldn't have a sentry walk around for no reason. The surprise was the laxity of their standards. They must feel very secure. The men of the French Resistance would have to disabuse them of this.

When still gathered in the village, Raoul had instructed his squad to use extreme caution. The forest was treacherous enough in daylight, but doubly so in the dead of night. His men were hardened veterans of many forays who often used darkness for added protection, but the reminder didn't hurt. Now they remained motionless and silent until the sentry's steps faded away.

Raoul's men rested during the next hour, their weapons held at ease but close, as they watched the sentry spiral closer to the compound's outer wall with each successive cycle. Time passed, and his weapon slipped lower until he slung it over his shoulder. At last, he slipped through a partially open stockade gate and disappeared. The prison now had no external guards.

Raoul scratched whiskery growth on his face and under a rolled, dark red cotton square knotted around his neck. His men trusted his leadership, glad they weren't the ones who had to make the important decisions. While this was like the war games they'd played in the woods as youngsters, they knew this was more important and dangerous.

Raoul was the one to decide whether or not to take action, and when that perfect moment arrived. The squad wore colorful scarves similar to Raoul's as a kind of uniform. The scarves came in handy for everything from mopping sweat to cleaning guns and blowing drippy noses.

Leaning out of the underbrush, Raoul squinted at the wall to roughly judge the structure's size, not easy to do in the dim light. He shrugged and shook his head. This was impossible. The dimensions of the structure were irrelevant and useless anyway. He thought it odd that he could hear no sound from inside the enclosure, and he was unable to tell whether the place was full of prisoners or completely empty.

An oppressive stillness all around seemed to indicate the living woods recognized the prison as something malignant. The *résistants* hadn't even heard the night calls of forest creatures as they'd approached the place.

Perplexed by the utter silence inside the stockade, Raoul's men crept closer. Why would sentries be guarding an empty prison? There was nothing—no talk, no murmurs, not a word from either prisoners or guards. If this was imposed silence, the discipline for noncompliance must be very severe or even fatal for anyone disrupting it.

Now that the sentry had completed his patrol, Raoul directed one of his men to approach the wall. The *résistant* peered through a narrow gap between two of the vertical tree trunks. With his nose mashed up against rough shredded bark, the man witnessed horror.

Prisoners sat shoulder to shoulder in still, silent rows, their shaved heads resting on their knees. He guessed there were as many as fifty demoralized French soldiers.

As he watched, a prisoner collapsed to the ground on his side. A guard with a black swastika band around his upper arm stalked over to the soldier, withdrew a garrote from his tunic, looped it around the unconscious prisoner's neck, and twisted it tight until even in the dark, it was obvious that the man's face was turning darker. The prisoner's tongue gradually protruded and his body spasmed in its search for oxygen. Within minutes, as Raoul's man looked on, it was obvious the prisoner was dead.

Only at the end was there a sound, a few grunts as the Nazi soldier dragged the corpse over to a heap of bodies stored against the far wall.

It was a scene the *résistant* would never forget. He crawled back to their hiding place, his cheeks wet with tears. The *résistant* swallowed bitter bile, mopped his face, and whispered what he'd seen: two soldiers standing on low elevated platforms at each of four irregular corners, holding weapons in the ready position; prison guards below them at ground level, sweeping flashlights across the packed dirt floor; and perhaps fifty prisoners.

Raoul's men shook their heads and scratched their scalps, their mouths set in tight lines. An attack on such a secure stockade would be problematic for the small group, controlled as it was by the well-armed *Wehrmacht* soldiers, who would undoubtedly use the prisoners as shields.

While the *résistants* had been successful with surprise attacks and rapid withdrawals, these were not against fortified positions. And their experiences had taught them to consider all possible consequences before choosing to attack. In this situation, a major adjustment would have to be made, beyond just tactics, before an attack could succeed.

Raoul beckoned his men deeper into the woods to talk over alternatives in whispered debate. They drank and ate (slivers of ham on rough-cut bread slathered with butter, boiled eggs, and fat red grapes) to provide energy and lighten their backpacks.

One man grumbled, "Let's go home. Get some sleep."

"… or we could blow up the place," one countered enthusiastically, making the other men groan. Explosions—the bigger, the better—were generally this man's suggestion for every raid.

Raoul slapped the back of the man's head. "Kill the prisoners, too? *Vous êtes fou.*" You're crazy.

Suddenly, loud gunfire tore a jagged hole in the night silence. The *résistants* dove to the ground for safety.

But guns were targeting others that night, others unprotected and defenseless. When the gunfire ceased, the sawing cicadas and hooting owls resumed their nightly serenades. The insanity of humans was none of their concern.

The *résistants* scrambled on their bellies up to the stockade and looked through chinks in the wall. Wide-eyed and open-mouthed, they discovered they'd missed their chance to rescue their compatriots.

The prisoners had been executed *en masse*. The place was dead silent but for the scuffling boots of guards who kicked at dead bodies.

The enormous gate began to screech open and Raoul's men scrambled back into hiding. Now through the open gate they could plainly see the massacre, illuminated by swinging flashlight beams that lent a macabre air. A haze of blood in the air and the odor of excrement contrasted with the polished boots of the guards.

Caught up in the horror, the *résistants* didn't notice the approach of a creaking, mule-drawn wagon until it was about to enter the open gate. The old driver wore a carefully neutral expression. He stepped down from a splintered wagon bench, letting his mule's reins drop to the ground. He looked away from the butchery, unable to hide a grimace, as soldiers slung limp bodies into the wagon until it could hold no more.

Responding to a peremptory command, the old man retrieved the mule's reins and climbed back up onto his perch, the wagon behind him heaped high with human meat, still leaking fluids.

The man's large mule, indifferent to this or any other burden, answered the driver's command, pressing into the traces to gather traction. The wagon trundled out of the stockade, a reeking coppery smell of blood and death drifting behind it. Once out of view of the Germans, the driver lost control and wept, his face contorted with rage and furious sorrow.

The *résistants* swallowed their horror, hardly able to manage their emotion. It took all the willpower they had to stay hidden, and not to charge into the stockade on a suicide mission.

Raoul's patience teetered between breath and death, but checked his emotions. There were already too many dead Frenchmen that night.

The gate's massive door screeched closed with the departure of the overloaded wagon. The dead French soldiers had escaped their prison at last. Heroes, yes, but now just as certainly corpses, in an anonymous heap on an old country wagon.

Raoul's stomach clenched at the thought that his caution had contributed to the massacre. Taking action, he ordered half his squad of ten men to follow the makeshift hearse. Perhaps they could salvage a miraculous flicker of life.

The mule, its heavy head low, was pulling a substantial load. Its plodding hooves echoing off the forest canopy created an oddly appropriate funereal dirge. Muscular haunches pulled the wagon, but each hoof covered no more ground than a man's walking step, making the wagon easy to follow. Perhaps there was a survivor, but in the crush of corpses, in the dead of night, could they tell the living from the dead?

The five unhappy pursuers dodged the drips falling in the wagon's wake. Moving closer, they saw dim outlines of bodies lying helter-skelter, bloodied and stinking. In the light of struck matches, they were saddened at grimaces frozen in their final agonies. A lifeless hand covered a vacant face not its own. Dulled blank eyes glistened eerily opaque. A heel of a shoe rested against another man's open mouth, deformed in a silent scream.

One of Raoul's men had gotten a good look at the driver when the wagon emerged from the enclosure.

"I know this old man," he said. "He won't tell the Krauts anything if I ask him to stop. We can look for survivors."

He trotted to the front of the wagon and called, "*Arrêtez, m'sieur. Arrêtez.*" Half-asleep in a stupor, the driver startled awake and began sawing back the reins. Pushing long wispy white hair from his face, he peered to the back over his shoulder. Though able only to see shadows in the darkness of the wilderness track, he recognized a familiar voice.

"*Alors*, Justin. It's you?" the old man exclaimed. "What are you doing out here in the dark?"

"Old man, you know these are *our* soldiers you're hauling in your wagon?"

The weary old man shrugged. "*Oui*, I know. It wasn't an easy choice, but I myself will die if I tell those pigs no. It's not me that killed them, *vous savez*. And they don't even pay me."

"*Bien sûr*," Justin answered. "Don't be scared, but I'm not by myself. My friends and I—we want to check if anyone still lives. We won't put you in danger."

The old man shrugged again. He gestured over his shoulder at the wagon bed.

"Look if you want," he shrugged. "I don't care about that. But don't take too long. Damn Krauts could speed up here on their damn motorbikes and kill us all." Snorting his contempt, he hawked up a wad of phlegm and spat it over the side of the wagon into the dirt.

The rest of the squad emerged from their hiding places at Justin's signal and vaulted into the wagon. With flickering matches held close to each face, the men checked for pulses. Instead of funeral oratory, the dead men were blessed with tears.

Miraculously, they found three survivors, seriously wounded. Retrieving them, they reluctantly left the others in the wagon to be buried in a common grave. Justin sent the driver on his way with his *merci*.

Justin and the other men used razor-sharp knives to fell small, flexible saplings. As they had after other fights, they fashioned litters by removing their tightly woven, durable cotton shirts and tying them across the saplings.

They carefully rested two smaller wounded men together on one litter, head to toe, with the larger man alone on the second litter. The four strongest men hoisted their burdens and set off through the woods at a right angle to the forest lane. A fifth man would periodically give the others relief whenever it was needed.

These country men, *des fils du pays*, knew every inch of the woods. The lane ran parallel to the main road. After a few steps into the woods, the lane was no longer in sight. It was no more than two hundred yards to the main road, and the four litter bearers with the support of the fifth could easily manage that distance through the woods.

As they emerged from the forest, dawn sunlight began to burnish the tops of the tallest trees and the highest tendrils of rising morning fog. The injured men on their litters were lowered gently to the ground and the fastest man ran to Vierville. He soon returned with a mule and cart. They concealed the men under a tarpaulin and carried them straight to the doctor's home office on the outskirts of the village.

Meanwhile, the *résistants* left outside the stockade were determined to make the Germans pay for executing the French prisoners, and they had a plan. They suspected the Germans were going to abandon the prison, and they knew they'd guessed right when a heavy vehicle ground into view. They melted back into the dense undergrowth and silently watched as the stockade swallowed a troop transport with tires as tall as a man and large enough to hold all the stockade's guards and soldiers.

In the typical German way, officers eschewed the troop transport. They had already organized more comfortable transport to lead the exodus. The Frenchmen had seen this before.

When the gate closed behind the transport, the *résistants* sprang into action, running far enough down the narrow dirt lane to be out of sight of the prison stockade.

Forming a chain, they quickly constructed a makeshift barrier of large branches and fallen tree limbs, one that extended across the lane and into the tree line so the Germans couldn't drive around the barrier.

The timing was excruciatingly close, but it worked perfectly as the gate creaked open.

A black Maybach luxury automobile emerged through the log doors. From its antenna fluttered a Nazi flag—a black swastika in a white circle on a bold red background. A heavily laden transport followed closely. Both drivers stared straight ahead as expected, not using their rear view mirrors to check the stockade. Had they done so, they would have seen a brave Frenchman with his back pressed against the heavy gate door, engaging all the power in his legs to shut it. This was to prevent a potential German retreat to safety.

As additional insurance, one of the men felled a small, fully branched sapling and muscled it across the gate, thereafter earning the nickname "Hercules."

The two German vehicles accelerated, seeming anxious to be away, but the shiny black Maybach suddenly braked as it came upon the unexpected barricade, raising a cloud of dust. Momentarily unable to see through the dust, the driver prepared to exit the vehicle to examine the barrier. Before he could, a fusillade shattered the car's windows. The driver and passenger felt the first few stings of shattered glass just before the bullets that killed them. They hadn't time to grasp their situation, and in that sense their deaths were far more merciful than those of the prisoners they'd executed.

As the *résistants'* rifles cracked, grenades thrown deep into the back of the transport detonated before they could be thrown back out. The resulting explosion was violent enough to overturn the truck. The surrounding earth shook with the onslaught, disturbing the tranquil life of the forest.

The ambush was lethal, brief and completely one-sided. The Résistance had avenged the deaths of the countrymen they'd been too late to save. The *résistants* turned for home, leaving a bullet-riddled car, its tattered Nazi flag fluttering in the breeze.

Germans bodies were left for scavengers to ravage. Civilian warriors faded into the woods, returning to their daily lives as silent and seemingly helpless villagers.

✳

Eyelids fluttering, Hattie revived, lying where she'd fallen at the top of the *auberge* stairs. She struggled to understand what happened and why she'd be lying on a wooden floor. A soft pillow cushioned her head and a warm quilt covered her body. Her boots, trousers, and underclothes had been removed and an absorbent cotton pad lay beneath her buttocks.

Beside her, Annette lay sleeping, her head also pillowed. She too was covered by a warm quilt. A pitcher of water sat within reach between them. Everything was illuminated in a shaft of early morning sunlight escaping an open door to cast light across the landing.

Hattie touched the other woman's shoulder. "Why are we on the floor?"

Receiving no answer, she groaned as she propped herself up on her bruised elbows. Pushing mussed hair from her brow, she recalled the previous day's events.

Annette opened bleary eyes, exhausted and craving more rest. She had been restless and far from comfortable during the night, but she was delighted to hear Hattie's voice. She reached over and patted Hattie's hand.

"How do you feel, *chère*?"

"All right, I think. Why are we on the floor? What happened? I feel naked."

That made Annette snort.

"You fainted right on this spot, bleeding through your clothes. I cleaned you a little, but you're too heavy for me to carry. I couldn't get you to bed."

Hattie grabbed Annette's hand. Fearing the answer, she asked, "Did I lose my baby?"

At Annette's sympathetic nod, Hattie began to sob. Annette felt the loss, too. She had relished the idea of a baby to play with and care for.

"Before I collapsed, I remember pain, but I couldn't stand. That must be when I fainted."

"I think that's right. It was very late and I thought it best to wait until morning to get the doctor. He'll be busy already, but I'll get him." Annette felt the aches of a night on the hard floor as she stood, and groaned, "I'm too old for this."

She looked down at Hattie. "Don't get up. Stay where you are until the doctor gets here. We'll help you up then." She pointed at the pitcher. "There's some water. Drink, if you feel strong enough. I'll be back soon."

Hattie whispered thanks and closed her eyes. She had known the possible consequences, but she'd had to search for Luke. Yes, she'd found the stockade, but she had no idea whether the *résistants* had conducted a search, if her husband had been found, or even if she'd given them the correct coordinates.

She'd lost Luke's baby because she fell in the ravine. Tears leaked from her eyes. The baby was the last thing she had of her husband.

Annette returned alone, in excellent spirits. Hattie lay in the same place, now curled in a fetal position on her side. She'd been crying, her nose red and swollen. Annette dropped to her knees and soothed her, rubbing Hattie's back.

"Your coordinates were perfect. Our men followed your directions right to the stockade, but they were too late to save everybody. Three men did survive and your Luke is one of them! He's badly injured, but he's alive." Hattie's face was transformed.

"My God." She breathed her thanks and ignored all her bumps and bruises and soreness, to sit up and hug Annette.

"Luke is alive and here in Vierville?" She had a hundred questions, but felt dizzy and lay back down.

"It's a miracle that three men survived! They're hidden outside the village because we won't take a chance that the Germans might find them. The doctor is still there. Their wounds are awful, so it'll be a while before the doctor is here, but his wife says he'll come as soon as he can.

"You can ask your questions then. I did find out that our men killed all the Germans at the prison. They told me it was a massacre."

"Do the Germans here know? Our villagers will suffer if they find out it was us."

"*D'accord*. It does no good to worry about that. Let's try to get you clean while we wait for the doctor. Can you stand?"

Hattie stood slowly with Annette's help, alarmed each time she felt a new injury.

Annette reminded her, "You're covered in bruises and cuts, *mon ami*, but your information saved three men. And our *résistants* were able to destroy the prison and its guards. But you paid a heavy price."

Hattie squeezed Annette's hand. "Thank you. I feel better—thanks to you. You and the others are so much more help than I ever expected. My body will heal. I'm happy to get the doctor's opinion, but there's not much to do, except rest.

For the tenth time, Hattie tugged on the wrinkles of her skirt, and pinched her cheeks. She'd been resting in Annette's *auberge* for a full week and hadn't seen her husband yet, not since the day he'd left the army base with his squad.

Luke was on his way to join her at the *auberge*. Excited and anxious, Hattie didn't know what to expect, though she knew he was in bad shape. Still, he was alive and she could dream about their future, certain that the minute he was well enough they would flee to safety and quit this war.

Sitting alone in Annette's pleasant parlor, she fidgeted, watching the play of the early morning sun through the parlor's two small blue and gold leaded windows set high on the eastern wall. She imagined Luke striding toward her, tall and strong, wearing a huge smile with his arms thrown wide for her.

She heard a commotion at the door and ran to the foyer, stopping only to allow two men to carry a litter through the door. On it, her husband's face contorted in pain.

Her heart drummed hummingbird fast. "Luke? Luke! Darling…" Her voice faded. Her husband wasn't ruddy or laughing or energetic. This Luke wasn't eager for her hugs…or more…. This Luke just lay on a stretcher, his skin sallow, his cheeks thin and sunken, round-shouldered and silent. He looked a decade older than he had a few short months earlier. Indifferent to Hattie's presence, he turned his head away, sending an arrow straight into her heart.

The doctor had debrided Luke's severe head wound and applied a liberal amount of the mercury-based orange Mercurochrome, before stitching torn flaps of skin back together. Then he and his wife had monitored Luke and the two other men in his own home for days. That had taken extreme courage.

Luke's expression was blank when he finally looked at Hattie. Mute, she returned his stare, both as awkward as strangers at first meeting. Neither spoke or reached out to the other. Their separate worlds had spun in different directions, and now Hattie wondered whether those worlds would ever spin together again.

Luke was in too much pain to wonder much of anything. Hattie shrugged off her overactive imagination and beckoned the litter bearers to follow her to Annette's kitchen.

Hattie opened the door to Annette's cellar. The men looked at each other as if to question her sanity, but she insisted they follow her down the steep steps.

She and Annette would hide Luke in the cellar, through a newly disguised door leading to a secret room. The men settled her husband on a cot. And starting right then, Hattie took on two roles, wife and physician, to direct Luke's recovery.

As hidden cellar rooms go, the one below Annette's *auberge* was a pretty special one. With typical French flair and excellent instincts, Annette had converted a small chamber that had been storing rows and rows of gleaming ruby red and pale gold bottled wines. The thick bottles rested in crisscrossed lathes built across the back wall, angled downward to keep their corks damp. A long inside wall of stacked, mortared, and whitewashed native grey and cream stone was an extension of the exterior wall of the dwelling above. It supported the polished wooden floor of Annette's *auberge* and the ceiling of the hidden room.

On another wall, more shelves held Annette's preserved fruits and canned vegetables that stood in regimented rows arranged alphabetically: *l'aubergine, la carotte, l'oignon, la tomate*. The two women and their patient would deplete the shelves by winter's end. Opposite the foods, a thin mattress, newly sheathed in cream linen, and a cased pillow lay atop a narrow cot. At the foot of the cot sat a neatly folded colorful quilt, in a pattern common to this region of France. Annette and Hattie expected enough heat would sift down through the plank floor upstairs to keep the patient comfortable under the quilt during cold nights.

After they settled Luke, Annette and Hattie dragged in a heavy hooked oval rug of carmine red, followed by a thin pallet for Hattie, who dropped a warm, dark blue blanket on it. At bedtime, she planned to roll into the blanket like a caterpillar's chrysalis, unfurling each morning like a butterfly.

The accommodations were far from the plush comfort of Hattie's bedroom in New Orleans with its four-poster bed with its ruffled lavender-dotted Swiss skirt. The spartan arrangement was even farther from Luke's upbringing. He had grown up in a mansion, wealthy beyond even Hattie's imagination, and of course surrounded by servants catering to his every need.

Hattie intended to sleep on the floor beside beside Luke's cot, but that very first night she thought better of it. Entering the normal cellar from the hidden room, she found a sharp, broad-bladed weapon similar to the machetes field hands used in the fields outside New Orleans.

Grabbing a corner of her pallet, she dragged it across to the closed door of the secret lair. If someone tried to hurt Luke, she would stop them dead in their tracks—emphasis on *dead*.

Luke and Hattie were fortunate to have Annette's support. Few others would undertake such a risk. The Krauts were always on the prowl, no longer complacent since the massacre at the prison.

Hattie nursed and doctored her husband. She changed soiled linens by lantern light, emptied his bedpan, and encouraged him to drink the sweet, fresh water that came out of the kitchen pump and to swallow Annette's delicious, restorative soups. When not occupied thus, Hattie hugged, kissed, and snuggled with Luke, gently tousling the graying hair on his healing head and taking whiffs of his soap-cleaned body.

She grieved, though, believing the Germans' increased inspections in Vierville-du-Mer were her fault. She had been afraid that the Nazis would retaliate and in that she was correct.

The Germans were infuriated by the massacre of their soldiers and guards at the stockade. They imposed a punitive curfew on the village and doubled surprise inspections, leaving invasive grit everywhere they stepped. The slightest infractions often resulted in serious injury and sometimes even death. Food became more scarce as the villagers were hard pressed to sneak away to their hidden communal farm. Before the war, French tables had groaned under cornucopias of foodstuffs; now there was little fresh milk and precious few eggs. German marauders intensified their search for hidden food stores, making concealment more difficult.

In response, *résistants* redoubled their sabotage of the invaders, and because Hattie owed them Luke's life, she fought with them.

At least one night a week, Hattie would slip away from the relative safety of the *auberge*, leaving Luke in Annette's capable hands, to join the fight. Fueled by their shared rage, she and the *résistants* interrupted communications, changed road signs, and damaged rails. All to impede the Nazi supply chain.

From a childhood of games and tree climbing, Hattie was agile and quick. She didn't hesitate to climb telephone poles to cut the lines, then fade with her cohorts into the darkness of the orchards and rolling fields.

As her strength returned, Hattie's value increased. She began leaving the *auberge* for days at a time. She never mentioned her miscarriage. Most of her companions had no idea she'd been pregnant at all.

To add to her expertise, Hattie began demolition training, starting with easy jobs. Her first job was heavy but simple: to unreel spools of large-gauge wire, connect the wire to explosives under bridges and rails, and then to the detonators that would set them off.

Along the way, the Resistance discovered that Hattie had a gift for organization, which became useful when the *résistants* captured a full Nazi warehouse. She arranged the movement of the food stores inside to a hidden warehouse, then arranged for its distribution to the villagers from whom it had been stolen. She did all this without being caught.

One morning before dawn, Hattie returned home exhausted by a night spent severing German phone and wire communications and sabotaging an electrical station. She made as little noise as she could manage, smiling at the thought of kissing Luke while he slept.

Lighting a candle and shielding it with one cupped hand, she tiptoed across the cellar into Luke's hideaway. As she shut the hidden door and approached, his eyes snapped open and he smiled.

"Darling!" she blurted, surprised and thrilled to see the smile that lit his face. Her voice quavered. Charged with emotion, her eyes filled with tears that glistened in the candle's light. Luke raised his head a few inches from the pillow when she reached his side.

"I'm so sorry I woke you, sweetheart," she said.

She set the candle holder on the floor so she could tangle her fingers in his hair. Luke's head dropped back to the pillow.

"I love you, my darling Hattie. Annette said you came to Vierville to find me, that every day you'd leave early to search for me and return very late."

His voice crackled, his syllables uneven. Those were the first words she'd heard from him in months. She flushed with happiness that he could speak, surprised to realize she'd been waiting to know his brain was intact.

She sat close to the cot, close to his warm body in the hoary chill of a winter dawn. He touched the back of her hand with his pale thumb. "And she told me the heavy price we paid for my rescue, darling. I'm so sorry."

Hattie only became aware she was crying as a tear hit her hand. Here was her Luke, back with her at last. This was the man she'd feared to lose forever.

"Luke." She sighed out his name, and it released all the tension of the past months. "I missed you so much, my husband."

They spoke quietly until well into the morning. She told him her miscarriage was only one of many adversities, many still in front of them. She lied about the significance of the loss, and she knew it wasn't a small lie. The miscarriage had come at a great personal and emotional cost, certainly physical, too. But here was Luke at last—alive—and, in time, might not another child be born of their union?

She stretched beside him, still in dusty clothes and dirty boots. Midnight skies that had earlier threatened rain now released their pent-up moisture. They snuggled close, holding hands and listening to the patter of raindrops falling on the gravel outside, talking until first Luke, then Hattie, fell sound asleep.

During the days that followed, Luke was able to sit up and hobble back and forth across the small chamber. The shelves of preserved foods gradually emptied, keeping time with the deep winter days of February.

Hattie pinched her lower lip with her teeth as she wondered how to tell Luke about Pierre Chennault's betrayal. His good friend's treachery had led to Luke's capture and his squad's execution. She would eventually have to tell him, but that could wait a while longer. For now, just act as his crutch and get him back to his cot when he was physically exhausted .

Luke's beautiful golden tan had faded long ago, but the sparkle was returning to his eyes and his ready smile had reappeared.

There were times when they heard the bell ring at Annette's front door and heard heavy boots cross the floor above them. That was their signal to maintain absolute silence, no movement, no speech, hardly breathing.

Luke asked not to be questioned about the treatment he and his fellow prisoners had endured during their captivity. Hattie could only guess his pain from the sounds he made in frequent nightmares. Hattie suffered with him during those nights; she would climb onto the narrow cot with her husband and hug him to her until the worst of his terrors subsided.

Afterward, she would try to find a comfortable arrangement of her limbs that would allow him restful sleep, searching for sleep herself and pondering how two pampered children had found their way to the middle of a vicious war. Growing up, Hattie had never given a moment's thought to the idyllic life she led in New Orleans. Embarrassed now at how little she'd appreciated her good fortune, she vowed to never be ungrateful again.

Hattie assumed as much responsibility for the household as Annette would allow. It was Hattie's way to thank her friend for her many kindnesses. And for the risk she was taking. They knew a thorough inspection would uncover Luke's presence and all three of them would be executed—shot or hung, most likely in public to cow any others contemplating resistance.

Their supply of food was growing increasingly desperate, and Hattie's latest plan had suffered a setback. Germans captured the coastal port city of Calais preventing the arrival and departure of most ships.

Now with complete control of the French coast, the Nazis began constructing beachfront bunkers. The bunkers had a twofold purpose: to defend the coast from Allied attack and as the first step of the Nazi's next initiative—to invade Great Britain. By sea, England was less than thirty miles from the western coast of France.

To compound matters for all those trying to leave, ships now refused to hazard German fortifications even at the smallest of ports, including the inconspicuous harbor of Vierville-sur-Mer. Germans allowed moorage only to fishing boats.

A whisper in Hattie's ear snapped her awake so suddenly her breath caught in her throat. *They found me,* was her immediate thought. Her eyes darted to Luke's dented pillow and empty cot. She surged to a sitting position, her heart struggling in her chest.

A fully dressed, unflustered Annette apologetically touched Hattie's shoulder.

"Sorry, *ma petite*. It's nearly time for lunch and I was worried. Will you come upstairs? Join us?"

Hattie unrolled from her warm blanket and stood shivering in the chilly air.

"Where is Luke?" She was appalled at her querulous tone, hopping on first one foot, then the other, as she tugged on wrinkled trousers.

Annette was using a long wooden spoon to absently scratch her back.

In an offhand manner that sounded suspicious, she said, "Luke made his way upstairs, *chère*—hours ago." Hattie searched her friend's smiling face, asking an unspoken question.

"Don't worry. Those *merde* Germans don't make their stupid raids until *après midi,* after the middle of the day. We're fine."

Hattie finished dressing and finger-brushed her tousled hair before bounding up the stairs, leaving Annette to follow more sedately.

She smelled the mouthwatering aroma of *osso bucco* in the kitchen, where a pale Luke sat quietly. He turned to Hattie when she walked in and returned her enthusiastic kiss. She pulled her chair close, blinking and nearly overcome that he was sitting beside her.

Annette smiled at them. Like so many of Vierville's young people, these two had the worn look of a dozen extra years.

Her cooking was even more inspired than usual, hard to achieve, and the food smelled and tasted especially delicious. Rosy-cheeked, Annette used a kitchen towel to carry a loaf of warm, freshly baked bread to the table. Red table wine, disguised in ordinary glasses, added a special celebratory air to the meal. Luke and Hattie toasted their hostess, telling her again how much they appreciated the comfortable warmth and good food Annette bestowed on them, not taking it for granted for even a moment.

But reality slowly crept in and Hattie's pleasure paled. Annette Rousseau's hospitality, and their acceptance by the cozy village of Vierville-sur-Mer, made her reluctant to leave, but she knew their presence put everyone in extreme danger. No one in the village would ever mention it, but Hattie couldn't avoid it.

She had done whatever she could to repay their hospitality—on a personal level with Annette, and for the village by using her medical skills to treat their neighbors. She'd also worked with the Resistance. But even with her help the local Resistance could only harass, not subdue the brutal Nazis.

Hattie knew Luke shared her concern. He had been the main beneficiary of everyone's protection. Not completely recovered, Hattie knew he would do what was necessary, and push his discomfort to the back of his mind. He broke into her thoughts, wrapping his cool, thin hand around her slender wrist.

"You wanted to wait until I was strong enough, Hattie, but I think we're out of time. The only way for us to protect our friends is to leave. We owe that to Annette and the villagers; it's too dangerous for them if we stay." Turning to Annette, he added, "We'll leave the minute we find a way."

Hattie nodded. Lacing her fingers with those of the man who'd found her in Paris, she welcomed the new strength she felt in his grip.

Now all they needed was another miracle to get them home to New Orleans.

Fate had a plan in store for the young DeValcourts. A few weeks later, on an early March morning just before sunrise, Annette left the *auberge*, tiptoeing into the chill outside air and softly pulling the door closed to avoid waking Luke and Hattie. Winter had begun withdrawing its frosty tentacles from across the land, but Annette's puffed exhales were plainly visible on her careful walk down the street's slick cobblestones.

Entering her friend Amelie's herb-scented kitchen, Annette stamped her shoes dry on a small mat, then greeted the chubby woman who stood with her big belly pressed against the table, already hard at work. No one could under-stand how the jolly woman remained overweight despite their restricted meals.

"*Allô, mon ami,*" Annette said. Not wasting time, she pulled a stool close to Amelie's kitchen table. Annette, in a spotless, freshly washed apron, had come to help Amelie shell harvested winter beans, to preserve them for the remaining lean months before the new summer crops matured.

"*Bonjour,* Annette." Amelie smiled. She then issued a cryptic comment. "You are here right now, but how long will you stay?"

Annette frowned, with no idea what her friend meant. "*Eh?*"

Excited to share news with the woman who had been her closest friend since they'd played together as babies, Amelie wiggled her eyebrows. Among the villagers, it was an open secret that Annette was sheltering two Americans, one of whom had escaped from a Nazi prison with serious injuries.

"Guess what, *chère?*" She didn't wait for Annette to venture a guess, and added, "Today there is an English scow sitting just offshore, wallowing very near Vierville-sur-Mer. It's hard to see because it's the same dark color as the sea. It's come to take refugees across the Channel to England. The crew is brave, *n'est ce pas,* to challenge the German cannons."

Annette's mouth rounded, her eyes widened, and her heart nearly stopped. She bounced back to her feet, the stool clattering to the floor behind her.

"This is true?" she demanded. When Amelie nodded, Annette spun distract-edly, the huge apron ballooning around her body, her hands pressed to her cheeks.

"You know what this means, Amelie?" Amused by her friend's gyrations, Amelie smiled.

"I'm sorry, I have to go home." Annette paused. "I think you had something to do with this. Thank you so much, Amelie. So much…"

Still apologizing and thanking Amelie, she ran out the door for home, the dawn mist swirling at her ankles. In her kitchen, Amelie continued to nod and smile, even as she looked at the mountain of unshelled beans she was left to conquer on her own.

It wasn't every day, these days, that she could make someone so happy.

Annette burst into Luke's shadowy cellar room without notice, but at least she carried a breakfast tray. Standing inside the doorway, her vague silhouette unsettled the startled couple, unceremoniously jerked from rumpled slumber.

"Wake up, *mes amis!*"

Had they been fully awake, they might have noticed that Annette's cheerful words held an undercurrent of loss—a furrowed brow and a mouth already downturned in sorrow. She blew at the strands of hair that had escaped her usually perfect *chignon*. Her face was flushed, not because of the heavy tray of ersatz coffee and thin-sliced cheese bread.

Luke looked down at Hattie, who already sat up on her pallet on the floor. Something had to have happened.

"Finally, *mes amis*, your chance *est arrivée*," Annette crowed. "A boat lies waiting offshore, but there's no time to waste. You must leave *right now*."

"Luke, *c'est vrai*, you're still recovering, but *mes chers*, you're both well enough. I hate to say it. For me, it's better if you go. Every day you stay, it's more dangerous."

Her voice trembled. Safer, yes; happier, no. These two people were her family now, and Annette would be returning to a lonely life once Hattie and Luke were gone.

"You're right, Annette, of course. We know." Luke spoke slowly, hesitantly, but his words were resolute. Hattie nodded. She agreed and reached to tear off a piece of bread, ignoring the "coffee" on the tray Annette had set on Luke's cot.

Hattie hugged Annette to her. "There's no question—we have to leave. You've been wonderful to us, Annette, and we want you to be safe."

Luke brought up a subject that he and Hattie had discussed. "Come with us, Annette. You'd have a good life in America. Where we're from, nearly everyone speaks French. You wouldn't have to learn a new language."

Hattie and Annette had become as close as sisters, sharing a bond made stronger by the hardships of war. Would separating jeopardize their friendship? The vast Atlantic Ocean would be between them and another thousand miles of *Les États Unis*.

"*Non*. I could never leave France. It is my home." Doing her best to not show her emotions, Annette turned away, her eyelashes batting tears from her eyes.

Abruptly she commanded them, "Take only what you can carry. Claude and I will ship your trunk after the war."

Hattie scrambled to pack two rucksacks, fighting against the feeling that her feet had grown roots in the French soil. A heavy mourning lay deep inside her, one she wasn't sure would ever go away.

Annette didn't want to go to the beach with them. It wasn't safe, she said. But mainly it was because she couldn't bear the wrench of their departure. And so they parted there in her doorway, hugging and clinging together. Annette watched Luke stagger from the warmth of her home on his weak legs, supported by Hattie's arm. She was still standing there when they turned to look back.

Luke and Hattie could hear the susurrations of the restless sea as they came upon early morning waves swarming a rocky beach. The sea snarled, wild in a strong, gusting wind. They stumbled over rocks in the murk of an early dawn, their rucksacks heavy on their backs, as they navigated to the small, wooden rowboat on the shoreline.

Nearer to the water, wet sand sucked and held tight to the soles of their shoes. The awkward rendezvous spot had been chosen because it wasn't visible from the harbor or the Nazi battlements. They faltered and tripped over stones as rain began to fall, obscuring a clear path to the boat. As they neared the water's edge, the crashing of waves on the beach grew louder, incoming waves seeming to fight for purchase against the swirling outflow. The violence of the sea was completely at odds with the placid Gulf swells Hattie remembered from the summers of her childhood.

Wind and morning warmth began to rip the maritime fog into wisps, the fog replaced now by rain that hid everything more than a few feet away. Seabirds flew from their presence with raucous cries.

Hattie stumbled to a stop as they came upon a small boat wallowing in the surf. *No!* She lost her nerve midstride and turned, intending to retrace her steps.

Who would trust themselves to a boat no larger than a low skiff in this wild sea? The boat was bobbing crazily in the thundering surf, at times disappearing in the rain then reappearing, always seeming on the edge of foundering in the waves.

The helmsman struggled to keep the vessel from skittering back to deeper water. He was more suspicious than the boat. This man was supposed to save them? He looked more like Popeye from the cartoons back home—a squat, scrawny, elderly sailor with an ancient pipe protruding from his toothless mouth.

An exhausted Luke wiped chilly raindrops from his eyes and tugged at Hattie's hand.

"Come on," he urged. "Don't be scared. Look out there—in the deeper water. This skiff isn't going to take us across the Channel, just to that bigger boat. That big one can't get any closer to the beach."

He put his hand on her shoulder, and Hattie leaned into his touch, glad to let Luke take charge. The warmth of his hand overcame her fear. What did she need to do anyway, but just get in the skiff and join the other couple already in it. She could do this.

Hattie found herself sitting on an unforgiving wooden seat, getting doused by rain and ocean spray. She lifted her eyes to cast a lingering, wistful glance at the village that had been her refuge, her only regret that it hadn't been during peacetime.

She said a silent goodbye to the tiny hamlet of Vierville-sur-Mer that had welcomed her with open hospitality and helped her rescue Luke. To all those brave and generous men and women.

From this vantage Vierville-sur-Mer lay as tranquil as a storybook village. But hidden behind those pristine starched lace curtains, she knew, were townspeople hiding their fears under their laughter.

The thatched roofs of the stone cottages looked otherworldly, burnished as they were by the gentle rain in the striated colors of dawn. The village appeared pristine, as if untouched by the vicious German invasion. But Hattie knew about the wounds, the deaths and slow starvation the people suffered. She wondered if she'd forget the bad times eventually and only remember the good.

Vierville's three streets rising inland from the rock-strewn shore receded more with each pull of the oars. Everyone in the little skiff prayed Nazi gunners in the battlement wouldn't notice them in the rain.

Hattie turned to Luke to voice her conflicting emotions, but was alarmed by his pale appearance. As raindrops skidded from the tip of his handsome nose, Hattie felt for and found an uneven pulse on his cold neck.

Hoisting her heavy rucksack, she rummaged in it, pushing aside other contents to find the remedy for Luke's nausea. Her fingertips found a carefully wrapped cylinder of thinly sliced fried potatoes, and she pulled it from her bag. Removing a few of the medallions, she tucked away the rest. Salt had disappeared from Vierville-sur-Mer's tables ages ago, except for the little recovered from evaporated seawater. Packaged salt and spices had all been appropriated by the Germans.

Annette had taught herself how to work miracles with very little seasoning. These potatoes were no exception. Hattie put two insubstantial wafers into Luke's hand. He refused them with a grimace, but she persisted, "I know it seems backward, my darling, but these *will* help your nausea."

She kissed his damp forehead and cozied in close to him. "We'll be at the bigger boat soon. Don't let this little rowboat make you sick."

In a flight of her always active imagination, the squat trawler that waited for them became a glorious Spanish galleon, its sails waiting to unfurl and catch offshore breezes. The galleon was a stallion, dancing, impatient to get away. She laughed, her eyes crinkling with amusement at her fancy.

What bobbed about in the deep water waiting for them was far from a Spanish galleon. It wasn't what anyone would consider large—no, more like a shrimp boat from back home.

The trawler neared with each pull of the oars. But less than a furlong from their destination, they heard shouts from the shore, yelling loud enough to be heard over the wind and waves. Hattie watched as a German officer in full uniform down to his tall polished boots pointed a stiff finger at their skiff. Two soldiers with him were pulling a mobile howitzer down onto the beach.

Wide-eyed, she watched as the soldiers furiously cranked the howitzer to adjust its trajectory until a projectile could skim over the waves and blow their little boat to smithereens.

The oarsman redoubled his efforts, his face an alarming shade of red. The trawler fired up its engine and a plume of dark smoke soared up, wavering in the misty air. The boat was pointed into waves that moved diagonally toward the beach.

Hattie and the other passengers were helpless on the skiff, afraid the trawler would abandon them to the open sea. The soldiers stopped cranking and lifted a heavy projectile requiring the strength of both men. The officer, of course, provided no help. The soldiers pushed the projectile down the weapon's muzzle, tamping it further down with a long, thick, padded stick. They then stepped aside and covered their ears. The skiff's occupants closed their eyes and prayed.

A thunderous explosion echoed across the waves. The shell hit short of the skiff, producing a huge spray of water on their small vessel before it passed harmlessly beneath them. The passengers were completely helpless as they awaited the inevitable adjustment of the Nazi gun. The oarsman's rhythm didn't change, and his passengers had been drenched by the spray. How many shells, Hattie wondered, already lay at the bottom of the sea? It was only because the gunners had to physically alter the gun's trajectory between firings that her story wouldn't meet its end in the waters of the English Channel.

Their stalwart oarsman pulled closer to the trawler. The gunner's aim was in front this time, but as the heavy shell glanced past their prow it caught the front edge of the wooden hull, just above the water line. Thick splinters flew and thin spurts fountained from the bottom of the weakened skiff. A pool of seawater began to spread in the flat hull.

Hattie leveled a glance at Luke. He would be no help to anyone; he'd lapsed into semiconsciousness with his lips blue. She had no time to check him more closely. The other male passenger appeared nearly as catatonic, his mouth hanging open. The other woman remained motionless. The oarsman grunted loudly to catch Hattie's attention, jerking his head to the bucket beside his feet.

She ducked under his oar and grabbed the pail. Turning to the growing puddle, she scooped seawater and threw it into the sea. It was a difficult chore and she tired rapidly, but she gritted her teeth and refused to quit.

On shore, the Germans celebrated the damage to the skiff, sure it would sink. They were reluctant to waste another shell, unaware a trawler lurked behind foggy wisps.

Hattie lurched when the skiff butted against the trawler. She read the trawler's name, *Le Bateau*, painted in an unsteady scrawl. Looking behind her at Luke, she saw him now lying on the seat with his eyes closed.

Their heroic oarsman exhibited unexpected strength in his scrawny body. His sinewy muscles maneuvered the slowly sinking skiff alongside the larger vessel. Bellowing, "We're sinking," he dropped his oars and threw a heavy line into the hands of a waiting crewman, who snugged the two bobbing boats close together by wrapping the line around a cleat.

Hattie raised her voice, "Luke! Luke!" He roused and half stood, painfully unsteady. The other couple was being helped up onto the larger vessel; she continued bailing. "Hurry, Luke, climb aboard!"

"I can't leave you, Hattie," he protested, but she screamed at him, "Just *do* it! The sooner you get aboard, the sooner I can stop bailing. Hurry."

As Luke was helped up onto the trawler, she dropped her pail and sloshed over to the strong arms of the oarsman, who handed her up to the waiting crew. The oarsman hauled himself up effortlessly, climbing the heavy mooring line hand over hand. Then using the heavy knife at his waist, he sawed through the rope and sent the skiff to its berth at the bottom of the sea.

Exhausted and shivering, Hattie settled Luke in a sheltered spot on the deck. Seawater dripped from her short hair down her neck and back.

Hattie felt herself suddenly trembling, and her eyes widened with alarm. She looked to Luke for comfort, then realized the sensation came from outside her body. The ship's engine had pulsed into a higher gear, burbling and coughing below the deck. A dark, acrid plume of smoke belched skyward from a midship smokestack. The trawler was underway. The howitzer team on shore spotted the trawler and launched one last shell that fell harmlessly beside them. It created a final spectacular *au revoir* splash on the starboard side.

Around Hattie, refugees slid across the inclined deck as the trawler came about to head for the open sea. A few unfortunates lost their balance and collided with crude bench seats that had been hastily nailed to the deck. The fog had dissipated and they were now easily visible to the battlement through the rain. The boat seemed to turn forever before it regained a level keel and steamed through rolling swells to the safety of deep Channel waters.

She wrung as much water as she could from her trousers before approaching their oarsman to offer her thanks. Grabbing his hand, she noticed wrinkles from years of immersion in seawater. She complimented his piloting skill and strength.

"You are my hero, *m'sieur. Merci mille fois* for helping us escape."

"*De rien, madame.*" He relaxed into the smoke of his pipe. "If I can't fight in the war, at least I can help people to safety."

"Now that your skiff is at the bottom of the sea, *m'sieur*, what will you do? Will you stay in England?"

He snorted, amused. "*Non.* I'll go back to France and help more refugees, *si le Dieu veut.*"

"But your skiff, *m'sieur*. Can you find another one?"

"The Limeys have plenty of boats. They'll put one on this trawler with me and a couple of oars. The trawler will drop me into the surf again, and I'll row to Vierville."

"You're brave, *m'sieur*, very brave. Thank you again for saving our lives."

He let a small smile leak around the pipe clamped between his teeth. He shrugged, saying, "You helped, too, *madame*." He nodded and walked away, as bedraggled as Hattie. Watching him go, Hattie realized she didn't know the man's name. Help, it seemed, was offered and accepted in this war without much fuss.

Luke was out of the wind near the bow, and his clothes were beginning to dry. Hattie took a good look at their fellow passengers. Hattie and Luke were the last to board this dilapidated scow, unceremoniously plopped alongside other cold, frightened refugees. How long had the other passengers had to cower in the cold rain, waiting for Hattie and Luke? A few resentful glances said they hadn't appreciated the wait, but most simply huddled in the cold.

Gulls squawked and circled above the trawler, providing an avian guard on snow-white wings. Occasionally a brave gull swooped to the bobbing deck in search of food, waddling among the huddled passengers. Hattie watched the birds, fascinated, while Luke lapsed back to semiconsciousness, shivering when cold sea spray dampened his clothes.

The sun continued its placid rise into day, the beautiful clear blue sky brightening. Hattie scanned for German planes, afraid they would be discovered, though there were enough low clouds to provide cover for one speck of a small boat that chugged through the waves. In France, she'd heard attacks on small boats were commonplace, as much for target practice as anything.

Their clothes finally dried, stiff with salt. The sun had passed its zenith and now shone directly in their eyes as they searched for a glimpse of land. At last, a dark edge appeared in the distance, and the rough waters of the Channel smoothed to low, undulating waves. The passengers chattered excitedly as their boat rocked on toward the growing land mass.

Less than an hour later, their skipper maneuvered a graceful sideways slide into a wharf that sat unmoving among gray swells. The trawler's rough diesel growl stopped abruptly, leaving only a noisy bilge pump to continue its struggle against a small leak in the hull. The passengers' ears were stunned by relative silence.

Behind them, France had disappeared. Out of sight, and the trawler's passengers hoped, soon out of mind. As they disembarked, the passengers shouted out their gratitude to the captain and his crew. They'd arrived at a secret anchorage under massive camouflage nets somewhere in the south of England. In first tentative steps, quivering legs fought to gain land balance. The refugees gazed at this new country.

But Luke and Hattie's goal lay across a vast, treacherous Atlantic Ocean. They were uncertain how to go about seeking passage home. And more immediately, where to stay. They owned only the clothes they wore. Their soggy French *francs* were worthless. Their few cherished belongings lay inaccessible in a trunk, under straw, in a barn miles away across the Channel.

Noisy crowds milled around the uncertain couple. An occasional man approached. The questions they were asked were often in languages they didn't understand. The couple soon grasped that the men represented different nations, and their job was to locate refugees from their home countries.

It wasn't long before the flat intonation of American Yankee English caught their attention. They turned to a young man with business card extended.

"Excuse me, folks? Pardon me, but are you citizens of the United States?" Surprised by his accent, Hattie gave a little yelp. Tears filled her eyes, but she held onto Luke's arm to keep him steady.

"*Oui!* I mean, yes. We're Americans. Can you help us?" The unfamiliar "Americans" caressed its way off Hattie's tongue, so that she nearly burst into tears.

"I'm Charlie Green, ma'am. I'm from the US Consulate, here in our British office. He took note of the woman's tremulous smile and imagined how lovely she must be when rested and well fed. It was the emaciated, unsteady man who clung to her arm that was a greater concern, but first things first.

"Do you have identification, ma'am?" It became obvious to Charlie that his question created some sort of agitation for the couple.

"No, Mr. Green. We burned our passports so the Nazis wouldn't know we're Americans. Can you possibly still help us? Our name is DeValcourt. We're both physicians. Luke's degree is from North Carolina and mine is from the Sorbonne in Paris. We're both from New Orleans."

"Wonderful." Charlie's wide smile creased his young freckled face, open and unaffected.

Luke and Hattie stood close together, protecting each other and basking in the unusually pleasant autumn afternoon. The sparkling waves of the English Channel refracted sunlight onto their faces, like casting freedom's jewels all around. Charlie began asking more thorough questions in his gentle way, and the crowd around them began to thin. By the time Charlie came to the end of his questions, he had their complete trust and the trio felt like old friends.

Hattie felt her French persona ebbing away until she experienced a curious sensation, almost like a rebirth, now again as thoroughly American as she'd ever been. Standing on an English pier without a plan or even a conscious thought, she and Luke, it seemed, had shed war-torn France for a safe future, thanks to the young man with them.

Charlie pumped their hands with vigorous handshakes, saying, "I'm happy you've made it this far. My assignment is to provide passage to the States for American refugees. It won't be long before I find a cabin for you."

Hattie doubted Charlie's task would be that simple, remembering her earlier attempts to do just that back in Paris.

"Are you sure you can find us passage?" It worried Hattie that they might be marooned in England indefinitely without proof of their identities. Would the British return them to France? She sniffed back her sudden fright. Her body itched with fatigue, her muscles aching from bailing seawater from the sinking skiff. She rubbed her eyes, caked with what could only be thought of as gunk. She needed a bath to melt away the dried salt on her skin. And then to put on clean clothes, though they only had what they wore.

Charlie's eyes and clean white teeth gleamed again. "I'll have to get it organized, but the short answer is yes," his words in an American accent like salvation to her ears, "I guarantee it."

Looking down at a clipboard, he continued, "In the meantime, let's get you to Southampton. A comfortable hotel room is waiting for you. That will be your home until it's time to board a ship for the U.S."

Relieved by Charlie's breezy confidence, Hattie and Luke straightened their spines and managed to return his smile. *Finally*, Hattie thought, *we're one step closer to home and safety.*

Before Hattie and Luke had fully recovered from the shock of their Channel crossing, they were aboard the *SS Seabreeze* heading for home.

Hattie pulled off her hat and tossed it on a narrow berth, one of two in their cabin. That hat and the simple dark dress she wore, plus a warm coat, had been purchased for her by the US consulate.

Hattie beamed and squeezed Luke around the waist, gently pushing him onto the other berth. He wore a new black flannel jacket, a blue, thin-striped, long-sleeved shirt, and dark flannel slacks that had also been provided by the consulate.

"Hard to believe, isn't it, that they found us a ship so quickly, darling? Especially one that steams right to New Orleans. We won't have a long, tiresome train ride home from New York. It's a good sign, don't you think?"

Not waiting for Luke's answer, she twirled around the tiny cramped cabin. It was much smaller than the suites her DuMond family had occupied on previous Atlantic passages, but the size of their quarters didn't matter—Hattie could easily ignore any discomfort, by now well used to uncomfortable situations. What was important was that they would soon be home.

Caressing Luke's shaggy head as he lay there exhausted, she leaned down for a grazing kiss. She was out of breath, too. It had been quite a climb up the long gangway, followed by two flights down a steep set of stairs to their cabin.

His mouth twitched at his wife's excitement, and he reached up for her. The wattage of Luke's smile prompted Hattie to bat her lashes. Despite his pale complexion, a *frisson* leapt between them that signaled the return of Luke's physical interest, but she would have to carefully monitor his activity.

Hattie's carefree days were gone, a casualty of war and growing responsibilities. Would she still wish all those youthful wishes, knowing everything they'd led to? She brushed away the thought. It was a *fait accompli*, and she'd rather look to the future than the past.

Luke's complexion might be as white as the pillow his head lay on, but he was still the most handsome, attractive man she'd ever known. He pulled her down to lie beside him.

"You are my heroine, glorious woman. You never gave up on me," he said. "And you are my beloved wife." He tangled his fingers in a wavy hank of her short, shiny, chestnut hair. Its silkiness slipped between his fingers. He murmured his plans softly in her ear, making her giggle and shiver with anticipation.

"And today is our anniversary," he added. "Did you know that? You made me the happiest man in the world eight months ago today. It's been a wild ride, hasn't it?"

"Really? Only our eight-month anniversary? How did we fit everything in?" Hattie pecked his rough, stubbled cheek. "You're a romantic man, husband."

Holding a finger to her cheek in mock thought, she pursed her lips. "It's more like eight years than eight months. Wait—that's not what I mean. That didn't come out right." Hattie's tinkling laughter was a delightful treat for Luke, a sweet sound he'd not heard for a while. Until now, laughter had been tamped down by the horror of war.

"What surprises me most," Hattie said, nuzzling his neck, "is how much more deeply I love you now than I did on our wedding day. Maybe that's because of the things we've gone through. My love makes it hard to regret some of what happened, now that we're well away from France.

"I feel sixteen years old in my mind today—isn't that funny? That's the same age I was the night of our very first dance." She scattered tiny kisses all over his face.

"We'll be home soon," Hattie added, "to fuss about hot weather and pesky mosquitoes. Won't that be wonderful?"

She burrowed under the warm shoulder that cradled her. Karl Schmitzer, the fiancé she had loved intensely for so long, had disappeared from her thoughts months ago and was only an occasional sweet memory. When she thought of Karl, it was with relief that she had released him from their engagement and returned his ring *before* she and Luke rediscovered each other.

Happy to be with her husband after the trauma they'd endured, Hattie felt a bittersweet melancholy when she looked at her husband, one she kept well hidden. With her medical background, it was becoming progressively more obvious that Luke needed expert medical help urgently. In a good neurosurgeon's hands, Luke's health might be fully restored.

As a general physician, Hattie could see evidence of severe brain damage, but he would require specialist intervention to avoid additional deterioration. The sooner that could happen, the better.

Her waking thoughts, and many of her dreams, were consumed by that urgency as the *Seabreeze* steamed across the Atlantic.

Hattie prayed Luke would survive.

In typical understatement, Hattie would later describe their voyage on the Seabreeze as "difficult."

In the mid-twentieth century, meteorology was a young science with relatively poor predictive tools, though the war had forced governments to push for better systems. Few people understood fully how or why weather changed from dry, still, and warm one day to wet, windy, and cold the next.

A lone ship carrying American refugees home held little meteorological interest… except to the passengers on board the *Seabreeze*.

Hattie and Luke were invited to sit at the captain's table on their second night at sea. Luke declined the invitation, electing to dine on trout amandine delivered from the ship's kitchen to their cabin, but Hattie accepted. Before she left for the spacious dining room, fresh and clean after an addictive long, hot shower, she gave her husband an appreciative kiss.

She wore an inexpensive, gauzy, black full-length gown, cut on the bias to hug her curves and swirl about her ankles. Hattie rushed upstairs, looking very like a luscious tomboy as she took the steps two at a time when no one was around. In a dress that showcased her toned, exceptional figure, she was escorted by the major domo to the captain's table, many admiring glances following her progress across the dining salon. It was the only other dress in their cabin's closet, both having been provided by the US consulate in Northampton.

"Thank you," said Hattie, smiling as the ship's captain pulled out the chair next to his for her.

"So sorry to keep you waiting." Her eyes and lovely smile included everyone at the table.

"Nonsense," he replied. Hattie was surprised to see the elegance of his table. There was a centerpiece of fresh red roses and white daisies and the snowy white tablecloth was set with crystal wine goblets and heavy silver-plate cutlery. The three couples already seated introduced themselves.

One couple, the Sliviks, were second-generation US citizens who had been trapped in Poland, there for a family funeral at exactly the wrong time. They had barely escaped being swept up by Hitler's army, escaping with little more than the clothing they carried in two small suitcases. The two other couples, the Andersons and the Fosters, worked for the US diplomatic corps. The two diplomatic couples, relieved to have been recalled stateside, congratulated the others on leaving Europe "unscathed."

Hattie looked around the salon. The walls were scuffed, the carpet threadbare, but it was filled to capacity, though subdued.

She recalled many happy shipboard evenings with Maman, Papa, and her brother in similar, but more polished, dining rooms. Her neck and arms prickled as she anticipated how wonderful it would be to hug them after so many years abroad. Jack, in particular, would have changed a great deal. He was a married man now. She could hardly wait to tell them that she had married Luke.

She noticed several differences in this particular cruise from her earlier voyages. No stringed trio played music during dinner. There was little evidence of extravagant jewelry, such as pearls or flashing diamonds. The mood and clothing of the passengers were far more somber, and the conversational static in the air, while still there, was undeniably restrained.

At her elbow, a steward laid a menu written in graceful calligraphy beside her salad fork. In her experience, beautifully unique menus would be provided each night of the voyage. Perusing her choices, Hattie's eyes lit up, thrilled that steak was on the menu. What a treat! Her mouth watered as she set the menu aside. Steak!

When the entree was set in front of her, she inhaled its wonderful aroma. This was the first sizzling steak she had seen in years—in fact, since she'd left for the Sorbonne in 1936. She moaned a happy little hum that made her fellow diners chuckle as she took the first bite of a perfectly broiled *petit filet de boeuf,* crowned with scattered bits of Roquefort cheese.

Hattie held her fork poised for another bite of succulent beef just as the *Seabreeze* lurched into a deep trough and was slapped by a fist of hurricane-strength wind. Howling winds began to slow the ship's forward movement. Her massive propellers could barely hold to their course as the *Seabreeze* pitched and rolled. Westward progress toward North American shores slowed to a crawl.

With the first tumultuous pitching, the more poorly seasoned passengers at Hattie's table excused themselves in distress, until only she and the captain remained.

She finished the steak, but lost her appetite for dessert. The captain's face was taking on an unbecoming shade of green and he showed relief when he bowed over her hand and wished her good night.

It was unusually early in the year for a hurricane. Nevertheless, the surprising storm was traveling unimpeded across the ocean, hitting the *Seabreeze* at the midpoint of her passage. Deep blue water transformed to craggy gray peaks that seemed as tall as mountains. Their ship was turned bow on to the gigantic waves, creaking, heaving, struggling, tossed about like a child's toy boat in a bathtub.

The *Seabreeze* was struggling. There was a real danger that the ship might break apart.

The storm had descended so rapidly that there'd been no time to stow deck furniture. Chairs and umbrellas were pushed, lifted, and blown over the side.

Swirling winds danced around the ship, keeping it company. Ferocious lightning and thunder were constant. The storm seemed endless.

The passengers and most of the crew, including a green-gilled captain, were finding it impossible to keep down food and water. A skeleton crew of hardy stewards stayed on their feet for double and even triple shifts, delivering soups and water to the cabins, helping seasick passengers and crew avoid dehydration.

During the second full day of the storm's banshee howls, the captain instructed his stewards to use their master keys when their knocks went unanswered so the ship's doctor, queasy himself, could attend those not responding.

Able galley hands forgot about elaborate meals. Nourishing soups and bland foods were substituted that had extra salt added to replace lost electrolytes. Countless servings of gelatin, clear soup, and aspic replaced the usual meats and seafood. The kitchen followed that routine for the five full days it took the ship to ride out the storm.

Luke was among the sickest of the passengers. He was unable to leave his berth without Hattie's help. She eventually succumbed to seasickness herself, but managed to keep Luke hydrated and his bedpan emptied, reminding her of these same things she'd done in Vierville-sur-Mer for her husband. She knew the ship's doctor could use her help, but taking care of Luke left her with nowhere close to enough energy to assist him.

Progress through the storm was agonizingly slow, yet by the evening of the fifth day the *SS Seabreeze* was finally able to veer out of the storm, leaving it to follow its mindless track.

Passengers began to stagger out of dank, stuffy cabins on weak legs. They discovered decks cleared of *chaise longues* and umbrellas, leaving only seating that was nailed down. Refreshed by softer ocean breezes, they were able to enjoy the flawless beauty of a starry, cloudless, navy blue velvet night. Stars reflected as pinpoints in the gentle, mindless swells of a tranquil sea.

On the sixth day, the *Seabreeze* rounded the tip of the Florida keys and turned north, its grateful passengers—and exhausted crew—finally entering the Gulf of Mexico.

It was the last leg of the voyage and they were all a bit the worse for wear.

✳

Hattie woke early. She had been pinned to the mattress for days with nausea and dehydration when not stumbling about helping Luke.

Her mouth had a terrible taste. Her breath smelled like a sewer. She hadn't brushed her teeth in days. Tentative fingers pushed lank, oily hair behind her ears. Her grossness made her shudder, but her nausea was gone. She rolled to the side to tell Luke she felt better, but he was sound asleep on his narrow berth.

Taking a moment, she scrutinized his handsome face in repose. The past months had chiseled away his remaining youth, leaving a man so gorgeous he would turn heads. Faded tan skin from his days under the sun in the Nazi prison lay taut across his classic nose. Dark curls, slightly too long, flopped over his forehead in a way that her fingers itched to touch.

Hattie's mouth curved softly. She celebrated her good fortune in having this intelligent, wonderful man by her side, recalling the months of worrying that perhaps she'd hugged and kissed him for the last time, of not knowing where he was or if he was still alive.

She and Luke were simply one incredible story of human perseverance. The other *Seabreeze* passengers had their own miracle stories. An entire boatload of war-traumatized people was steaming home.

The tragedy of the many millions of people left behind in Europe sobered Hattie. The world outside her foul-smelling cabin would never appreciate, could never appreciate, the extraordinary efforts it had taken from so many people for her and Luke to be there. So many heroic lives.

Hattie was grateful her dizziness and vertigo had disappeared. Pushing back her covers, she crawled out of bed and experimented with the steadiness of her footing. The reassuring thrust of the ship's pistons thrummed deep and steady in the hull below her.

The *SS Seabreeze* rode higher in the quieter waters of the Gulf as the ship burned fuel and her passengers emptied more of the larder. Hattie's good health reasserted itself. She was almost home.

In their cabin's minuscule bathroom, she scrubbed away weakness with a restorative shower. She shampooed hair that had grown almost to the curve of her jaw and stepped back into the cabin wrapped in a towel with her skin and hair gleaming. The Atlantic crossing had cost her at least three pounds. That was on top of weight that had melted away in France from her work with the Resistance and her miscarriage.

Feeling rejuvenated, Hattie opened their porthole so the sea breeze could scrub staleness out of the cabin air. Her towel dropped to the floor, revealing a slender Venus who enjoyed her nudity and was reluctant to cover herself. She looked over at Luke, trying to will him awake to see her standing there at the foot of his berth, ready to be gathered into his arms.

Knowing her desire was futile, she sighed and pulled on the dress she'd worn the day they boarded the *Seabreeze*. Metal hangers on a bare rod clanked discordantly, begging to be used. Hattie, claustrophobic in the confined space, hurriedly dressed, tugging at the plain white slip under her wrinkled dress.

Both garments had been bought in Southampton, out of a store soon to be demolished by a German bombing onslaught.

A hint of salt-laden ocean air poked through the open porthole and cleared the cobwebs from Hattie's brain. Encouraged, she left the cabin and circled the upper deck in the warm sunshine, mingling with other hardy passengers. Beneath their feet, the ship engines changed their growling pitch. The *Seabreeze* slowed to advance to the mouth of the treacherous Mississippi River. The ship idled, waiting for tugboats to guide it up the main channel of the river.

The mighty river's tons of outflow had slowed their ship's lengthy approach to New Orleans. Hattie was impatient. She'd been desperate to get home for months, and attempted to contain her excitement by observing the dark green palmetto fans and the raucous wildlife along the shore. A glossy mink family caught her eye as they bobbed in the ship's undulating wake snatching up the edibles brought to the surface by the turbulence.

A red-tailed hawk skimmed the cloudless cobalt sky, waiting for a mink morsel to separate from its family long enough to become her next meal. Her nest was empty, her fledglings flown. There were no babies to feed. Her own hunger spurred her pursuit.

Balanced on both forearms, Hattie inhaled the scent of greenish-brown river water. A short month ago, she'd thought she might never again breathe that muddy smell of decay. She lifted her head to the light breeze. It tousled hair dry enough for sunlight to reflect its auburn highlights. Her skirt swirled in the constant breeze and she gathered it modestly against her bare legs.

Euphoric to be near home, she grinned at any passenger who had recovered enough to join her out in the bright sunshine. Struck by a thought, she looked for a ship's officer.

As it happened, the duty officer stood fewer than thirty feet away, looking in her direction. His thoughts seemed far away, his eyes unfocused and he jumped, shocked when Hattie strode up to him. He blushed and stammered before he regained his poise.

"G…good morning, ma'am."

"Indeed," she replied, a lilt in her voice. "May I ask a question?"

Hattie had lived in France, and had spoken the language for so long—all the years of medical school—that her English carried a charming accent. The young officer slipped easily into French, as did Hattie.

"*Certainement, madame.*"

"Will you… the ship… provide a wheelchair to take my husband ashore after we dock? He has wounds from the war."

"*Alors!* A wounded warrior?" The officer was astonished and smacked his broad forehead with the palm of his hand hard enough to knock his billed hat back on his head, which gained him the treat of a lovely smile.

"Why we didn't know this, *madame*? A wheelchair is not a problem, of course. Just your husband's name and cabin number, please. He *is* your husband, is he not?"

Slightly offended, Hattie blushed and narrowed her eyes.

"Of course he is. My husband's name is Luke DeValcourt, and he was badly injured. If I gave the wrong impression, I apologize." She remained determinedly cordial, not the least bit sorry. "Weren't you the duty officer on the bridge last night who helped me send my parents a message?"

The officer eyed the alert, vivacious woman. She looked nothing like the haggard, lank-haired woman on the bridge from the night before, but he remembered his manners.

"That was you, *madame*? How could I forget that pretty face? It's stupid of me and I apologize for my thoughtlessness. You have caught me at the perfect time. Walk with me. We must get your husband up on deck before the other passengers clog the corridors."

With Luke strapped in for safety, two stewards rolled him through the corridors in a wheelchair. The men's strong arms worked in practiced concert and hoisted him effortlessly up the narrow stairways backwards in the chair, one man pulling, the other man pushing.

Weak as he was, the ride still delighted a laughing Luke. Hattie ran to keep up with the jogging stewards. By the time they spun Luke to a halt before his tickled wife, pleasure had transformed him. His eyes sparkled and were completely alert.

She rewarded the men with the last bit of their hoarded money. Luke's happiness delighted Hattie, and she wished she had more money to give them. His laughter was a treat; her poor husband had had so little to laugh about.

She squeezed his shoulder and admitted, "I'm nervous, Luke. We're home—well, almost. It's exciting, but scary to tell our families our news."

Anticipation fizzed in Hattie's core until it was impossible to stay still. She combed Luke's tousled hair with her fingertips until it lay in docile waves. He laced his fingers with hers and pulled her down for a kiss. His free hand stroked the faint freckles across Hattie's nose from her walk on deck.

"My Hattie—my heroine." His baritone crackled with strong emotion. "First, you saved my life. And now you've brought us back home."

Home. Neither could remember a childhood without the other being part of it.

Hattie mused of a future when she'd think back to France and the war, her wedding, her days in Vierville-sur-Mer, the nightmare hurricane on board the *SS Seabreeze*. She'd marvel that so many important events took place in so few months. She'd recall how thrilled they'd been to finally be safe in America, how they'd paused before leaving the ship to speak together of Annette Rousseau's friendship and hospitality and of the vital assistance of the French Resistance. And how, without that help, Luke would surely have died. And, Hattie thought, she might have died right along with him of a broken heart.

Hattie's message reached New Orleans and was then conveyed by telephone to both families. No one of either family slept much that night, and the next day excitement grew until it was time to meet the ship.

Their parents assembled on the wharf, watching while the tugs moved the big ship to its anchorage, and waiting for Hattie and Luke to disembark. Both mothers dabbed at their eyes, hankies pushing up their spectacles. The two fathers surreptitiously pinched the inner corners of their eyes at the bridges of their noses.

Luke disembarked first, ahead of all other passengers, rolled down the gangplank—mostly under control— by a steward. Hattie stepped smartly behind them, her hand grazing the rail. Luke raised his arm in salute, sleeve flapping on an emaciated arm.

Their parents, appalled by Luke's appearance and Hattie's slenderness, couldn't disguise their anxiety.

Overcome by the sight of parents he'd thought he would never see again, Luke covered his eyes. His shoulders shook. His parents had aged dramatically, as though they'd intuited his capture and the botched execution, and were aware of his severe injuries.

Luke's father had cancelled his patients that day so he could meet the ship. Immaculate in an expensive deep charcoal suit and dark red silk tie, he twisted at the tail of his jacket. Fannie, Luke's mother, pressed her kid-gloved hands over her mouth in a prayerful attitude. Her eyes were wide, glassy with unshed tears. She wore a rosy red bouclé suit and a pearl choker. There was a small gold lapel pin secured over her heart, the first present her son had ever given her. Snow white curls peeked from under her feathered hat. When the wheelchair rolled up, Fannie clung to her son's shoulders, her cheek pressed to his. Luke felt her slight tremor, recognizing it as emotion. He closed his eyes and inhaled the familiar fragrance she had always worn.

Luke's father, Dr. Abner DeValcourt, hovered beside Fannie, compulsively patting his son's arm. His parents had completely shed the remoteness they'd shown Luke during his childhood. They had missed their son from the moment he had informed them he had joined the French army. It woke them to their neglect of him as a child and they were determined to make amends…if he made it home. Now that he had returned, nothing would stop them showering Luke with as much love and attention as he would tolerate.

Hattie had lingered beside Luke's wheelchair, which left her parents confused. They glanced at each other and didn't understand why she hadn't run to them for a hug, but they were secure in their love and waited for the chance to welcome their daughter. They thought it fortunate that Luke had been on the ship with Hattie, knowing he would have been good company for the voyage.

The DuMonds were well-dressed, though not as resplendent as their friends, Luke's parents. Maman and Papa noted that Hattie was slender, nearly as thin as the DeValcourt boy. Her cheeks were pale, but compared to Luke they could see now she looked quite healthy. Her rosy lips curved in a small contented smile.

Maman noticed that Hattie's beautiful auburn-highlighted tresses had disappeared, replaced by a short, choppy gamine haircut that looked particularly French. She touched her fingers to her mouth, a mannerism that reflected her dismay.

Their daughter wore an ill-fitting, cheap, dark blue cotton dress stamped with a faded floral design. The dress was badly wrinkled and of inferior fabric that was far different from the fine clothing Maman had sent with her to France. The thin garment did little to disguise Hattie's gaunt frame. Maman concluded that the dress had simply been at the top of Hattie's trunk. Hattie wore no hat or gloves, in contravention of ladies' fashionable attire, nor did she carry a purse or wear the slightest bit of makeup.

The feathered plume in Maman's hat trembled, as though ready to take flight if necessary, as she and Papa approached Hattie. Their expressions telegraphed loving concern. Where was that vibrant, confident girl they had packed off to France more than five years ago? No one would think this woman a fresh-faced girl. This worn apparition looked folded in on herself—as though determined to limit movement to save some energy. She was thin as a wisp of evening river fog.

Hattie raised her eyes and offered her mother and father the wide, generous smile that had always defined her. Here, then, was their daughter. Her eyes, with new crinkles at the corners, livened with a familiar sparkling glint. In those amber eyes, her parents glimpsed reminders of the precious child who had hugged them goodbye on this very wharf. They also saw an ineffable sadness in the depths of those lovely eyes, even as she offered her smiling cheek for their gentle kisses.

"Welcome home, *ma petite*. We worried so about your safety," said Papa.

Such an understatement. Hattie's father wrapped his warm arms around his daughter. Hattie knew his words meant that the family had been agonizing over her presence in a Hitler-invaded France, but he wouldn't want his darling girl to feel the slightest bit of guilt.

Papa DuMond's mellow voice covered Hattie like a warm breeze on a freezing day. She took a deep breath that felt like the first she'd taken in months. Her shoulders relaxed. She inclined toward her parents, and her spine straightened to the erect posture so familiar to them, as vast relief like a soft, cushioned cocoon enveloped Hattie. She was home at last, and everything would be all right. Her parents would hold her and Luke safe, and she wouldn't have to pretend to be strong any longer. She wept tears of joyful release.

"Maman," she whispered. "Papa. I missed you so much." She tried to dry her eyes with the collar of her flimsy dress, and looked for her brother.

"Where's Jack?"

Before they could answer, Luke stood from the wheelchair and interrupted the DuMonds' reunion. Surprising their parents, he took Hattie's hand in his, and cleared his throat. His reedy voice reflected fatigue, but he was determined to get this done.

"We're happy to be home."

The word "we" was the first clue of what was to come. He smiled at his parents first, then at the DuMonds.

"We have much to say, but our most important news unites our two families." Their parents looked at each other with their eyebrows elevated. What could Luke mean?

"How, you might be asking?" Luke had seen their questioning eyes. Maman DuMond smiled, on the verge of speaking, so Luke quickly answered his own question, raising the hand he had linked with Hattie's.

"Almost a year ago, we were married in Hattie's parish church. Our official marriage certificate lies in a trunk hidden under a load of hay at the back of a French warehouse." He shrugged. "We have no idea if we'll ever see it again.

"The parish priest in the Fifth *Arrondissement* church closest to the Sorbonne declared us man and wife. The pastor himself performed the ceremony and signed the registry alongside our signatures. Unless Hitler destroys the records, the proof we are husband and wife is in that church."

Their parents were thrilled by Luke's news and looked at each other with expressions that could only be called triumphant. Both couples had hoped, years before, that their children would unite, but Hattie's engagement to Karl Schmitzer had led them to abandon that hope. This was a time to celebrate. Their children's unexpected news called for another round of hugs and kisses. Certainly it was no time to mention old commitments.

Transformed by flushed cheeks, Luke's happy grin pushed aside his pallor. Standing close to him, Hattie saw her parents' delight and felt a deep gratitude. Her lips softly upturned, she took pleasure in everyone's good will.

They, Luke and Hattie, were the most fortunate of children, both born into enduring, loving marriages. Hattie's family, full of happy fun, enjoyed a warm, loving environment.

Luke's upbringing had been relegated mostly to faithful and kindly family employees while his parents occupied themselves with their own activities. Fortunately, his mother, Fannie, had an excellent staff. Because she treated them exceptionally well, they were happy and gave her a stable household. Luke tolerated all the kisses and hugs, before sinking back into the wheelchair. His marriage to Hattie, a *fait accompli,* had been unexpected. It had lacked the pomp and ceremony—and the parties—their mothers had dreamed of, but Luke knew the result was perfection.

In the background, the *SS Seabreeze* steward heard it all, patiently waiting to deliver the wounded warrior to his father's motor car and to his destiny. He would have quite a tale for his shipmates that night as they prepared the ship for its return voyage to Great Britain.

The group departed in two cars from the wharves along the Mississippi into the diminished wartime traffic of New Orleans. Hattie had joined her parents, with her father behind the wheel of his shiny new Ford. He had loved to drive from the moment he sat behind the wheel of the first car he'd ever bought.

The DeValcourts piled into their limousine with Luke. Their chauffeur, who had hugged Luke hello, doubled as the family's full time gardener. He had known Luke all his life and lived in a small one-room cabin on the family property. The two cars caravanned to the grand DeValcourt mansion on St. Charles Avenue that nestled beneath picturesque mossy oaks.

They mounted Fannie DeValcourt's immaculate front steps and settled in the gracious drawing room. The home, furnished over many years with exquisite one-of-a-kind pieces meticulously selected by Fannie, had become a mini-museum. Its drawing room had always been the center of their family life. Upholstered in soft fabrics, comfortable furniture provided plenty of seating. The walls were decorated with original art that reflected the couple's interests. The bookcases were stuffed with volumes that helped create a pleasing room that fit the DeValcourts well and satisfied their guests.

As soon as they entered the house, Dr. DeValcourt had requested champagne for everyone. Once it was served, Luke again took the floor, now in the midst of familiar surroundings. The others quieted their conversations when he clinked his simple wedding band against his champagne flute.

Luke's nostrils flared as he breathed in the familiar lemony polish and old book smell of his parents' drawing room. Hattie walked to him, offering her support. He steadied himself, his hand on her shoulder, her warmth reaching him through the thin rumpled cotton of her dress. Luke thought fleetingly that Hattie should keep that dress as a memory of the day they'd bought it in a small English store.

The convalescent was exhausted by the short trip from the ship to the house. His relief at being home was palpable, as was his struggle with strong emotions. Luke found it difficult to speak past the lump in his throat, but he had several questions, such as where he and Hattie would live now that they were home.

Luke's father, a medical doctor like his son and daughter-in-law, viewed Luke with some alarm. The boy's mouth had a pinched whiteness that signaled fatigue from just the effort it had taken to climb the wide stone steps to the door of his childhood home. He made a mental note to thoroughly examine him later.

Luke was saying, "Our priorities right now, Hattie's and mine, are for food and shelter. We certainly plan to find our own home, but until that happens, we need to rest and recuperate more than anything else." He looked at his mother.

"We—Hattie and I—talked, Maman. If you'll have us, we'd like to stay with you here, at least for a while. We know it's an imposition, but maybe we can find space in the servants' quarters below stairs."

Fannie glowed with delight, looking younger by a decade. Luke smiled, his expression tender. He'd always thought his mother was the most beautiful woman in the world. She was perhaps at this precise moment more beautiful than she'd ever been because many of her involvements earlier in life had fallen away, leaving her more relaxed.

"Of course, my darling. Of course." She looked to Luke's father. Though more restrained than his wife, Abner DeValcourt was pleased, and nodded his agreement.

Hattie's hand covered Luke's. He had taken charge in the gathering and said just the right words. This was a new side of Luke, one she hadn't known, but one she found admirable.

Luke addressed Hattie's parents. "Your daughter has missed you terribly, you know, and we love your home, too. And of course you remember me spending half my childhood within your walls," a remark that left everyone laughing as they recalled the mischievous boy he'd been.

His arm swept wide. "This house, though, has unused space on the ground floor… that is, I hope it's still unused." He turned back to Fannie.

"I think you have enough help to handle the extra work we cause. If something has changed, Maman, please tell me." His mother flushed with pleasure and nodded, making a *moue*.

Luke turned to his father. "Hattie and I both know medicine, but until we're recovered, we need your help, Papa." Dr. DeValcourt acknowledged his son's request with a small nod.

Next, he took Maman DuMond's hands and said, "We miss Cook's wonderful meals, *madame*." Her eyes twinkled at Fannie and she interjected, "Please call me maman, Luke. I'm your other mother now!"

Luke grinned. "Yes, maman. We want you to know we'll be at your table with our napkins on our laps more than you expect…if you'll have us."

The mansion was a sensible choice. It could absorb far more additional occupants than one young couple. They would have comfortable privacy downstairs without intruding on the elder DeValcourts.

Hattie's family home was gracious, but only half the size of the mansion. There was certainly far less space to give the young couple real privacy. And the DuMond's Octavia Street bungalow was close by, only seven blocks down the uneven, cracked sidewalks of St. Charles Avenue, an easy walk from the DeValcourts.

Fannie rang a small silver bell that sat beside her on a table and summoned help. While her guests chatted, she issued quiet instructions to prepare the basement suite, speaking in a patois of French and English.

Luke saw the woman arrive and his eyes lit up. Standing slowly, he walked across the room and interrupted his mother.

"Coco!" She turned, surprised by Luke's voice, and covered her face with her apron to hide her emotion. Her shoulders shook briefly before she recovered and reached out.

"Luke! Thank God you've come home. So thin, my sweet boy. So thin."

Fannie flicked her fingers, telling Luke to move. He smiled, transported to his childhood by his mother's sign language. Her gentle hand settled on Coco's arm to get her attention, and she resumed her instructions.

"Hattie and Luke are married, Coco, and they've had a difficult ocean crossing. They need rest, so please hurry the preparations. We hope they'll live with us for quite a long while, and you'll have time to visit with Luke later.

"Oh! And Coco? Please tell Cook—on most nights from now on, there'll be four for dinner, including tonight."

"Yes, ma'am. Right away." Coco's rich voice held a joyful lilt. "She'll be glad. We'll all be happy Mr. Luke's home, but his white hair is a shock."

Coco turned to Luke like he was her own child despite her innate shyness. The colorful scarf over her dark curls tickled Luke's ear as she hugged her boy. He had been her special charge since his birth. They had always loved each other, hugging and being hugged every single day. She was his second mother.

She had cuddled and wiped away little boy tears and slipped him treats between meals. Leaning against Coco's knee, Luke had learned many common sense life lessons from her.

Relieved to have her boy back home, Coco was overjoyed to learn that he and his pretty new bride would live with Miss Fannie, under her own watchful, maternal eye. She hurried off, unaware that everyone, including Hattie, was staring at Luke.

Caught up in the excitement of their earlier big news, no one had paid any particular attention to Luke's hair.

"It's true, Luke." Hattie marveled, breathing the words. "Your hair is sprinkled with white—like you stood under a rain of white ligustrum blooms. It's very distinguished. Salt and pepper makes you a grown man—and more handsome than ever. It must have happened so gradually I didn't notice. It's as though your hair always looked that way."

Luke pushed his fingers through his thick, longish hair. He didn't care a fig about his hair. He thought his difficult days in the French army and as a prisoner had probably caused the change in his hair color. He decided to give a full accounting this once, and never again. He gained everyone's attention by clearing his throat, then told his story.

Hattie listened closely while Luke spoke, hearing some of the information for the first time. Until this very moment, her husband had refused to talk about those traumatic days of captivity.

The atmosphere in the room began to weigh heavy as Luke's parents heard about the stockade prison that confined him, an enclosure that he and the other prisoners had been forced to build themselves. He talked about extreme hunger and deprivation, of living under both hot sun and rainstorms without shelter. His voice trembled as he conveyed the fear and apprehension that had culminated in such an unspeakable way— staring into the muzzles of a firing squad, waiting to die with the other prisoners.

He remembered nothing after that—didn't know he'd fallen to the dirt, didn't know he'd been thrown for dead into the back of a meat wagon. He couldn't imagine his rescue by the French Resistance, or remember how he'd hovered between life and death. There would never be a memory of that time, but he had listened closely to discussions in Vierville-sur-Mer to finally grasp all that had happened.

Luke became aware of excruciating pain in the home of Vierville's kind country physician. He hated the thought of enduring more torture until he realized he'd been rescued by the French Resistance.

Holding her hand to his heart, he told their families of Hattie's heroism in the Resistance, and of her dedicated, unwavering search for the secret prison that held him captive. And what it had cost her to find it. Even while he recuperated with Annette at the *auberge*, Hattie had continued to fight for many days alongside the other village *résistants*, her days fraught with danger, the *résistants* refusing to be defeated.

Hattie protested when he called her a heroine.

"What else should I have done, honey?" responded Hattie. "I had to repay the Resistance for your rescue. It was no more than anyone else would do, was it? No one gives up on the ones they love."

Wanting not to hear about her very own personal loss, she jumped the story to their frightful sea crossing through the terrible storm the helpless *SS Seabreeze* encountered. She told how sick the two of them had been, along with the other passengers and most of the crew, including the captain.

Distressed to hear about Hattie's rough Atlantic voyage, Maman crossed the room to sit with her daughter. The two women snuggled, happy to be together again.

Maman whispered, "I'm so sorry you had to go through all that, darling. It's worse, knowing I wasn't there to help."

Luke picked up the thread of the story and backtracked a bit. His voice roughened as his eyes reddened. It was important that their parents understood the perils they had experienced.

He told of the day Hattie had nearly died at the hands of a Nazi sentry, and of her survival despite a precipitous fall that resulted in a miscarriage and a severe concussion. She'd known the risks (and had willingly taken them) in long days of searching for him in the French forests.

Hattie listened to Luke tell her story, thinking it ironic that her pregnancy had survived so many grueling searches but couldn't overcome her terrible fall. She had lost her baby but regained her husband on the very same day.

She thought of Luke's recovery, so much longer than her own. She remembered the day she'd told Luke that Pierre and Marie Chennault, whom they'd thought to be friends, were traitors to France and that Pierre had cost Luke's comrades their lives. She thought of their unspoken agreement not to dwell on ugly memories— that this was probably for the best.

The indolent summer days slipped past. Free from the fear of goose-stepping Nazi patrols, Luke and Hattie soaked up sunshine on Fannie's lovely patio, surrounded by the midsummer abundance of lush, aromatic blooms and murmuring to each other in lyrical French.

They grew closer, with more time to learn each other's idiosyncrasies. Luke's parents delighted in their company, and all four often dined at Hattie's childhood home with her parents. At the dinner table, they spoke a patois of French and English, in which everyone including the household help was fluent.

Fannie presented her "children" with expansive new wardrobes from the gentrified shops of uptown Magazine Street that had been a seedy part of town when Hattie left for France. They'd gratefully relinquished the frayed clothes from their arrival, and the household staff outdid themselves helping the young couple physically and emotionally recover, and reacclimate to a New Orleans not quite as they remembered it.

Hattie's skin and hair soon glowed with good health and she regained enough weight to smooth out her hollowed cheeks. She refused comment on things that couldn't be undone, but in private she mourned the loss of her baby.

The basement apartment was now personalized to Hattie and Luke's taste and she cast about for ways to keep herself busy. Hesitantly, she asked her father-in-law if he thought Hôtel-Dieu hospital's medical clinic could be convinced to add her to their staff.

The hospital was founded in 1859 by an order of nuns, the Daughters of Charity. It had functioned for less than two years before the country became enmeshed in a ferocious Civil War. It was the sole private hospital in New Orleans that remained open throughout the war, and its name meant "House of God." The hospital was pleased to accept Hattie's services.

Thoughts of Annette Rousseau and the friends she fought beside in la Résistance would come unbidden. Hattie enjoyed the more pleasant memories and learned to let the others go.

Luke chafed, watching Hattie set off to see patients. His recovery moved slowly. Besides the horrendous gunshot wound caused by the firing squad, Luke had suffered vicious beatings by sadistic Nazi guards who pounded the defenseless prisoners unconscious with their heavy weapons. Few men under Luke's command had survived Pierre Chennault's treachery.

Despite their awful memories, the couple enjoyed several pleasant new routines, but forgot to celebrate their first wedding anniversary.

Hattie had begun to wonder if sexual intimacy was gone forever. It wasn't for lack of private time. While she waited for Luke to show interest in her, they enjoyed each other in other ways, frequently laughing at themselves.

After months of limited meals in France, the abundance in both homes startled them. Their parents couldn't believe the dietary substitutions their children described, but often heard praises for Annette's culinary skill. No one in New Orleans, hearing their stories, could imagine roasted and ground acorns, chicory, and beechnuts replacing their beloved Morning Call dark roast coffee. Luke agreed that the substitute was unsatisfactory and bitter —and the only sweetener available had been unsatisfactory, too—ground beet flour.

Coffee heresy.

Odd, how Luke's decline began. Odder still, the signs went unrecognized by Luke, himself a physician, and by his physician wife. By any measure, Luke's father, an excellent physician and well regarded locally should never have overlooked his son's obvious symptoms.

One afternoon, four months after Luke and Hattie's return, Luke and his father sat in deep shade on the patio drinking Sazerac cocktails as the sun dropped below Fannie's brick garden fence. At the patio's fringe, dusted rays of the declining sun fell onto leggy flowers. Softly splashing water rippled in Fannie's indulgent marble fountain. Twittering finches evoked all that was best about being home in New Orleans.

Rustling leaves curled in a pleasant end of summer breeze and provided background music for comfortable conversation between occasional sips of the cold Sazerac in condensate-coated glasses. Lazily drifting clouds reflected breathtaking glorious salmon and gold hues from the setting sun..

Luke was telling his father he thought their patio was a slice of heaven just as he grimaced. A momentary, sharp, numbing sensation traveled below Luke's right eye down the side of his face. He bent over and pressed a finger to his nose. A drop of blood quivered at its tip, a minute amount easily blotted by the clean handkerchief Luke pulled from his pocket.

His father exhibited little concern. "You all right, son?"

The rested and tanned young man nodded his reassurance. Abner DeValcourt saw not the wounded warrior, but the athletic son who'd excelled in sports during his high school days.

Such a minor thing, a transient nose bleed. So common. And, after Luke's dreadful injuries in France, a nose bleed was laughable to him, easily forgotten as the dinner bell rang.

So Dr. DeValcourt Senior put aside his uneasiness, making a mental note to examine Luke thoroughly in the next day or two. At the dinner table, Dr. DeValcourt enjoyed Luke's spirited conversation, which allayed any concerns his father may have had.

The good doctor listened proudly to the younger man's intelligent, incisive comments that reassured him Luke was fine. He'd been looking forward to the future when they would practice medicine together as a team. To make that happen, Abner DeValcourt had inquired about adding both his son and daughter-in-law to the clinic's staff.

The hospital sorely needed their help. With the distinct possibility that the country might be forced into the European war, the federal government had begun to bulk up its armed services in earnest. Hôtel-Dieu's clinics had lost several doctors to the US Army. As a result, the hospital was drastically understaffed and the physicians who remained were desperately overworked.

Following the meal that night, Hattie and Luke retired to their cozy apartment on the ground floor of the raised mansion. Its low ceilings and small windows cut into creamy plastered walls, creating dim, cave-like rooms in stark contrast to the expansive chambers above stairs. The couple thought the rooms were perfect. They reminded them of Annette Rousseau's *auberge* and the hidden cellar room that protected Luke during his first days of recovery. Here in New Orleans, the stripped-down, insignificant apartment may not have had shelves of wine and canned vegetables, but it cocooned them and gave them little reason to seek another home.

Hattie kicked off her shoes and swung onto their bed, then propped the dog-eared novel she'd chosen from Fannie's library on her thighs. She tucked its bookmark between two pages in the back, and settled in to read, digging her bare heels into the mattress. Nearby, Luke slowly rotated the dial on his new, matte red, Bakelite radio. It was amazing, Hattie mused, how many uses inventors could find for these new light plastics.

Luke searched for overseas news of the war every night. They worried about their French friends, aware that silence didn't necessarily mean good news. She and Luke would be delighted if the United States finally joined the Allies to fight against the Axis powers—though they worried it might be too little, too late by the time they did. Still, they kept up by listening to the news and reading whatever they could find on the war.

After an hour, Hattie closed her novel and sat with Luke on their old sofa. Draping her legs across his lap, she snuggled with him, her head on his shoulder.

"Any more nosebleeds, beloved husband?" She stroked Luke's nose and grinned. Their months together had dispelled Hattie's worry that perhaps she hadn't married him for love, but for security. Every day, she fell more deeply in love with this man, with a surprised emotional ferocity. Kind and funny, he was so relaxed he could have talked to a pecky cypress board about all its knots without becoming the least bit restless.

"No, wife." He returned her smile, then buried the aforementioned nose in Hattie's fragrant, silky hair. "No nosebleed, just a really bad headache. Hay fever, I think. I'm a damn sissy—always something to complain about."

"One thing for sure," Hattie nuzzled his warm neck, as intoxicated as she had been on that first day in Paris. *God*, she thought, *he feels good. I love this man*, "you're not a sissy, sweetheart. I'll tell the whole world how virile you are—just let me know and I'll say the word."

She reached across him and turned the radio dial to a music station, then nibbled his neck and ear until he turned fully into her embrace, his headache be damned, and began to prove his virility.

Later, they once again listened to the news, lying side by side on the rumpled bed.

Hattie asked Luke, "Do you remember our first date?"

"The one here, or the one in France?"

He shushed her response, his finger across her lips, while he listened to a news report. She snuggled closer. Never had she believed she would marry Luke DeValcourt. She lightly stroked his hand and reminisced, her finger holding her place in the novel she had again picked up. Casting a sidelong glance at her husband, she intended to mention something about their first date, but, just like that, he fell asleep before his news program ended.

Hattie set aside her book and reminisced about the first of their many dates. She had been such an innocent in high school, unaware of, and uncaring about, the larger world.

In that year of 1930, Hattie's beautiful formal gown and shoes cost more than most people could afford during those dire times. A financial depression had gripped the nation, but the teenage Hattie was oblivious. Perhaps she was more immature and self-involved than she should have been. She had been blessed with a father who'd had the financial foresight to protect his family, and thus the means to let his daughter play the role of a Southern belle.

Hattie had finally accepted that she had an excellent intellect. As she progressed in school, she thrilled with each new morsel of knowledge, particularly if it related to the human body. She developed ambitious plans for herself. Her delighted parents encouraged her, but on this particular night, she primped, completely preoccupied with her appearance. It would be years more before she understood how special a role this night would play in her life.

"I want to wear this dress like it is, Maman," Hattie whined. "It's perfect."

"No, ma'am, you can*not,*" Maman said. "That would send the wrong message, and you are *not* that sort of girl." She held up a bolero sewn of gossamer lace that was dyed the same deep royal blue as the strapless dress Hattie wore.

Maman shook the bolero at her daughter like a toreador challenging a snorting bull.

"Remove this, and I'll hear about it. That would make tonight your last dance living under my roof. And don't think you can do whatever strikes your fancy, just because women won the right to vote. You're too young to be un-chaperoned and the *only* reason you're going out tonight is because Luke didn't ask anyone his own age soon enough."

Hattie wrinkled her nose. She'd prefer another escort tonight. This date wasn't even Luke's idea. And worse, *she* hadn't been asked at all.

Luke's *mother* had begged Maman to allow Hattie to go with him to the dance. Luke had decided to go stag to his senior formal at Fortier High School, but the idea had scandalized his mother. Fannie DeValcourt was all about proper behavior and her son needed a date. Without Luke's knowledge, his mother asked Hattie's mother to help rectify Luke's lapse.

Hattie stomped off when Maman told her she had accepted the dance invitation on her daughter's behalf. Maman implored Papa for his help, and he insisted she go. Maman further enticed her with the offer of a full-length evening gown, which was irresistible to Hattie, as much as she hated to waste it on the obnoxious Luke.

The event was so soon, Hattie and Maman had been forced to shop for a ready-made dress. Society women rarely bought inferior ready-made garments, relying on their dressmakers for bespoke clothing. Ready-made was suitable only for school uniforms.

It felt magical when they found the perfect garment, like finding the one four-leaf clover in an entire field. The moment she had touched the dress, Hattie loved how the blue taffeta crackled between her fingers. Shameful though it was to waste this beauty on a grubby boy she'd known all her life, she resigned her new dress to its fate.

She rolled her eyes at her reflection on the night of the dance, but had to admit she liked the way the gorgeous blue helped her unfortunate brown hair that Maman called "chestnut." At least her hair was thick and shiny and smelled good.

Shrugging on the lacy bolero, Hattie grudgingly approved.

"I like the bolero, Maman." Not that she wanted Maman to notice, Hattie felt it added an allure that revealed as much as it hid. She flicked a glance at Maman, who often intuited her daughter's thoughts.

Luke was the only fly in Hattie's ointment. He'd been an intolerable mess—odious, unkempt, and smelly—the last time he'd visited her brother. And it was Luke's *mother* who arranged the date. She whined to herself, *What was this, the Middle Ages?* What made it worse was that *Papa* had insisted she go because Luke was the son of their good friends, the DeValcourts. Anger was making her so dizzy Hattie tried to faint. She couldn't force that much fury, but the idea of a swoon was so interesting that her mood brightened.

Her height concerned her. She was already tall and would be taller than usual, wearing kitten heels the same blue as her gown. Unless Luke had grown taller than the last time she saw him, she would tower over him like a knock-kneed stork. She'd probably end up staring down at the top of his head.

That would serve him right.

The doorbell downstairs chimed, making Hattie jump, her skin prickling. Had the chime always been that loud?

She had meant to ask Maman how to act on a first date, but now it was too late. Her heart thudded in time with Papa's footsteps as he walked to the door. She frowned at the moistness in Maman's kind eyes.

Hattie clutched her tummy.

"I feel sick, Maman. I can't go." Her hands trembled, but Maman shook her head.

"You're fine, *ma petite.*"

"I'm not fine! Just look at me."

Maman held out a pair of long white kid gloves, helped her little girl pull them on one at a time, then spun her daughter around by the shoulders to give her a final appraisal.

"You're beautiful, my adorable Hattie." She nodded, her lips pursed, as she admired Hattie's smooth shoulders, barely visible through the lace bolero. She approved of her daughter's tiny waist. Both happy and sad, Maman realized her baby bird had fledged, no more saggy diapers, no more childish pudgy legs. She gathered her tall daughter close for a last squeeze.

"You remember we talked about the ugly duckling when you were little?"

"Yes—you called me ugly."

"*Mais non*, Hattie!" Maman gasped. "You believed I thought you ugly? *Ce n'est pas vrai*. Not true! You missed the point of the story."

"The point?"

"Yes. Little girls grow into their loveliness like awkward cygnets mature into graceful, beautiful swans. You *are* a swan—you *are* so very beautiful."

Maman had never considered that the story might have hurt her child's feelings. She took a breath, because there were other, more vital, things to convey.

"This is your first dance*, ma petite*. You must be ladylike. Tomboys are everyone's friend, but girls who act like ladies are the ones who become wives and mothers. Boys can take advantage, so behave." A personal memory revealed a glimpse of Maman's inner self and made her blush.

"You taught me that long ago, Maman. But this is just Luke."

Maman wagged her finger. "No, *chère, not* different. He's like any other man—and he *is* a man. He'll soon leave for college. A friend, yes. He's a friend, but he'll see your behavior like he'd see any other girl's. Don't be fooled."

Maman spoke louder so that Hattie, who was already running to the stairway, would hear her last words. Her voice trailed away as her little girl swept down the broad staircase.

Downstairs, Papa opened the door wearing his favorite disreputable, snagged brown sweater, always his first choice to ward off cool weather. His bent-shouldered appearance made quite a contrast with the relaxed posture of the tall mesomorph in a summer tuxedo at the door.

Their companionable French greetings drifted up the stairs. The deep timbre of Luke's voice startled Hattie and a tingling *frisson* curled at her core. Not believing that could possibly be the odious Luke, she searched the doorway for a nonexistent second person.

Luke's voice might have changed, but his devilish grin was the same. The only difference for Hattie was her degree of interest—which could only be called heightened.

Papa's greeting, with affectionate pats of the taller young man's shoulder, was more like the welcome for a family relative, not to his daughter's date.

As she descended, Hattie's taffeta dress rustled and reflected the overhead chandelier's glowing light as its hem caressed the step risers. Her coquettish red crinolines peeked out as she floated down the stairs, and her blue satin shoes showed flashing glimpses of feminine feet and shapely ankles.

Light from the chandelier showcased Hattie's smooth, olive-toned tan. Her smile widened into the old tomboy grin to acknowledge the men's admiration as they watched her shimmering in blue iridescence.

Their reactions looked quite different to Hattie. She heard Luke whistle under his breath—that was gratifying. Luke's eyes were stunned wide open, his mouth perfectly rounded.

Papa's expression confused her. He looked proud, but in the next second, melancholy.

Hattie stepped from the stairway and was pleased to look up at Luke, taller indeed. Later, at the dance, she would notice that his height outstripped not just her own, but that of nearly all his friends. Unnoticed by his contemporaries, but certainly remarked upon by the tailor who sewed his family's clothing, his shoulders had grown broader and his lean, ropy muscles, strengthened by his beloved school sports, had tapered his torso to a narrow waist in a strong, fit body.

On Luke's most recent visit to Jack, Hattie had noticed that his floppy light brown curls had been replaced by short, wavy hair of a darker brown—still unwashed, but with hints of gloss.

His appearance pleased Hattie. Luke looked elegant and handsome in a white tuxedo jacket, his black trousers trimmed with broad black grosgrain ribbon down the outer seam of each leg. This person was far from the grubby boy she remembered. Comparing him to her father, she saw Luke stood a full head taller than her darling Papa.

Upstairs, Maman tried to blink away another blur, swiping dampness away with the heel of her hand, and newly aware that she and Papa had tonight launched their baby bird on her first step out of their nest and into her future.

Hattie warbled, "Right on time."

Unable to break all her old habits, she added, "and you clean up well," then mentally kicked herself for acting so stupid. Her spell broken, Papa chortled at Hattie's tomboy words and patted his daughter's cheek.

"Do I look all right, Papa?"

She twirled and the long, full skirt flared about her slender ankles. Beautiful and thick, Hattie's hair nestled at the nape of her neck in a low bun secured by sparkling barrettes. Her arms in their long white kidskin gloves raised in a graceful pirouette.

"You are very beautiful, Harriet Therese." Papa's voice shook when he uttered her full name. She knew that meant the moment was serious and her smile wavered, but she recovered and kissed him.

Luke offered the glossy white beribboned corsage box that teetered on his fingertips, to which she showed genuine delight.

"For me?" She smiled up at him. "So thoughtful." Her exotic amber eyes, fringed with thick black lashes, seemed to glow when they met his intense dark blue gaze. The brief, subtle glance thumped his heart like a physical blow, and he began the long fall into love.

Hattie's unconscious made a note of her effect, though consciously she was oblivious. Extending a gloved hand for him to tie the dainty white orchid to her wrist with his abnormally awkward fingers, she graced him with a smile.

Leaving the empty box behind, she blew a kiss up the stairs to Maman, who was hiding her reddened nose.

Hattie's first date was wild. Luke's football buddies stood outside the entry to the dance and gaped at his gorgeous date until he introduced her.

The young men took a step back, reverting from jocks back to regular boys.

"This is *Hattie*? C'mon—you kidding me? *Hattie*?"

They had known the little tomboy all her life, many having lost foot races or marbles to her when they were younger, but now they scrawled their names on her dance card.

The band struck up its opening tune and she mentally noted she should thank Maman for insisting she go to the monthly cotillions that taught her how to dance.

Inundated by a kaleidoscope of laughing young men and colorfully dressed girls crammed on the dance floor, Hattie thrilled to the new experience. The drummer's heavy bass thrummed in her core and added excitement. Colored lights and decorations transformed the gym into a New Orleans honky-tonk.

Luke plucked Hattie's dance card from her fingertips, shocked that Karl Schmitzer's name appeared on every other line. Karl was an excellent athlete, and as tall and strong as Luke. He had gotten to know Hattie well as her next-door neighbor during the summers their families spent on Biloxi beaches.

Karl's freshly barbered hair was straight and blond. The contrast with Luke's brunet curls and others in the dark-haired crowd made Karl noticeable. Everywhere he moved in the room, he was easily seen, as though a personal spotlight shone down on him.

Hattie and Karl's first dance together was remarkable. The moment Karl touched Hattie's waist an invisible spark leapt between the two young people, and his wide-eyed reaction made her blush with charming innocence. The music and the colorful pageantry of the evening entranced Hattie, and her excitement made her more beautiful than ever.

The warmth of Karl's strong hand breached Hattie's kidskin gloves. She tingled with a sensation that nestled deep inside, delighted that he would be her dance partner as often as Luke.

Toward the end of the evening, Karl pressed her closer and whispered, "May I call on you at home?"

His warm breath tickled Hattie's ear, and that gave her delicious shivers. She had a moment to say "yes, of course" before the band leader announced the final tune. Luke materialized at her shoulder as if by magic and tugged her clear across the dance floor. She looked back at Karl one last time before the house lights dimmed.

Luke held her far too tight. Hattie squeaked, "Luke, please," and socked his bicep using her knuckles. He flinched and vigorously rubbed his arm.

"Ow! That *hurt*."

"Who taught me how to do that, huh? I wonder…" Tomboy Hattie emerged from the beautiful young woman in front of him, grinning. She looked up at him through her impossibly long eyelashes.

Smitten, Luke's heart collapsed, completely in love with this adorable girl. He carefully gathered her to him, wanting to be close.

The room's energy and the drummer's swishing brushes blended hypnotically, but Hattie was thinking of Karl when Luke inched his fingers under her lace bolero up her back until he touched her bare skin. He was Karl in her imagination and she sank against Luke's chest.

Her young molecules vibrated, giving Luke a subliminal impression that she was as entranced with him as he was with her. A vague groan came from somewhere, and Hattie thought it could've issued from her throat.

Luke stepped back and shook himself. He murmured, "Hattie, Hattie, Hattie."

Deep in her imaginary world, Hattie answered. "Hmm?"

"Never mind…want some *café au lait* and *beignets*?"

She had barely the sense to remember she had a curfew. "Do we have enough time? I'm supposed to be home by midnight."

Luke's head snapped up.

"Good God. This is the last dance. The band *quits* at midnight. We have to leave! Right now!" Holding Hattie's hand, he strode off with long steps, jerking her along. Hattie snatched her tiny purse from a table and scurried to keep up.

Beneath the starry sky, the midnight air felt cool and refreshing. Luke had borrowed the old DeValcourt horse-drawn open carriage to get to the dance, rather than drive his father's faddish new motorcar. The horse and groom waited at the curb with the carriage, the groom's chin fallen to his chest.

The carriage had waited for Luke many times this past year, though never quite this late. Its springs made the carriage dip as Luke handed Hattie up the step, which woke the dozing groom. He harrumphed and straightened as Luke followed Hattie up to sit close beside her. The groom earned extra wages for Luke's evening excursions, and he knew never to mention anything he'd seen or heard. Should one have occasion to ask the horse, however…

"Sorry, James. We lost track of time. Miss Hattie has to get home in a hurry." Without a word, James snapped and sawed the reins, clucking to rouse his mare. The mare trotted off, eager to reach her fragrant hay-strewn stable, pulling the carriage into its usual swaying motion.

It had been an evening of "firsts" for Hattie—first real dance, first time "alone" with a boy—and the first time she'd been awake so late. She relaxed and closed her eyes, lulled by clopping hooves and the carriage's rocking motion.

Feeling as adult as her mother, Hattie recalled Maman's advice to show some restraint. It was easy to see that Luke was no novice when it came to girls, but Hattie forced herself to ignore the tantalizing, starry night and gently stirring breeze that were so seductive.

"Can I tell you something, Hattie DuMond?"

Luke's breath tickled her ear. Her eyes snapped open, on guard, as he pressed her gloved hand to his lips. Had she been thrust into the pages of one of Maman's purloined romances?

The second-most handsome man of the evening, Luke leaned close. Hattie had no idea what he would say. Regardless, it was Karl Schmitzer's handsome—no, beautiful—face that flashed through her mind and her mouth softened into a small secret smile.

"Certainly, Mr. DeValcourt. Spit it out."

"Tonight is the best night of my life so far." He tugged the collar of her bolero, rubbing its soft lace between his fingers.

Hattie could smell whiskey on his breath, a whiff that smelled like her father's goodnight kiss. Whiskey? How had she missed that at the dance? She wanted Luke to leave her clothes alone and squirmed her collar out of his hand. She sat up and tried to regain her focus.

If only it was Karl who sat beside her under the starry sky in the open carriage. Her body thrummed. Overwhelmed with confused thoughts and new sensations, the young teenager experienced the world turning topsy-turvy, and she knew she was ill-equipped to handle her emotional state.

"I'm serious." Luke dredged halting words from some newfound depth, astonished as he spoke them. The creaks and slips of the wooden carriage wheels on the bricks of St. Charles Avenue formed an uneven backdrop to Luke's fervent whispers. Out of nowhere, he began to laugh, confusing Hattie.

"I've had a crush on you since we were children. Remember the day you showed me that red Jujube smile?" Hattie's expression was inscrutable, difficult to grasp in the gaslights flickering along the Avenue. Luke might have seen her blush had there been more light, but Hattie didn't want him to, grateful for the darkness.

It was her natural instinct to be agreeable and put others at ease, but Hattie wondered how she should respond to Luke's confession. She was completely inexperienced. Searching for the proper words and not finding them, she said the wrong thing, unaware that those few words would shape their lives—her life, and Luke's life, too.

She could've stayed quiet and not complicated things, but Hattie was not used to dealing with other people's emotions—so she uttered a fib, hoping it was what she was expected to say.

Squeezing Luke's muscled arm, Hattie murmured, "I've liked *you* since then, too."

Lying beside the man who had become her husband all these years later, Hattie understood how poorly she had handled things that evening, all to pretend she was more worldly than a young teenager should ever be. How fortunate she was that "things" had finally turned out well for them.

Things in young Mrs. Dr. DeValcourt's life were about to change again—and not for the better.

Hattie inspected her husband's handsome profile as Luke, asleep, nestled warm against her side. She loved him with all her heart, a good and loyal man. She regretted the grief she'd caused him when she favored Karl Schmitzer and sent him away when they were young.

The summer following her date with Luke, he and Karl had both courted Hattie. She alternated time with the two young men until Maman said she was being unfair to them and forced Hattie to choose.

Hattie chose Karl. Even so, during her enjoyable days with Karl she missed Luke. He had stormed from her life after that, leaving the city to attend college in another state.

She was happy that Luke had never forgotten her and had persevered. In Hattie's mind, it was partially her fault that Luke was so badly wounded in the war. She doubted he would have joined the French army at all, had she not been stranded in Paris during the German invasion.

But Hattie could never regret the path her life had taken. All her memories were tucked away, secure in the vault of her mind, and retrospection couldn't do a thing to change the past.

That's not to say there weren't some memories she would prefer to forget. Ah, but those others… she would enjoy them many times over. Scattered through those good memories were thoughts of her infatuation with Karl Schmitzer—the man she had planned to marry. But Hattie had moved past Karl and was deeply in love with Luke DeValcourt.

Hattie drifted off to dreamland, her body touching her husband's from shoulder to toes.

The early sun shone on Luke's closed eyes through a narrow gap in the bedroom curtains. He squeezed his eyelids and turned to snuggle against his sleeping wife. Burying his nose on her warm neck, he dozed, aware he had an intense headache.

The apartment's rusty screen door hinges screeched, startling Hattie awake. She slipped from under Luke's heavy arm. Her toes probed for her slippers. The screech meant they had slept through breakfast again. Someone in the kitchen must be taking pity on them by delivering coffee and breakfast goodies to their minuscule living room.

Adding prayers of thanks to her already long list of gratitudes, Hattie again thought how happy she was that they were home safe with Luke's parents and their plentiful sustenance.

She would never take breakfast for granted again, though, after all the deprivations she had seen in France. Hattie liked most food, but the first meal of the day had always been extra special. Shrugging her robe on, she followed the tantalizing aromas, padding to the bistro table in their living area. She poured steaming coffee from a hefty insulated carafe into a flowery oversized cup.

Adding a splash of milk and a spoonful of sugar, she carried the cup into the morning's warm dappled sunshine, juggling it with a plate of warm buttered croissants. Carefully setting everything on the black wrought iron table under the leafy live oak tree, she sat on a matching wrought iron chair.

A hummingbird had detected the sugar sweetness in her coffee and zoomed to hover above the table, its wings audibly and invisibly buzzing, its tongue probing the air. Dismissing its chances as too dangerous, it zoomed away and disappeared, to Hattie's disappointment.

She loved Fannie's patio, regardless of the time or the weather. Her eyes canvassed the walled garden, grateful for the peaceful flow of New Orleans' mild seasons. Seeing life, whether trees, flowers, grass, or animals, soothed her spirit as much as exercising her medical skills soothed her psyche.

Fannie had had the foresight to hire a gardener with an artist's eye. Unschooled, he arranged the beds so that flowers bloomed year round. Today, Hattie enjoyed the espaliered yellow roses that rambled across the brick privacy wall, climbing high above the lavender blue blossoms of mounding plumbago. The effect was very Monet.

A heavy crow sank onto a branch, flapping its wings for balance, reminding her unhappily of a bird seen on a dusty street of the French army base in Nantes. He was an unusual sight in urban New Orleans. His feathered iridescence swayed above the fragrant clematis and jasmine that twined together along the top of the wall. Pungent gardenia blossoms filled the air with their heady aroma and floating pollen tickled Hattie's nose.

The crow's obsidian eyes calculated the possibility of stealing a croissant, judging Hattie to be an interloper between him and something tasty. His caws made her skin crawl like fingernails across a chalkboard, but the muted clatter behind her followed by faint laughter made her relax. The well-oiled DeValcourt household work was well underway.

Both arms crossed behind her head, Hattie thought of other breakfasts at the bistro near the Sorbonne. Fannie's peaceful garden was a sharp contrast to those over-pruned Paris hedges. In New Orleans, wherever Hattie looked, the city rewarded her with beauty and uninhibited color. Paris was unique—more restrained in black and white, its tight displays of color corralled beneath striped awnings and in corner flower stalls.

The air in Paris was in marked contrast to the humid New Orleans atmosphere, a difference between temperate and subtropical.

Hattie loved both cities. She appreciated their differences. Closing her eyes, she recalled her memory of Luke strolling down the cobblestone street in a French Army uniform. Nostalgia washed over her. Those days, those cobblestones, were an ocean and a world away.

Hattie had been a serious student at the Sorbonne while still enjoying her friendships with the other students, who invariably dressed in black. Happy to have become the physician she'd always dreamed of being, she wondered if she'd ever be able to put her skills to full use. In the United States, women physicians were not well accepted. They remained a distinct minority in the mid-twentieth century, but the war was changing that.

Hattie's arms stretched wide to figuratively embrace her beloved city, happy to enjoy a day free of storm trooper boots and bursts of gunfire.

She and Luke planned to visit her parents today and meet Gertrude, a widowed friend who helped people like themselves find a home. It buoyed Hattie to think they could soon have their very own love nest, comfortably feathered with their favorite belongings.

Peering at the angle of the morning shadows, Hattie estimated it must be close to time to leave the house. Inhaling a last deep breath of garden perfume, she swallowed a final bite of croissant and drained her cup of coffee. Time to rouse her sleepyhead husband.

PART FOUR

HATTIE CLOSED THE door and blinked so her eyes could adjust to the dim basement light.

Luke sprawled in the twisted sheets across their bed and Hattie "tsked." The man could sleep away the days. She exhaled coffee breath in his ear, but he didn't move a muscle. She ruffled his hair, then shook his shoulder to rouse him. He murmured something unintelligible.

"Luke? Darling? Rise and shine, sleepyhead." His eyes remained closed.

Shrugging off her robe, Hattie clattered around, making noise and singing at the top of her voice while she dressed.

She watched Luke, who barely stirred, from the corner of her eye. His left hand rose to his forehead, his right arm remaining strangely immobile.

"You okay this morning?" She leaned over for his kiss, but straightened with alarm at his appearance.

A resentful thought of Pierre and Marie Chennault flicked through Hattie's mind, gone as quickly as it had appeared. She would forever attribute Luke's poor health to their treachery.

"*Mon Dieu*, Luke! What's wrong?" Fear speared through Hattie and she grasped his chin to gently turn his head for a look straight on.

One eye, the right one, had swelled and seemed to protrude. Its sclera was no longer white, but was bloodshot red. A pinkish teardrop trembled in the inner corner.

Time stopped for Hattie. She held her breath and catalogued more abnormalities. The fingers of Luke's right hand quivered, faintly blue against the rumpled sheet.

"Luke, honey? What happened?" She begged him for a response, struggling to subdue her alarm, aware that time could be Luke's enemy. He mumbled a few garbled words through teeth that clicked and chattered despite the warmth of the room.

Hattie knew his shivers were an instinctive effort to keep his body oxygenated. She checked her husband's vital signs, the typical first step for her clinic patients, and acknowledged Luke's multiple irregularities. Her own heart began to speed.

Not trusting herself, she said aloud, "I'm running upstairs to get your father," hoping he hadn't already left. Abner DeValcourt would be more thorough, and perhaps offer Luke a more optimistic prognosis. "Be right back."

She ran up the stairs two at a time, her heart thudding. She didn't dare examine the likely diagnosis.

She spied Fannie in the foyer pulling on a pair of creamy gloves. She was about to leave, the car and driver waiting curbside for her. Hattie's breathless arrival startled her, so that she asked, "Where's the fire, honey?"

Hattie latched onto Fannie's hands, squeezing tight. "I-Is Dr. DeValcourt here? He has to check Luke."

"He's already left. Can I help?" Fannie yanked off her gloves and threw them with her purse on top of the Biedermeier chest.

Raising her voice, she sent Coco to cancel the waiting car. For the first time in many years, Luke needed his mother. Her bridge game was trivial. It could wait.

"Luke is sick." Hattie's pretty eyes flashed her alarm. "I want to be wrong, but I'm afraid he's dangerously ill."

Mrs. DeValcourt eyed her daughter-in-law. During Hattie's time in Fannie's household, she'd learned the girl was an astute medical practitioner. Fear galvanized the older woman, who'd been a ward nurse when she met young Dr. Abner DeValcourt.

"I'll call for an ambulance. Let's get Luke to the hospital first." She turned Hattie back to the stairs.

"You get him ready and I'll wait for the ambulance." Picking up the hall phone that sat on the Biedermeier, she called emergency services, then dialed the hospital and paged her husband. Praying the entire time, Fannie cancelled her bridge game and removed her hat.

Her bridge buddies of many decades were dear friends who understood all about family emergencies.

Downstairs, Luke stumbled to the bathroom with Hattie's help. It was a relief that he could at least shuffle on his own. Unshed tears clogged her throat when she saw his right arm swung useless at his side. He'd suffered a stroke! She couldn't make sense of the things he mumbled, but he understood Hattie, docile and much too quiet as she dressed him. She was reassured that Luke had recognized he had a problem. She hung her hopes on that.

Preoccupied by her thoughts, Hattie hadn't heard footsteps and was startled when ambulance attendants burst into the apartment, preceded by the competent Fannie.

The men had expected the worst and were astonished to find their patient fully dressed and sitting quietly. Thinking their time had been wasted, they gave each other an exasperated look until they noticed Luke's pallor and his red eye, now more pronounced. They repeated the check of his vital signs, which continued to be abnormal.

They were confounded when Luke refused to lie on the stretcher, wasting more valuable time. It was impossible for him to climb the stairs, so the medics improvised and carried him up on their strong, linked arms. They lost more time at the ambulance, Luke resisting until he collapsed. He was then strapped in and the ambulance, its siren blaring, sped the mercifully short mile to Hôtel-Dieu.

Abner DeValcourt paced across the covered ER entrance, its awning flapping in the morning breeze as he waited. Dr. DeValcourt, chief of surgery, had left the operating room when Fannie called. He wore a surgical gown, his silvery hair tucked under a sterile cap. Fear radiated off him despite a conscious struggle to remain impassive.

"My God, Luke!" His first sight of his boy dispelled Dr. DeValcourt's bland professional affect. He needed only one glance to recognize the signs that a blood vessel had ruptured in his son's brain.

Abner couldn't know how bad the rupture might be, but the staff neurosurgeon would soon answer that question. The attendants loaded Luke into a wheelchair as Dr. DeValcourt ordered the intake personnel to notify the surgeon they were on their way.

Dr. DeValcourt hurried beside Luke as the wheelchair careened along the corridors, until they whooshed through a last set of silent double doors, coming to rest in the neurosurgeons' bailiwick.

Luke was semiconscious, barely aware of his headlong rush through the corridors. Luke's profound lassitude frightened his father and other hospital staff. His eyes were shut, and his chin bobbed loosely on his chest.

Sleep. Luke wanted, needed, nothing more than sleep, but one after another, people pried up his eyelids and shined brutal lights in his eyes. Someone, an orderly maybe, roughly removed his clothes, and the too-thin hospital gown was leaving him cold. Then orderlies manhandled him onto an icy hard surface that chilled him and made him shiver.

Strapped to a gurney and immobilized on his back, someone gave Luke the blessed relief of warm, heated blankets. He was vaguely aware of movement, lights speeding rapidly overhead, and bumps and faint rumbling from the gurney beneath him. That he should perhaps be concerned swam into his thoughts, but he couldn't sustain the idea and it faded away.

Subdued conversations rumbled around him, disturbing his deepening reverie. Once, a loud voice commanded, "Don't move."

Not wanting, or able, to move anyhow, Luke remained still.

Immense heaviness in his chest caused breathing already difficult to become more laborious. Luke believed he was back in the filthy Nazi stockade, again imprisoned, though at some level he knew that was no longer the case. His head squeezed in a vise ever more tightly until the pain became unbearable and he began to thrash. He dimly understood that the thin, whining moan he heard came from his own throat.

Luke's head pain throbbed, severe and merciless. His world had become hazy and smudged. His fatigue had no bottom, his surroundings were unbearably cold, and his exhalations endlessly deep. He gulped his progressively shallower inhalations, now spaced farther apart.

It was Hattie he needed, and he thought he called out for her. Those arrayed around his gurney only saw that his tongue lolled with garbled sounds. His eyes wouldn't focus, and his nonsensical utterances gradually faded into silence.

From a great distance, Luke heard Hattie's soft voice echo, and a feathery pressure grazed his cheek. Vastly relieved, he struggled up from an infinitely deep well to a murky consciousness. He relaxed, all his tension gone. Was that what he had waited for? This touch? That soft caress?

Luke wanted to hear more of Hattie's voice, but he couldn't respond as a vortex of impossible fatigue pulled him into its grip.

A tear slid from the corner of Luke's eye and the battered warrior exhaled his final breath.

Cradling her husband's head, Hattie cried, panicked, "Luke! Luke! My darling love."

Luke died from a weak blood vessel that bulged into an aneurysm, then ruptured, flooding his brain. That paradoxically starved the brain of oxygen and caused irreversible damage to his autonomic functions, which led to his death. Her medical understanding of this cascade of events did nothing to ease Hattie's grief.

Helpless to arrest Luke's demise, the hospital staff faded from the room. Awful keening leaked through the door when Luke's parents briefly stepped away, leaving Hattie privacy to mourn the loss of her handsome, laughing lover. The man she'd braved her own death to save was irretrievably gone. Ironic that she lost her warrior only after they reached safety with their families.

Hattie would often wish, during the rest of her life, she had stayed awake that last night to constantly remind her husband how much he was loved.

Abner and Fannie DeValcourt joined Hattie in grief. Fannie caressed the lifeless face that still held the warmth of a beating heart. Luke's family huddled, numb, as an orderly shrouded his vacated body with a sheet and trundled it from the room. Their wistful eyes followed the silent gurney until it disappeared around the corner.

Luke's light had been extinguished and their world went dark.

Dawn each day approached the summer's heat by throwing stunning pinks and salmons across fluffy drifting clouds. Sleepless, Hattie shared the spectacular sunrises with thoughts of Luke.

To his parents, the passing hours remained interminable, each minute borne grudgingly. All three, Abner, Fannie, and Hattie, tiptoed around in silence and mourned in private. Luke's parents retreated to politeness, showing Hattie distant courtesy once they realized she preferred it so.

The young widow wanted solitude to reminisce about Luke and their shared memories. Not contemplating all they had shared would be worse than forgetting. Hattie felt responsible for Luke's death. He'd gone to France to find her, and she was certain his parents also blamed her for his loss.

Beneath the grief, she bore an additional terrible, unbearable secret—a trace of relief that though the worst had happened, it had happened to Luke, not to her. Relief conjoined with guilt led to a profound depression that defeated Hattie's normally sunny disposition.

The pounds she had regained upon their return now fell away for a second time. Skin draped loose over jutting bones and her shoulders bowed with unbearable, desolate weight. Her dull eyes were red-rimmed with the tears that woke her every morning, their lively sparkle gone. At the DeValcourt table, food was something to push around a plate in an imitation of eating while she waited courteously until she could return to her solitary bed.

Hattie endured the burial ceremony in Metairie Cemetery, standing immobile before the cold white marble of the DeValcourt mausoleum. A succession of chiseled dates, some two centuries old, were blurry, as were the names of Luke's ancestors. The eroded numbers and letters cut into the stone only emphasized the starkness of the newest engraved name. Luke Abner Lambremont DeValcourt, M.D., the stone proclaimed, a life extinguished far too early. The harsh whiteness of the inscription brought tears to her eyes.

The years of Luke's life carved below his name said nothing of the man. It was intolerable that a man so full of life was reduced to scratched hieroglyphs. Hattie's family supported her, thinking they understood her loss. Hattie knew she would never experience that all-consuming love a second time.

Hattie had measured her life in terms of their time together, fewer than two years. She twisted and kissed the simple ring he'd given her, vowing no other would ever replace it. Surrounded by her caring family, thunderstorms of loneliness drenched Hattie.

This was far worse than sleeping on the hard damp dirt of a French forest alone and hungry. Worse even than losing an unborn child. Of all the difficulties she'd undergone, she was sure she wouldn't survive this one. Her husband was imprisoned again, this time forever, behind the bronze doors of a massive sepulcher.

Stoic at his son's death, Abner DeValcourt returned to his medical practice, wasting little time. He, too, felt responsible for Luke's death. He had neglected Luke's symptoms. If he had paid attention, he could've prevented the outcome. His guilt hastened an irreversible decline in his health.

As a ward nurse long ago, Fannie DeValcourt understood the rhythms of life and death with a philosophical acceptance of that yin and yang. Fannie handled her son's loss objectively, but her husband's rapid decline so soon after was difficult—too much, too soon.

One afternoon she found a morose Hattie outside on the patio and patted her daughter-in-law's arm.

"I'm sorry to be a bother, Hattie, but can we talk?" Hattie looked up, her eyes dull.

"Of course, Maman."

The simple "Maman" forced tears to Fannie's eyes. She shook them away.

"It's just—I'm worried about your father-in-law."

The concern on Fannie's pretty, faded face roused Hattie and made her aware that she wasn't alone in the world. Her hand was gentle on Fannie's arm.

"Why? What's wrong?"

Hattie watched as Luke's father declined. He was a man she loved and appreciated, who freely shared his medical knowledge. Less than a year after Luke died, Dr. Abner DeValcourt succumbed. He joined his son in the family tomb. His heart had failed. The two survivors knew he died of a broken heart, believing he didn't deserve to live. The gentle, brilliant man's death hit Fannie and Hattie hard.

As the months passed, Western Europe suffered and starved, and died in ferocious battles. Hattie, home in New Orleans, worked hard, but felt alone.

The DeValcourt patio remained her refuge. Daily on clear mornings she winced barefoot in her nightclothes across gritty, punishing bricks to a curlicued wrought iron chair.

She lost herself in nature and imagined Luke's caresses in every breeze. It was her way to escape the news of war, of Axis cruelty, and on the patio she began the long task of emerging from her grief.

The kitchen staff brought out Hattie's breakfast, which she appreciated. She would take small sips of *café au lait* and bite into a warm *beignet*, enjoying them as if a new experience. The return of Hattie's appetite gratified the cook. She thought the lovely young woman was finally taking her first steps to recovery.

Hattie began to appreciate again the people and experiences that had once populated her world, finding they were still immeasurably enriching her life.

From time to time, thoughts of Marie Chennault popped into Hattie's head and her skin crawled. The duplicitous Frenchwoman was as close to an enemy as Hattie had ever had. Ironic that she wasted any thought on the woman. She and her husband Pierre had cost Luke his life.

One such day, Hattie wondered why she'd thought of Marie at that particular moment? Was it a premonition? She knew many people believed there was no such thing as coincidence, or that humans have a sixth sense that gives them a certain awareness.

Hattie shook her head and refused to entertain the farfetched theory. Her mouth twisted. Why let these thoughts into her head? She challenged herself to stop the self-pity and follow Annette Rousseau's example.

She recalled that Annette's longtime lover had been killed in the first days of Germany's invasion. Annette had mourned, but knew that holding onto her sorrow wouldn't change anything. Instead, she took each new day as a blessing with unfailing humor and Gallic practicality.

Hattie knew neither Luke nor his father would have wanted her to waste her days as a recluse. So she shook off her depression and asked to take over her father-in-law's clinic work at Hôtel-Dieu Hospital, leaving his surgeries in other hands.

Fannie DeValcourt smiled from her upstairs window to see the younger widow DeValcourt set off for work that first morning. She dropped the edge of her lace curtain and glanced at an ornate ormolu clock on her tall dresser. She had scheduled an important appointment with her attorney and had to hurry to not be late.

Each night, Hattie tuned the Bakelite radio to the national news. She listened to the war news out of respect for Luke's role in the fight against the Germans. She was appalled to learn that scores of innocent French citizens were being arbitrarily executed. The nation's population was decimated and perilously close to starvation. French Jews, the target of Hitler's genocide, suffered greatly as they died.

The French museums were gutted of priceless art, taken by Hitler's officers as the spoils of war. Thousands of young Frenchwomen were raped and impregnated by thuggish Nazis. Elderly men and women, wanting only to live in peace and grow old with their neighbors and friends, were brutally killed, thought of as a drain on resources.

Hattie clenched her fists. She didn't understand why President Roosevelt hesitated to join the war in Europe. And on that day in December of 1941, she screamed when the Japanese had bombed Pearl Harbor. Had the tiny Asian nation attacked, thinking a weak United States was a viable takeover target? How much more war would her country tolerate?

She itched for the United States to retaliate, but could they now, suddenly threatened on both coasts? Within days of the Japanese bombing in Hawaii, both Germany and Italy declared war on the United States. That seemed finally to be the tipping point.

The United States at last battled back, committing thousands of soldiers and sailors and a never-ending stream of foodstuffs and powerful weapons to fight the Axis in the east and the Japanese in the west.

Hattie's fugue dissipated with her country's challenges. She had to regain an emotional balance to handle the hectic pace of her medical practice. Hôtel-Dieu needed her more than ever. The clinic was sorely undermanned now that many doctors and nurses had been drafted into the military.

She stumbled through long days, never getting enough rest, doing what she could while trying to boost the morale of an exhausted hospital staff.

There was no time for grief.

PART FIVE

AFTER CONFIRMING TO Hattie that she and her husband were Nazi spies, Marie had fled the army base before the commandant could organize a group of soldiers to follow her.

Before reaching the village, Marie stepped from the truck she'd hired, frightened that she was being followed by French trackers. She gave the driver everything she and Pierre owned, with only her baby left in her arms. An abandoned shed served as her protection as the sky grew dark. It was there that Marie first began to lose her grip on sanity, imagining pursuers all around her in the stubbled fields.

After dark, Marie set off carrying her baby son. Her silk stockings were soon tattered and her shoes dampened as she flapped across two miles of uneven open fields before finally reaching the home of Pierre's parents in Chennault village. Her sanity already slipping, she forgot that Hattie had promised her time to leave before she would alert the Nantes commandant, only remembering her ignominious departure.

When the fortunes of war changed and the Nazi occupiers of Chennault were forced to retreat from the village, they burned all its buildings and executed everyone, children included. That Marie survived was a fluke. She had been scavenging for food in fields too far from the village to hear the murderous gunfire and screams. The odor of burning human flesh nauseated her well before she reached home. Once there, she discovered only smoldering destruction. She fell to her knees in the formerly picturesque town square in front of the little stone church.

The sight of her child's still body lying in Pierre's arms overwhelmed her. Her family had given the Nazis their allegiance, but in the end it made no difference. After all they'd done, this was the ultimate betrayal. Already teetering at the edge of a mental breakdown, the perfidy of the Nazis tipped her into insanity. It was the *coup de grâce*. Her husband, his parents, and her beloved son were gone.

Marie seized on Hattie as the person responsible for her losses. She was sure Pierre's commandant had had her followed when she'd fled the base. The French army had been sent after her, the Germans knew it, and that was why Chennault village was destroyed. Everyone would be alive but for Hattie.

Numbed and unhinged by loss and betrayal, Marie remained lucid long enough to appeal to the international Red Cross on a humanitarian basis for entry to the United States. Accepting that the devastated young woman deserved rescue, the Red Cross added Marie Chennault to an overcrowded ship of refugees that sailed to New York, where a sympathetic United States government welcomed her to America.

Ellis Island immigration processed Marie into the country without a passport as they did for thousands of other undocumented refugees fleeing the European war. Marie obscured her identity, telling authorities her *prénom* was Jeanne and adding a noble French surname to become Jeanne Beauvais.

Plucking the valuable dark blue U.S. passport from the fingers of a compassionate immigration officer, she mentally sneered at the "sloppy" process. The officer hadn't seen the wild insanity in Jeanne's pretty eyes.

Uninterested in the spectacular scenery passing the window of a speeding southbound locomotive, Marie Chennault swayed from side to side. She fell asleep sitting upright when darkness fell.

Her choice of her favorite red silk dress proved to be impractical for travel. It had become a mass of wrinkles, another annoyance in the fastidious woman's life. Her smooth, dark bun had loosened, increasingly untidy as the jerky miles sped past under her feet.

Marie could've packed bags of fashionable belongings, but she hadn't. She wanted to set a certain tone, and the lack of luggage gave her authenticity. That's what she was after. That and revenge, of course.

New Orleans, Louisiana, with its French heritage, was the logical destination for French-speaking immigrants fleeing the war in Europe. At least, that was what she'd told overburdened officials when she arrived at Ellis Island.

The long train ride south from New York gave Marie ample time to invent torments for Hattie to suffer before she killed the woman. Other passengers avoided eye contact and conversation with the wild-eyed woman whose mouth contorted in cruel grimaces.

In her smelly boarding house bedroom, Jeanne studied her reflection in the small cloudy mirror that hung above the sink. With a sigh, she dunked her head in the bowl, stripped her dark hair of color, and became a champagne blonde. Having done as much as she could to transform her appearance, Jeanne decided it was too soon to confront her archenemy, though the time would soon be right.

Fannie insisted her household continue to celebrate Christmas, which was somewhat easier this year with Luke two years gone and his father dead a year later.

Christmas was almost upon them. Hattie and Fannie had toasted the coming holiday with the household staff in front of Fannie's beautiful tree, and had distributed the customary annual bonuses while the radio played traditional Christmas music in the background.

Hattie pulled back her bedroom curtain on the view of a dead brown world outside. The movement of the curtain stirred chilled air that penetrated her nightgown. New Orleans had cycled into its usual brief, mild winter. Hattie decided to step out for a breath of refreshing cold air.

The bare branches of Fannie's pecan tree thrust across a gray morning sky like bony fingers, and Hattie looked in vain for new buds. Each fall, Fannie's pecan trees were the first to drop their withered leaves to the ground for the next spring's mulch and the last trees to leaf out in the spring. Crackling leaves and overlooked nuts crunched under Hattie's slippers.

Two evergreen oaks shared Fannie's yard with the pecan tree. Dying leaves blanketed the ground, their chlorophyll factories having fed their hosts only to be unceremoniously pushed out. Unlike pecan trees, oaks repeated the cycle twice in a year, growing new leaves both winter and spring.

Back inside, Hattie bounded up the stairs in her warmest clothes.

She opened Fannie's bedroom door and poked in, saying, "I'm off."

Fannie, still snuggled in her big bed under the quilts, held out her arms for a hug. "A shame you have to leave our warm house."

Hattie's eyes crinkled. "Want to settle in your chair before I go?"

At Fannie's nod, Hattie helped her shuffle to her favorite chair by the window in the oversized master bedroom. Her mother-in-law settled a warm shawl over her increasingly bent shoulders.

Hattie looked around a room filled with a lifetime of treasured mementos. Her entire basement apartment would fit in this one chamber. She still lived in Fannie's basement, in the rooms she'd shared with Luke. Hattie liked its privacy and refused to move to grander rooms upstairs.

This morning there was no impatience. It hadn't been easy to carve a large enough sliver from her hospital duties to shop for gifts, but she'd managed. Their celebration this Christmas would include Hattie's parents and her brother Jack and his wife for the first time.

Jeanne Beauvais—the former Marie Chennault—had been hired as a temporary sales clerk despite having no prior sales experience. It was the Christmas season, and her looks and sibilant French accent had carried the day. She'd found the job soon after arriving in New Orleans.

It was a drastic comedown in status for the former German spy. Her low status and equally low wages hadn't improved her mood. Her earnings were barely enough to keep a roof over her head, and she was annoyed that anything left over after rent and food had to be spent on personal care products.

It was Christmas Eve and Jeanne slogged down the ugly, wet, cold sidewalks of a bad neighborhood in New Orleans, and grumbled as she shivered. She kept her eyes averted from the storefronts and the garish American decorations, so overblown and different from those of her beloved France. Angry, alone, and lonely, she reached her shabby boarding house.

Mlle. Beauvais was tidying merchandise and, as always, glanced up whenever a customer entered the shop. Startled, she coughed and angled her head toward the floor.

In an undertone to the other clerk, she said, "I have to take a break. I'll be back in a minute," and walked rapidly to the back holding her stomach. Her annoyed associate, busy with multiple customers, gave her a sidelong glance, but said nothing.

Jeanne's enemy had come in to the very shop where Jeanne spent her miserable days.

Hattie had pushed open the door and entered the fragrant and warm Magazine Street boutique, smiling and greeting people by name. One familiar-looking clerk hurriedly walked away. Hattie couldn't quite place the blonde woman.

Hattie was in a hurry and dismissed the thought.

"Merry Christmas, everyone," Hattie called out. Popular with the clerks, several tried to chat with her, but she headed straight for the package pick-up area in the rear of the shop. She paid for her purchases, grabbed her wrapped packages, and rushed out of the store, there and gone in less than fifteen minutes.

Jeanne watched Hattie leave, then returned to her sales station.

"Who was that woman?" she asked, trying for an innocent voice.

"Hattie DeValcourt." Her fellow clerk answered. "Isn't she beautiful? Poor thing. Her husband was wounded in the war and died only a few weeks after they came home. They were very close."

"Too bad," Jeanne shook her head, her expression and tone acceptably dismayed, but internally she was thrilled, delighted at Hattie's pain and loss. She was surprised that Luke had survived Nazi imprisonment; not many men did.

Jeanne patted a curl into place, missing the sleek dark *chignon* she had worn for so many years. She blamed Hattie for that loss, too. She'd had to scissor off her beautiful long hair, and bleach what was left into short, riotous curls— *à la* Jean Harlow—that was disgustingly American. It worked, though, and she hadn't been recognized. Her new hairdo and expertly applied heavy makeup would hide Jeanne in plain sight in New Orleans, right under Hattie's nose. All she needed now was that hated woman's address.

Maybe the ignorance of these clerks could help her after all. "Where does Mrs. DeValcourt live?" They shrugged. No one in the shop knew Hattie's address. *But the day's not a complete loss*, Jeanne thought. *Hattie's husband is dead, that's good. She should endure as much pain as possible before I kill her. Maybe first kill her relatives, if she has any. And make Hattie look like the killer.*

The planet was becoming a world of women as war killed off the men. No doubt there were some women who deserved to lose their lives, too. Who that should be depended on a person's point of view. Jeanne knew one woman in particular she wanted dead. She would do the killing, but before that she'd do everything she could to make Hattie suffer.

The January sun hadn't yet cleared the horizon when Hattie tapped at Fannie's closed door and entered the bedroom. Visiting with her delightful mother-in-law for a few minutes each morning before leaving was one of Hattie's favorite habits. Their holiday had been excellent, though it had been shadowed by the loss of their husbands.

She tiptoed to the bed where Fannie nestled in her warm covers. She was awake, her eyes twinkling.

Hattie laughed. "I didn't mean to wake you."

Fannie was delighted by Hattie's laughter. Leaving a dent across her forehead, Fannie pushed back her thick hairnet and grasped Hattie's smooth hand with wrinkled, age-spotted fingers.

"Honey, Abner was a doctor. This early hour is a lifelong habit. I've been waking up with the chickens for longer than you've been alive."

"Of course, what was I thinking?" Hattie's brow wrinkled. Her mother-in-law had shared this comfortable bed for many, many decades with a warm and loving husband. Yet she could still present a cheerful face to the world. What remarkable emotional strength, Hattie thought.

"I'm about to leave, but I wanted to check on you first. My clinic hours are beginning much earlier with all these winter colds and flu. I swear my days are longer than ever. I have no idea whether I'll get home before you're right back here in bed. Please don't wait supper for me."

Hattie shivered a little. Fannie, snugly covered by blankets and quilts, liked the room kept cold at night. Though not the robust social animal she had been before Abner died, she remained alert, active, and interested in the medical world she'd been part of for so long.

Fannie answered, "I will *too* wait! Our talks about medicine are the high point of my day. You'll just have to put up with this old woman because it makes me feel relevant." She looked Hattie up and down.

"You look especially nice today, dear."

Indeed, Hattie's appearance was another indication of the pleasure she derived from her medical practice. She'd eschewed her black clothes in favor of beautifully tailored suits. It was not that her grief didn't linger, but it didn't need to be displayed. Today she wore a gray heathered wool jacket with a skirt hemmed just below the knee. Before she left the house, for warmth she would slip on a fox squirrel fur cape and a matching cloche almost the same color as her short hair.

She swept Fannie's hair to the side and kissed her grooved forehead gently.

"You're so sweet to me, Fannie! Thank you. Now, what I can do for you before I go?"

"Help me to the bathroom, please? My old knees hardly hold me up these days. Will you have time to help me to my chair, too?"

"Of course, Maman. Ready for some breakfast? I'll call down while I wait for you, and have it brought up." After she made the call, she wandered around Fannie's room. It smelled just like her—sweet and powdery from decades of perfume and makeup. The walls displayed family photographs. Hattie studied the images of Luke, growing from child to man. Some of the photos included Fannie's servants, but she and Abner were rarely shown. Hattie shook her head at their absence, knowing they'd been the heart of the household.

Fannie's comfortable nest of a plush ruby velvet bergère and ottoman waited for her beside a small table, close to the window that overlooked her garden.

Hattie turned when Fannie spoke, moving across the room by grasping various pieces of furniture.

"Can you believe the stairs intimidate me after all the years I've traipsed them up and down?" It was difficult to watch her irregular gait as she approached. Hattie reached out and helped Fannie to her nest.

"Want Kitty?" Hattie asked, then handed Fannie her warm, fluffy cat.

"Thank you, yes. Sorry to be a bother."

"I've told you a dozen times that you're not a bother. I can never thank you enough for helping me through the dark days. You're wonderful."

"Time well spent, Hattie, you with that good heart all your life."

Fannie had given Hattie her unconditional love and support after Luke died, her generous spirit providing buoyancy that probably came at some personal cost. The holidays this year, though, seemed to have stolen much of Fannie's physical strength. Now she was using a cane or a walker to get around, difficult to accept for a woman who had always been energetic.

Hattie tucked a blue and gray knitted cashmere throw over Fannie's knees before leaving to see her waiting patients. She trotted through the cold January air to the waiting car and driver, her collar held tight to her throat.

Staring unseeing through the car's side window, she thought sadly that Fannie was much weaker now than she'd been when she and Luke came home.

Even a strong woman couldn't overcome advancing age, especially after suffering double blows when her son and husband died.

She mused about the difficulty Fannie was having getting around, and vowed that tonight they would discuss hiring a companion to help her during the day. Hattie had set aside her own emotional life, though she sorely missed Luke's loving arms and the satisfaction of their sexual union. She might not have another experience like that.

Little bombs of sleet exploded against the car windows all the way to the clinic. Busy with her reflections, Hattie barely noticed there was only one bundled-up person outside on the St. Charles sidewalk, braving the day's bad weather.

That morning, Fannie enjoyed a good breakfast, crunching a triangle of buttered toast as she sat watching icy sleet build up on the windowpane with quiet glassy sounds. She had become so decadent these days. She snickered to herself that she didn't miss her youth at all. Often she didn't change into day clothes unless the day warranted it.

She dabbed her napkin to the corners of her mouth and set aside her tray, then rearranged her warm throw. She picked up the mystery she was reading, soon to become engrossed in the story. After an hour, she drifted into a nap, glasses askew, her head slumped against the chair back. The Dorothy Sayers novel lay open on her lap. Kitty purred in her sleep, curled next to Fannie's warm hip.

The bedroom door edged open inch by tentative inch. Having stealthily climbed the servants' backstairs unnoticed, a figure tiptoed quietly into the unheated room. On the level below, no floorboards creaked over the heads of Fannie's industrious household. They were oblivious to the activity taking place in Fannie's bedroom.

The trespasser's gloved fingers slipped off the unlit gas heater's spigot, unable to gain purchase. One glove removed, the spigot opened fully but was deliberately left unlit. A tripled cloth covered the intruder's nose as gas escaped, softly hissing. Lethal fumes gradually displaced life-giving oxygen in the room. The prowler quietly closed Fannie's door, trapping the poisoned air in the room with the napping woman, and left the house, never having been seen or heard.

Her servants knew not to bother Fannie until she rang for them, and they continued with their other duties until it was time for lunch.

Fannie and Kitty napped undisturbed, until their rest became eternal. They had become the first casualties of a wicked plan.

Her elbows propped on the chest-high counter at a ward nurse's station, Hattie took in the muffled sounds that swirled around her. Most people thought hospitals were quiet places, but the truth was they were busy, though work was conducted as privately and unobtrusively as possible.

She enjoyed the hushed footsteps, the swishing mops and brooms, the distant laughter, metallic clinks, and more. Hattie's small smile reflected her pleasure at being right there, right then. She felt she could burst into song from sheer exuberance.

The hospital had been told there might soon be an armistice. She wondered what would happen to her when the hospital's former employees returned.

A chilly loneliness swept through her with the thought she could be asked to leave. This was home, and these people who chose to heal injury and battle disease were her people. She would fight to stay here. Like Hattie, others had invested years of time and vast energy to be here in this building. Along the way, they'd jettisoned old wives' tales and outmoded ideas and replaced them with medical facts. They had lost their ignorance and self-absorption, and learned through experience to give good care to those who were broken and in pain.

Carrying a heavy stack of files, she pushed away from the counter and started toward her small office at the very moment the hospital paging system blared.

"Paging Doctor DeValcourt. Doctor DeValcourt."

The obnoxious tinny voice was much too loud in the hospital corridors. She hesitated in the act of pushing open her office door, letting it swoosh to a close as she turned back to the ward station to answer the page.

Patched through, she listened to the caller. Her files scattered unnoticed on the counter while her face lost its vibrant coloring. She sagged against the high counter, needing its support. Since eavesdropping was the ward clerk's chief pleasure, Annie easily overheard loud wails from the receiver pressed against Hattie's ear. Hattie interrupted abruptly, her questions silencing the caller. At the ward clerk desk, Annie's countenance changed from curiosity to alarm.

"What? Gas? Did you call the police? Well, hang up and call them right now—and don't touch anything. Hear me? Don't touch *anything*. That's important. Yes, Mimi, I know you had to open the window. But starting right now, none of you—you, Coco, too—no one—goes in Fannie's room unless the police say it's all right. I'm on my way."

When she touched Annie's shoulder, the woman felt Hattie's hand tremble through the sweater.

"Get an ambulance to my home right now, Annie. When you've done that, call scheduling. Cancel my rounds and appointments for the rest of the day. And apologize for me. This is a family emergency and I have to go home. I may not be back for several days.

"Oh. Right after the ambulance, call a cab for me."

"Yes, doctor," said the wide-eyed Annie. Hattie added a "thank you" from halfway down the hall.

The clerk watched Hattie's figure recede as she dialed. She'd never seen any doctor scuttle down a corridor, and certainly not at that speed. Unseemly, Annie's expression seemed to say, especially for a woman in a medical world of men.

Hattie peered through the windshield from the back seat of the cab and groaned at the congestion in front of her home.

The driver grumbled, "Looka dat. Them ambulances and p'lice cars choked da whole street. Somethin' big hasta be hapnin'. Lookit all them blinkin' lights. Tell me *that's* not a waste, it bein' broad daylight an' all."

"This is close enough. I'll get out here, driver, thank you."

She thrust a few folded bills at the man and jumped out, her squirrel cape open. It flapped as Hattie dashed along the sidewalk. The heavy medical bag that had once belonged to her father-in-law thudded against her leg. Later, she'd find a large bruise there, with no idea from what.

Hattie prayed she had misunderstood Mimi's urgent call. Except for advanced age, Fannie was healthy. Surely the emergency response team had revived her by now. In her mind's eye, Hattie saw Fannie looking around like a bright-eyed bird, questioning all the fuss.

Despite the prayers, foreboding settled heavily over Hattie. Sniffling her tears into submission, she scaled the marble steps up to the front door.

A policeman blocked Hattie from entering Fannie's house. With an imperious hand raised, he demanded Hattie's identification, saying "And you are…?"

Hattie skidded to an off-balance stop, breathless from the dash up the icy steps, slick with sleet.

"This is my home. I live here. I'm a doctor, and I have to see my patient."

He showed the common skepticism that women could ever really be doctors. It was still extraordinary, despite all the male doctors displaced to active military duty on two fronts.

The policeman snorted. "Prove it, lady. This here's a crime scene. That means you can't go in until I see your identification first, and then I check with my sergeant."

"A crime scene?"

Hattie frowned and dropped Abner DeValcourt's heavy bag to the steps, sorry it hadn't hit the man's foot and ashamed of the thought. Trembling fingers scrabbled in her purse for ID. She thrust it out to the man, who looked very cold.

While she waited for the sergeant to give the go-ahead, she wondered what happened, and whether the twinkle in Fannie's lovely eyes was truly gone. Despite Hattie's trepidation, her mouth curled at the way Fannie waited each night for Hattie's return, her violet eyes so like Luke's dark blue ones.

It almost seemed as though Fannie would have two goblets of wine waiting, eager to hear about Hattie's day.

Fannie had been enthralled and amazed at how quickly the medical field was changing these days, thanks to the government's involvement. The recently developed penicillin and sulfonamide medicines were truly miraculous, and she applauded the new commonsense standards for a sterile workplace, required now in all hospitals, and how particularly helpful those standards were in the surgical suites. As was her way, Fannie kept Hattie on her toes by asking a multitude of questions about all the procedures.

What was good? What was bad? Was it better now, with more women physicians in the medical field?

Approved for entry, Hattie ran up the littered back stairs, gritty and covered in slush from police brogans and the shoes of emergency techs. Reacting on the run, without thinking, she stuffed paper trash from the stair treads in her pockets. Ludicrous to care about trash, she thought, when there was so much more to be worried about today.

Fannie had become Hattie's second mother. She was a real confidante and a non-judgmental listener. Hattie could turn to her parents or to her brother and his wife, but that didn't matter at the moment. She had lost a friend, a beloved and rare woman who understood Hattie's life and profession.

Hattie shook her head, hardly believing she was the only surviving member of the DeValcourt family. It happened so quickly, and nothing made sense.

The heavy pall of darkness from when Luke died now draped itself over her a second time. Tentacles of despair entered her deepest thoughts.

Stopped by a hallway sentry at Fannie's bedroom door, Hattie couldn't get to her mother-in-law. The man summoned the detective in charge, who sauntered over. He looked Hattie up and down before he spoke, and when he finally opened his mouth, he was far from sympathetic.

"You can't be in here, ma'am. We have work to do." He turned to leave, but cocked his head and turned back. "Who did you say you are?"

Hattie identified herself.

The man nodded. She tensed when he lay a hand on her shoulder. "If you'd give us an interview at headquarters, it would be a great help to our investigation."

"Of course, officer," Hattie answered. "I'd be happy to do that. I want to help. Just tell me…" she forced out the next words, "…is Mrs. DeValcourt—?"

"Dead," he interrupted. "And it's *detective*, not officer." That brusqueness put him on a fast track to become Hattie's least-liked person in the entire world.

She allowed him to sandwich her into the squalid back seat of a waiting police car. The detective slammed the door and slapped the car roof to signal the driver to leave.

As the cruiser bleated a signal and U-turned, Hattie could see the rope festooned with fluttering red fabric strips that was tied between the two saw-horses that blocked Fannie's front door. She craned her neck for a final look as the mansion receded from view.

Claustrophobic alarm added a layer to Hattie's fogged haze of stunned grief as she looked around. A grimy metal screen pinned her behind the driver in front. A strange, nose-tingling ammonia smell rose from the seat. She squirmed, finding comfort impossible on the butt-sprung bench seat. She needed some fresh air, but there were no window cranks nor door pulls. Was she being treated like a prisoner?

She was ashamed to need some creature comfort. Instead, she should be more concerned for Fannie's employees than herself. The poor souls had to be as stunned as she was, and paralyzed by this awful catastrophe. Thinking of them, Hattie began to cry. All of them had been in tears, corralled like sheep in the drawing room by the police.

They had to have heard the emergency crew's conjecture that Fannie had been murdered. Being questioned would make matters worse for the household if the police believed she died from deliberate gas poisoning. Such deaths were common in cold winter weather, but most were accidental. Hattie ached to think that someone deliberately killed Fannie. Who could have done such a thing?

When the squad car pulled to a stop at police headquarters, Hattie exited. She squinted, her mind still foggy. A cool breeze reminded her she'd left her jacket behind. Hattie hardly noticed the two officers flanking her until she tripped and one of them caught her by the elbow. They were courteous as they escorted her to a poorly vented, malodorous room no larger than an oversized closet. She was looking around when they closed the door behind themselves and she heard an unusual double click.

She could choose one of three splintery, uncomfortable wooden chairs bolted to the cement floor. Two chairs sat on one side of a narrow table liberally carved with initials and obscene words. The table was scarred with burns and was also bolted in place. A third chair sat alone across from them on the other side. A poorly cleaned anomalous mirror was on one wall, practically within reach. It was the only item on any wall.

Hardly aware of time passing, Hattie sat quietly, deep in thought and occasionally weeping. She welcomed the silence, though thoughts of Fannie flew through her mind.

Fannie and her husband Abner, ten years her senior, had met in a hospital corridor during her first year as a registered nurse on the ward. Friendship sparked to marriage, and Luke was born a year later. Fannie devoted herself to Abner's comfort and, through their friends, to promoting his medical practice. She didn't regret shelving her own career. Being with Abner and loving him was far more important to her.

The lovely Fannie was thoughtful and kind. To her everlasting regret, she'd left her son in the care of others more than she liked, but her evenings were spent doting on her "two men."

Fannie's hair had become snowy white by the time Hattie and Luke returned to New Orleans, but she was still a beautiful woman. Hattie's one glimpse through the doorway that morning revealed death hadn't dulled Fannie's beauty.

Startled when the room's poorly hung door scraped, Hattie jerked out of her reverie and dashed away her tears. An unkempt bear-like man shambled into the room. Could this be someone who'd sworn to protect his city?

He smacked a thin file down, disturbingly loud on the table, and cleared his throat. It was a growl that reinforced the bear image. Slouched onto the chair across from her, his legs sprawled wide. She struggled to remain objective rather than wary. What impression did he want to convey?

A peek at her watch surprised her. She'd been in the tiny room for close to an hour. He noticed and snorted, amused.

Hattie thought about her abandoned patients. The nurses would be tearing their hair out parrying questions about her absence and the nature of her family emergency. They must be wondering what happened.

Under red-rimmed lids she eyed the detective, unimpressed with the city's police personal appearance guidelines. The man's hair was messy and too long, accentuating a head that was larger than the norm. Beyond grooming, his mouth was too small for his big head—a rosebud, currently screwed into a scowl. The man's hands were disproportionately small compared to his skull.

She remained silent, with nothing to say. Some men, she thought, favored bright plaids, but they were usually comedians or circus clowns. The man's gapping jacket showed a shirt straining across his gut as though he'd suddenly gained considerable weight. Shorter than average, he might compensate with pugnacious behavior. His expression was off-putting and unpleasant under the starbursts of broken capillaries on his florid face. Was he an alcoholic? Maybe diabetic, too.

He gave no indication that he felt her inspection, and didn't look up until he asked the first question.

"*Exactly* who are you, Mrs. DeValcourt? This time I want your full name."

Hattie frowned, confused. This was the same fellow who had asked her the identical thing at Fannie's house. Had she missed something? Unsure if this was a trick question, she rubbed her arms, then answered.

"I am *still* Harriet DuMond DeValcourt." Misery and grief had exhausted her, and in the clammy room she was in no mood to be particularly polite.

"There ain't *no* record of *no one* in New Orleans with that name," he snarled. "Nowhere in the whole country, for that matter."

He suddenly slapped the folder with an open palm, the loud crack echoing off the cement walls. Hattie quivered, skin sensitized by her alarm's electricity.

His glare glinted, skeptical. "I ask you again. Who are you, really?"

"That *is* who I am, officer." She sniffed back tears.

He stiffened. Hattie wondered what she had done to offend the obnoxious man.

"*Detective*," he grumbled, jabbing his name tag. "Not officer—detective. Detective Breaux."

He glowered, until she shrugged. She didn't act or look like any doctor he'd ever seen, dressed in a spotless white silk blouse tucked into the waistband of a circular pink-checked skirt, pretty unusual garb for a so-called physician.

"Prove you are who you say," he demanded. "Where were you when Mrs. DeValcourt died?"

"You already asked me that, and I answered the question. You wrote my answer on your little notepad, *Detective Breaux*. Can you not read your own handwriting?" Hattie had let the buffoon get to her.

His cheeks flushed dark crimson. "Don't get smart with me, lady. I'll lock you up with the drunks and prostitutes. That what you want? Answer my questions."

He considered her a suspect, Hattie realized, and this was not an interview. Maybe she was his prime suspect, at that. In the small room's fetid air, the longer he peppered her with questions, the more she felt like a victim herself, one not allowed to mourn her dear Fannie's loss, not for even a moment.

Regaining control of her animosity, Hattie listed those people who could vouch for her identity. On a second list, she named the Hôtel-Dieu doctors and nurses who could corroborate her presence at the hospital that day.

He picked up his file and notes and stood, rapping the table hard with his knuckles. "Was that so tough?"

When Hattie stood, smoothing the wrinkled and limp pink-checked skirt, he frowned. In an ominous, threatening tone, he asked, "What do you think you're doing?"

"Leaving." She was disconcerted. Breaux shook his head, trying to provoke her.

"Nope. In fact, maybe I'll arrest you right now for Fannie DeValcourt's murder. See how you like sitting behind bars, waiting to be put on trial. Unless something better comes along, you can bet I'm gonna talk to every person on your list. I doubt you'll get out of here." He slapped the tabletop with the folder, dust and grit scattering.

He pushed her out of the room roughly between the shoulders, walking her down the hall to be fingerprinted. Before Hattie fully understood what happened, she was sitting in a cold, bare cement jail cell, her clothes replaced by baggy, ill-fitting and scratchy, black-and-gray prison stripes.

Under her breath she said, "Bully." The enormity of the situation hit hard. Hattie sat on the cleanest edge of a thin stained mattress that had been laid haphazardly on a concrete platform. She fumed at the bulldozing detective who'd put her behind bars.

The cell was smaller than the interview—no, interrogation—room. Not frantic yet, she suspected she soon would be. Outside the bars the corridor echoed with plaintive cries and phlegmy coughs. Hattie was struck that the sounds were so similar to the hospital ward she'd left hours ago. What differed completely was the urine-splashed grime and sour, unwashed body odors that had replaced her antiseptic hospital.

Thirst shortly became paramount in Hattie's mind, giving her a break from thoughts of Fannie's death. Before she'd thought to ask for water, that metallic snick had locked her away from the world. She knew she would get thirstier, and it was ironic that as thirsty as she was, she needed a bathroom. She eyed the grimy toilet in the far corner of her cell, but wasn't about to use something that was visible to everyone who walked by in the corridor.

How could they keep her in here? She couldn't catch anyone's attention.

Hattie blinked, her eyes not used to natural light. She was chilly and unsteady, stunned to breathe fresh air free of institutional odors. She wore the clothing, now wrinkled, that she'd worn early that morning when she'd left the house. The sour smell of the police station permeated everything she had on. She'd throw all of it in the trash, shoes included, before taking a hot shower until the water turned cold, and she had soaped herself clean and shampooed the smell from her hair.

It felt like a week had passed rather than less than a day. She'd been in the claustrophobic cell for only a few hours.

Someone had anonymously dispatched the city's most prominent criminal defense attorney for an arraignment so Hattie could be bonded out of jail until a criminal trial date could be set. She was in great danger until Fannie's killer was caught, but she would rectify that. Otherwise, it would be a struggle to prove she wasn't guilty of murder. She had thanked the gracious attorney who had freed her.

Why should I have to prove a negative, she thought. *Whatever happened to innocent until proven guilty?*

A January breeze kicked up, the kind of wind that could only be called *welcome* when one was as far south as New Orleans. It swirled the pink checks of Hattie's skirt around her knees, and its gentle eddies helped brush away unpleasant memories of damp cement walls. She stepped to the curb where Fannie's car and driver waited.

The unpleasant detective had fought Hattie's release, reluctant to let her go despite multiple witnesses who'd corroborated her presence at the hospital that morning. It didn't matter to him what they said.

He was there at the hearing to stare at the judge, saying over and over that she was the "smoking gun." Breaux was convinced Hattie was after the family fortune.

True, Hattie could possibly have the most to gain from her mother-in-law's death. But she'd never given that a single thought until the detective mentioned it.

It was the first time Hattie had ever heard anyone say she might be a beneficiary. The thought was macabre, and she discounted the possibility. Fannie and Abner were a charitable couple. She was sure the bulk of their estate would be distributed to the charities they supported.

Breaux was a dogged man. His suspicions meant he would chase every possible lead that could implicate her. He would waste time and taxpayer money, allowing the killer to slip the noose of justice. That bullheaded determination made Hattie want to wring the squatty man's thick neck, but that would put her in prison forever. He certainly wasn't worth that.

Whether or not Detective Breaux liked it, Hattie would mount her own private investigation. She would find poor Fannie DeValcourt's murderer and turn him over to the disgusting detective.

Breaux might get the credit for solving Fannie's murder. That would be fine, because Hattie would be rid of that odious man once and for all.

It was Fannie's housemaid, Mimi, who smelled the rotten-egg odor of gas. It hit her nose the moment she strolled into Fannie's bedroom wielding her feather duster. She gagged and became dizzy right away, but saw Fannie and her cat lying inert. She ran back to the hall for a deep breath of good air, then returned to the bedroom heater holding her breath to turn off the heater spigot.

Her nose pinched between her fingers, Mimi unlatched the bedroom window and threw it open. She leaned out and took a deep breath. Though the air outside was winter-chilled, she left the sash up to flush the poison gas from the room. Then she ran from the room and slammed the door shut. Fannie and her precious cat hadn't moved a muscle. It seemed too late to save them.

Weeping convulsively, Mimi ran down the back stairs to the kitchen, barely able to talk, but within moments Fannie's dazed cook called the hospital for Hattie. Only after that did she pacify Mimi, so traumatized she had gone into shock.

The DeValcourt household trusted that the police would identify Fannie's killer right away. But that didn't happen. The search was slow going and so far fruitless.

The crime scene police who processed Fannie's bedroom also fingerprinted the household staff. They dusted the heater spigot, of course. Mimi's thin fingers had obliterated other prints, though not completely. Surprisingly, those prints belonged to no one in the house. Initially, the police thought that was a stroke of good luck for the investigation.

Back at headquarters, it was torture to compare prints with those of known criminals in police department files. No one relished the task, so generally it was the last thing done and often by the newest member of the department.

Without automation in 1944, fingerprint comparison was time-consuming and tedious. In this case, several well-defined fingerprints had been lifted from the heater spigot. Because the impressions were relatively small, the consensus was that the killer was probably female. That didn't bode well for Hattie, but her prints didn't match any of those on the spigot. The spigot prints had then been matched against the household staff, and finally against the ten-finger inked cards on file locally. Two weeks elapsed before the New Orleans police knew two of the lifted prints matched nothing in their files.

At mid-century, an unidentified imprint was first manually compared to local fingerprint repositories. If no match was found, a copy could be mailed to Washington, D.C. where dozens of clerks searched the national archives. It was a labor-intensive process of flipping through fingerprint cards sorted by a combination of whorls, arches, and loops first, then alphabetically. The search was often unsuccessful, but not always, and the national archive was growing day by day.

The work of the clerks in Washington expanded when the U.S. government in a brilliant wartime protective measure mandated that immigration authorities fingerprint all European refugees accepted into the country. These prints were now routinely bundled and sent to FBI headquarters for inclusion in the national registry.

Finally following protocol, the New Orleans Police Department sent a copy of the unknown prints from the DeValcourt spigot to the national repository. The city had wasted weeks by not sending the file right away.

In the meantime, Fannie's body in the refrigerated city morgue could not be buried until the disposition of the murder case was decided. Her cat, Kitty, had not had to wait, having been laid to rest under Fannie's favorite rosebush, covered by mulch and sprinkles of January's unusual sleeting rain.

New Orleans police worked to develop suspects, interviewing everyone who worked at the DeValcourt house, and others like Hattie, who were part of the household but not present when Fannie died. The interviews expanded outward to include those whose lives Fannie had touched, rippling across the city. One thing was certain: Hattie's fingerprints were nowhere on Fannie's gas heater.

In the end, two unidentified fingerprints remained.

To Detective Breaux's disgust, the New Orleans chief prosecutor dismissed the criminal charge against Hattie "without prejudice." The bond fees were refunded to the attorney who had represented her on behalf of a still anonymous benefactor.

Despite Hattie's request, the attorney steadfastly refused to identify who had stepped in to aid her. Hattie assumed Hôtel-Dieu had been her benefactor, which later proved to be mistaken.

Thin nearly to emaciation, Hattie stood quietly at the DeValcourt mausoleum for the third time in as many years. The same funereal garments worn when Luke died draped loose over her diminished frame. She'd worn them a second time when Luke's father was buried. Her life had become enmeshed with death.

Months after Fannie's death, the police released her body and Hattie scheduled a private graveside service. On Hattie's lapel glinted the small pin that had been Fannie's gift from her son. She glanced at the heads around her lowered in prayer. Fannie's closest friends and all the household employees gathered at Metairie Cemetery to bid her farewell, together now for eternity with Abner and Luke, the men she loved.

New Orleans was deep into a warm early spring, but the DeValcourt mausoleum was in the shade of a live oak. Around the marble tomb, a well-tended garden of Fannie's perennial flowers and shrubs was in full bloom. Hattie leaned against her father and sobbed. Maman's warm hand patted her as Fannie's walnut coffin slid into place. She had known and loved the DeValcourts, and she wasn't alone. Everyone's tears attested to Fannie DeValcourt's gentle, loving nature.

When at last the heavy door of the mausoleum closed, Hattie trailed her fingers across the deeply engraved names of husband, mother-in-law, and father-in-law, knowing she would miss them for the rest of her life. She turned to leave. Left in her wake were masses of beautiful flowers that would wilt and fall into the dirt to nourish future blooms.

Hattie tried to picture the impossible. Who would want to kill Fannie? It was a murderous unknown in a hateful jumble. And now the city police had announced they were moving on. Their investigation had exhausted every lead and there were other cases to investigate.

That incensed Hattie and in her limited free time she continued her personal search for Fannie's killer. The tragedy stayed at the forefront of her thoughts—she wouldn't be deterred. The walls of her basement apartment became cluttered with notes of possible clues and connections.

Time-consuming and difficult, her investigation continued.

Hattie lay spread-eagled across the bed she and Luke had shared so briefly. She was exhausted by another long day filled with patients who needed her help. She punched a groove in her pillow and stared at the low basement ceiling. This had been Hattie's lonely bed for three years. Despite her housekeeper's plea, she refused to move upstairs to the echoing spaces of the main house.

It wasn't that she preferred living in the basement. Rather, she still clung to her last moments with Luke, in this bed, in this room. She missed him terribly, and sighed. As usual, her attention wandered from memories of Luke to memories of his mother.

Ideas of ways to find Fannie's killer scudded through her mind. She grasped at an occasional wild idea to examine it, then let it slip away. What could she accomplish that the police hadn't already tried? Was there something they'd missed? Was Fannie's death a case of mistaken identity?

Hattie couldn't ignore her clinic work or put it on hold. The hospital was shorthanded with the war, overwhelmed really, and Hattie's dedication wouldn't allow her to abandon her patients except for her weekly day off. It grated on her that Fannie's killer might get away with murder simply because she didn't have the time to track him down.

Uneasiness nibbled at the edges of her mind. She felt like she was missing something obvious, something hazy, something of utmost importance.

Fannie had not had a single enemy. No one wanted her dead. What other reason could there be to kill her? She thought her investigation was going in the wrong direction, but she had no idea what might be the right way.

She heard a knock, followed by Mimi's voice.

"Miss Hattie? Phone call, ma'am."

Thinking it a hospital problem, Hattie groaned. "Oh no. Tell them I'll call back."

"No, ma'am. I can't do that. It's the po-lice, Miss Hattie." The police?

"All right, I'm coming."

What the heck do they want? The dratted police will hound me forever. She rose reluctantly and made her way up to take the call.

"Mrs. DeValcourt?" Detective Breaux's abrasive voice made Hattie shudder.

"This is *Doctor* DeValcourt. Who's calling?" As though she didn't recognize the hateful man.

A pause, then the voice continued, its tone conciliatory.

"Ma'am, this is Detective Breaux. The chief wants you to know we're re-opening your mother-in-law's investigation."

Hattie decided not to annoy the odious man, but that didn't mean she had to help him out.

"You're investigating Fannie DeValcourt? Why? What did she do wrong? Was her cat unlicensed?"

"Now look here, ma'am. Just listen. We have new evidence, and we—I—could use your help."

That captured Hattie's attention, and she abandoned her taunting.

"New evidence?"

"Yes. The FBI fingerprint repository sent us a letter, saying they identified a partial fingerprint from the gas spigot—from a refugee named Jeanne Beauvais, who was admitted into the U.S. from France. You know her?"

The back of Hattie's neck tingled. France?

"No-o, not that I recall offhand."

He sighed. "It was worth a try. Will you think about it and let me know if anything changes?"

Hattie agreed, then disconnected. She wandered downstairs deep in thought, and threw herself on the bed and tried to empty her mind, wondering if a stab at self-hypnosis would help.

In the midst of thinking self-hypnosis was an impossibility, Hattie had a brainstorm. Was she, not Fannie, the killer's real target? After all, *she* had been the one who'd spent all those years in France. She sat up, thinking hard.

Could Hattie recall anything unusual about the day Fannie died? She squeezed her eyelids shut and went over her actions that day as minutely as she could. She bounded from the bed and rummaged in her crowded closet. The jacket she'd worn home from Hôtel-Dieu that day hung in a dry cleaner's paper bag. Her heart plummeted... The paper scrap she'd picked up on the back stairs. At the time she'd thought its presence odd, knowing Fannie's employees would never leave a mess anywhere, even on the back stairs. Then she'd crammed it in her jacket pocket as she climbed. Had the cleaners thrown away the scrap?

Her fingers found a crumpled paper enclosed in a glassine envelope tucked in the jacket pocket. Was there any writing? Could it help find Fannie's killer?

Hattie murmured a prayer, removed the creased paper, and spread it flat on her knee. Disappointment welled up. It was very common paper that could be found anywhere. Her house address was written there, but nothing else.

The writing looked different from the styles seen in the United States, more reflective of how the French wrote—in a narrow, slanted and looping penmanship.

Fannie had no enemies, but her daughter-in-law certainly did. Hattie snorted at the possibility—her one enemy was too far away to be the problem, across the ocean. Besides, the French army must have chased her down. But a chill foreboding swept down Hattie's spine.

She paced around the room while she thought, her intuition on high alert. The US authorities had embraced as many European wartime refugees as they could. Everyone in the country knew that.

Was Hattie's enemy in America? It was true she had threatened to expose Marie and Pierre Chennault as the German spies they most certainly were. The two women had argued, but Hattie's confrontation with Marie had given Marie time to escape military apprehension. Had she in fact been pursued?

Had Marie sneaked into the United States and traveled to New Orleans? Hattie had often shared stories about New Orleans. If Marie, or someone paid by her, had killed Fannie, how could she possibly benefit from the death of an innocent woman? How had she discovered where Hattie lived?

Hattie stood in Fannie's house and wept tears of guilt and suffered the recriminations of hindsight. It had to be Marie. None of this would have happened if she hadn't confronted Marie. Could she have turned a blind eye to the woman's espionage against France?

No good deed goes unpunished.

Hattie cinched her robe sash and grabbed a pen and a notebook. At the patio table in the shade of Fannie's oak tree Hattie ignored the verdant outdoors, the flowers and fountain, and strained to recall where she had shown her face for the last six months Fannie lived. Her pen poised above the clean page ready to jot down the list of places she would visit to question their staffs.

Remembering the places wouldn't be difficult. Not much had taken her away from home after Hattie's life shrank to caring for her patients, Fannie, and herself. She'd barely tasted the cook's good fare, despite Fannie's pleas to enjoy leisurely meals with her.

However, there had been several exceptions. Hattie had made several rushed shopping forays to buy Christmas gifts for her family and others before the holidays began in earnest.

Who had she seen? More importantly, where had *she* been seen? Where had she shopped, and what else had she done? Would this be a useful angle to pursue, or would *this* be a dead end, too?

Hattie blew a bothersome curl off her forehead. She stood outside the fourth store of the day, hot under the New Orleans June sun and damp with perspiration. Cumbersome packages weighed her down, and she wondered why she'd purchased bulky items at her previous stops when she could've chosen smaller ones instead. Her hungry stomach growled. She was discouraged and very thirsty. And with all the walking she'd done, her feet were hot and swollen.

So far, Hattie's search had been spectacularly unproductive. She was starting to think she was like a female Don Quixote, tilting at windmills—except she was horseless, and moving at a snail's pace. And this was the one day each week she had free to chase connections between her and Fannie's killer. She snorted at herself for the silly metaphors she had lumped together.

She'd never been much of a shopper, anyway, and this search confirmed her dislike of the process. But Hattie thought she should buy at least one item from each store, for good manners as much as hoping to make her many questions more palatable to the shop clerks. And to make herself memorable, too.

If Fannie's killer had any money, there would have been time to leave New Orleans to escape capture. That worried Hattie, though she knew that refugees often had little money to spare. Lack of funds would make escape difficult for a foreigner, and the killer could still be hiding in the city in plain sight.

This would be her last store for today. Exhaustion made Hattie huff a hot breath, as she put her hand on Kreeger's gleaming upscale brass door pull. This is one store too many, she thought.

She had traversed the length of Canal Street, her feet again burning through the soles of her shoes on another hot June day. She'd struck out at Godchaux's, her personal favorite store, a half hour ago. The store in front of her, Kreeger's, was another favorite when she ever bothered to shop, its buyers in tune with Hattie's taste in clothes. She'd exchanged her black widow's weeds to join with other New Orleans women, donning clothes in patriotic reds, whites, and blues to support their country at war. It was a tradition now for the women of New Orleans.

Hattie's focus was not on fashion. She was targeting French immigrant saleswomen working for stores like Kreeger's. The entry-level clerk positions would be available to Frenchwomen without any particular expertise.

Pulling open the heavy door, she entered the store's faintly perfumed, cool air. Hattie plastered a smile on her face, self-conscious as she skirted the cosmetics area. Exposure to the sun for hours today without makeup probably meant more freckles than ever. The perfectly made-up sales staff would be horrified, she was sure, so she avoided them.

She approached the *Guerlain* perfume counter instead, and caught a quick glimpse of a short-haired, white-blond woman scurrying away. She was struck with a sense of *déjà vu*, as if repeating something already done, along with an intense sensation that she was being closely watched.

She turned a complete circle and a smiling brunette clerk standing behind the counter asked if she needed help. Hattie rested her packages on the counter and smiled back, shaking off the strange sensation.

Speaking French, Hattie said, "*Bonjour.* I'm looking for a new cologne. Can you help?"

"*Certainement, madame.*" The young clerk's hand swept wide in a gesture that beckoned Hattie to follow her to the end of the *Guerlain* counter where a sparkling artistic array of perfumes and colognes in all shapes and sizes waited.

"You see we have a wide selection." Disappointed right away, Hattie had to eliminate the clerk as a suspect because of her underlying American southern accent. Could she have faked an American accent in her spoken French? Hattie thought no, she would be able to tell the difference.

The clerk offered to spritz Hattie's wrist. She accepted and Hattie bent to sniff the tiny spritz. She glanced up.

"I hear that Kreeger's had hired a French refugee. Is that true, miss?"

A fleeting expression of distaste crossed the clerk's face before she hid it, first looking down, then up at Hattie.

"Why, yes, as a matter of fact." The words didn't disguise the clerk's distaste. "*Mlle.* Beauvais. You must've heard about her. She works behind this counter with me. Only a second before you walked up, she left on a break."

A pulse stuttered below Hattie's ear. Detective Breaux had reported the name "Beauvais" to the fingerprints lifted from Fannie's gas heater. She wouldn't get ahead of herself, but the new information that a refugee of that name worked at Kreeger's certainly got her attention.

"That blonde that walked away? Is that who you mean?" Hattie's heart plummeted. Marie had a *chignon* of beautiful long dark hair. She had struck out once again and inwardly cursed her bad luck.

She had to keep searching, but she made one last stab.

"I've been looking everywhere for my cousin," she lied. "Maman wrote that she'd come to New Orleans, but she's not a blonde. She has long, dark hair."

"I know you're kidding, *madame.*" The clerk laughed, unable to mask her scorn.

"Jeanne dyes her hair. You know like Jean Harlow's champagne-colored finger waves. But her roots are dark," she added.

Hattie had no idea who Jean Harlow might be, but the clerk's comment quickened her breath. Though she was completely ignorant of this woman Jean Harlow, not surprising in her little world of a hospital and sick patients, maybe this blonde woman was a possibility.

"Ah," she said with raised eyebrows. "Has she worked here for long?"

"Not as long as me. I've been here since before Christmas. Jeanne, the store hired her away from a small boutique right after the New Year. I can't imagine why she hasn't come back, she's been on break long enough."

Hattie could imagine a reason why, but she made no comment. She pointed at the spritzer in the salesperson's hand, and said, "That smells lovely, mam'selle. I'll take it," and she pulled her change purse from her handbag.

She couldn't think of a way to get "Jeanne Beauvais" to the police station, where her fingers could be rolled in black ink and stuck to a ten print card. But could she get her fingerprints some other way? She lit on an idea.

"I have another question, mam'selle...," wishing she could tell this young woman exactly what she needed, but thinking better of relying on the clerk's discretion.

"Oui, madame?"

"My maman usually orders her cologne from France, but this time I want to give her a surprise gift. I don't know the name of her cologne or who makes it, but I have an empty bottle scenting my lingerie drawer. If I bring it to you here, do you think the Frenchwoman could identify it from the shape of the bottle or the scent? Then, perhaps you could order it for me?"

"Of course we can try, madame," the clerk answered, as she counted out Hattie's change and gave her an elegant Kreeger's bag containing the wrapped cologne. The clerks worked on commission, so the prospect of a future sale would work in Hattie's favor.

"Don't mention this to anyone, please, not even your colleague. Let me find that bottle and then you can show it to Mlle. Beauvais. I don't want either of you to wait unnecessarily. I'll bring it as soon as I can."

Nodding, the clerk bid her goodbye and moved to a waiting customer, Hattie's comments already dimmed in her mind.

Hattie feigned an interest in other merchandise as she made her way to the door, taking plenty of time as a customer would, aware she might be under close scrutiny.

Twice she returned to Kreeger's, once to leave a brown paper bag containing a spotless perfume flacon, all fingerprints removed; and a second time to retrieve it, bag and all. A note written in beautiful European cursive with the brand name of a French perfume and its cost was taped to the outside of the bag. As best Hattie could tell, the writing looked like that on the note she had found on Fannie's back staircase. Fine hairs at the nape of her neck stirred, but she'd need to find someone to compare the two handwriting samples for an expert opinion. Her heartbeat accelerated in anticipation.

She'd ordered the expensive scent and paid for it in advance. When she asked to thank the French clerk, she was told that Jeanne Beauvais no longer worked there. *No*, Hattie thought, her spirit plummeting in panic.

She had been so close to her quarry, but "Jeanne" had slipped away again. But she'd handled the perfume bottle. Maybe the police could find a fingerprint match? And the handwriting specimens—at least it would be worthwhile to compare them.

Disheartened, Hattie managed to keep her emotions to herself. She gathered her things to leave, but the cooperative saleswoman leaned closer. Firmly clutching Hattie's money, she whispered, "I know that Godchaux's asked our store for a reference on Jeanne. Maybe I shouldn't say so, but I'm happy she left. She didn't strike me as being a very nice person."

"I understand, *chère*. Thank you for sharing the information." They smiled at one another, complicit.

Hattie felt her energy returning.

Hattie smacked a fist into her other palm.

"Won't you at least *check* and see if there are fingerprints on the bottle?"

Frustration made her voice sharper than she'd meant it, and she mentally kicked herself. Her tone would only make Detective Breaux defensive. She was already angry at herself for taking extra time on her hair and clothes for this ignorant oaf.

Breaux shook his obstinate, overinflated head and used his fingertips to push away the paper bag she'd placed on his desk, rejecting it and not gracious enough to thank her for her willingness to help resurrect his "dead" investigation.

"You ask too much, Mrs. DeValcourt. We don't undertake arbitrary fingerprint tests simply on someone's vague suspicion." He flicked his dismissive fingertips against the thin brown bag to make a crinkling sound.

Not once had Hattie been addressed by the honorific Doctor she deserved, but she let its absence slide—as usual. This man was too chauvinistic to accept that women could be medical doctors, let alone as proficient as men.

Perplexed by Breaux's reflexive reaction, a vertical line appeared between Hattie's bunched eyebrows. He needed her help, he'd said, but his attitude didn't reinforce those words.

She stared into his eyes and rapped the detective's desktop by the bag. "These fingerprints probably belong to the German spy I uncovered and reported to the authorities in France. If it's her, it doesn't matter how she sneaked into America—she's our country's sworn enemy. The last time I saw her, she vowed vengeance against me."

"Why were *you* in France? *You* could be the spy." Detective Breaux cocked his head, his mouth pursed. Hattie's opinion of his idiotic comment showed despite the effort she'd made to hide it.

Using her fingers, she ticked off her answers.

She had lived in France to study at the Sorbonne for her medical degree. She'd been stranded in France when Germany invaded. Her husband was a French intelligence officer who had been killed by the Nazis.

"That's three somethings," she added. You already know all that from the extensive research you've done on me. Am I right, detective?"

Breaux had hardly enough good grace to show embarrassment, but he snatched the bag holding the perfume bottle off his desk.

"Just to show you I'm a good guy, I'll get this thing dusted, but you're wasting my time and city money. I'm drawing the line right here, lady. Don't try this again."

Hattie's shoulders relaxed, lips twitched into a smile too small to reach her eyes. It was a miracle that she had changed Breaux's mind. *And,* she thought, *he called me "lady." That says something, though I'm not sure what.* "The prints on the bottle will match, detective. That woman's an immigrant and her handwriting matches the sample I gave you. She was on the stairs the morning Fannie DeValcourt was murdered. You haven't found a local fingerprint match yet—but these will. She's Mrs. DeValcourt's killer. Look at the Jeanne Beauvais card from the FBI; she's using that name now.

"My tax dollars cover the cost of the tests, detective. But if I'm wrong, send me an itemized invoice and I'll pay a second time. I'm confident if there are prints on that bottle, you won't need anything else.

"And keep an eye on this 'Jeanne Beauvais.' She's good at slipping nooses."

Her patients were cheered with Hattie's return to work. As was she. The rustle of her starched white coat as she moved between rooms, a stethoscope draped around her neck, was her own kind of music. Surrounded by like-minded professionals during the day gratified her. But nothing eased the isolation and loneliness of her nights in Fannie's huge house.

Hattie had never felt more alone. The building was full of the family's ghosts.

"DeValcourt residence."

A youthful female voice asked, "May I speak to Mrs. DeValcourt, please?"

"I'm sorry," Hattie answered. "Mrs. DeValcourt passed away some weeks ago." Each time she said that, she felt wounded, though she knew she'd repeat those words often, and for a long, long time.

"Oh! That's awful. What happened? She was so young." The words sounded like polite convention, without real emotion to back them up.

Annoyed by the vacuous comment but restraining the rude retort bubbling to her lips, Hattie for a moment held the receiver away from her ear and clenched her jaw. She was furious at herself for answering the phone at all. She was running late and becoming short-tempered. She wanted this girl to hang up.

Hattie struggled to modulate her voice. "Is this call for me? There is only one *other* Mrs. DeValcourt, and that's me." Hattie's voice tailed off, her fingers creeping up to massage her temple.

The lilting voice said, "The police dismissed the charge that you murdered Mrs. DeValcourt and we're ready to settle her estate."

So, this call concerned Fannie's will, and these disembodied comments meant Hattie had been finally cleared of Fannie's murder.

"Wait… Did the police arrest someone?"

The woman's response was unintelligible, but Hattie wouldn't have grasped it anyway, as caught up as she was in her own thoughts. It was no surprise that the curmudgeon detective hadn't given her the news. Though tempted to dress down the fool man immediately, she decided to call him during this morning's first break. Breaux thought a silly tin badge gave him carte blanche to persecute innocent people. On second thought, why should she waste her valuable time? A call would only inflate his self-importance and the man wasn't worth her time or her attention.

She tuned in to find the woman still speaking on the other end of the conversation.

"I'm sorry. Could you please repeat that?"

The young clerk cleared her throat. "Yes, ma'am. Can you come to our office at noon tomorrow? Mrs. DeValcourt stipulated that you must be present when her will is read." She rattled off the firm's address and Hattie jotted it on the pad kept by the phone.

Agreeing to be there, Hattie disconnected. Her emotions were in turmoil again, heartsore and missing Fannie. The call brought Fannie's death back to mind. A mind, she thought ruefully, only just returned to functional.

She knew she'd been vindicated. The Jeanne Beauvais fingerprints stored in Washington D.C. must match the ones lifted from Fannie's heater. And Detective Breaux knew Hattie would be able to identify Jeanne Beauvais as the German spy Marie Chennault.

Dear Fannie's death had been so unnecessary, just a crazed woman's way to hurt Hattie. Thank goodness the police had arrested Jeanne Beauvais.

Hattie called her brother Jack to go with her to the will reading the next day for a little support. She wanted the whole thing to be over, but instinctively felt she'd feel better if a family member was with her. Tomorrow's visit to the lawyer was only the latest onerous, painful duty in a long string of hurtful things.

The disposition of Fannie's estate would likely mean Hattie would have to leave her home of the past three plus years. She took for granted it would be sold as part of settling the estate.

Luke's parents had been famously philanthropic all Hattie's life, frequently supporting the arts and other worthy organizations. Their substantial wealth was managed by an attorney who specialized in investments and estate management. It must have been that lawyer's office that had called. She hadn't caught the firm's name during the call, but she didn't need it, having jotted down the street address.

The DeValcourts' estate would go to charity, she thought.

She couldn't have been more wrong.

The DuMond siblings boarded a streetcar similar to one they'd ridden to school years earlier. Together they dropped coins in the hopper and smiled at each other as the coins rattled and clanged.

Jack's wife and young daughter were at the beach house with Maman and Papa in Biloxi, but he had returned to New Orleans and spent the night at the posh DeValcourt mansion with his sister. Hattie's call for Jack's support was unusual, and he was delighted to act as her crutch.

Brother and sister each wore business suits. His was pinstriped dark blue linen, worn with a starched white shirt and a claret-colored necktie. It was late in the season for linen, but New Orleans weather was notoriously fickle and the temperature was quite warm.

Hattie's suit was a somber matte black twill. She'd found it impossible to wear a lighter color when it came to anything associated with her beloved Fannie DeValcourt.

Her jacket featured a petal peplum lined in a muted red, and was closely molded to her small waist. The calf-long skirt was sleek, as narrow as an accountant's pencil. Above a narrow gold choker, Hattie's lovely face was pale, its only color a rosy lipstick that gave her mouth definition. An unadorned black hat and veil and a pair of dove gray gloves completed her outfit.

The electrified streetcar clacked and swayed down the uneven rails, pushing aside weather so humid it was almost visible. Strands of mosses suspended from the oak trees fluttered as the streetcar picked up speed. Both DuMonds thought of the past as they traveled, memories unspooling as they rode.

In earlier days, Jack and Hattie had seated themselves at opposite ends of the car, as far apart as the streetcar allowed. Today they shared the same wooden bench and caught up on family news until they reached Lee Circle and their destination, an imposing building beside the traffic circle.

The centuries-old building smacked of the Spanish architectural influence typical of New Orleans two hundred years before. It struggled to represent an earlier, a more gracious time amid atrocities built more recently. After purchasing the building, Karl Schmitzer arranged for its red brick façade to be cleaned and meticulously restored, and the building looked as good now as it had when first built.

Hattie confirmed the address against gold-embossed numbers on an outside wall as Jack pulled open an inviting, gleaming and elegant, varnished black door. He ushered Hattie in ahead of him. Neither noticed the bronze plaque on the outside wall that listed the partners.

Approaching the polished antique desk and the smiling receptionist who sat behind it, Jack gestured to his sister.

"Mrs. DeValcourt has an appointment this morning."

"Of course, sir. We've been expecting you." The receptionist lifted a receiver at her right side.

"Someone will come for you. Would either of you like coffee or something cold? It's quite warm today."

Jack answered as Hattie shook her head. "No, ma'am, thank you."

They looked around the room. Jack and Hattie were used to fine furnishings, but everything here teetered at the edge of being too special, a huge contrast to the medical clinic's emphasis on functionality.

They lowered themselves onto the nubby blue silk of the anteroom's upholstered chairs. Their dusty shoes were visible through the polished glass of a low table sitting on a handwoven jewel-toned rug that anchored the room.

Hattie paid no attention to the beautifully framed Audubon bird and plant paintings that hung on the walls, each lit by its own light. The upcoming meeting was on her mind, and she feared it would be unpleasant for her.

While they waited, she catalogued her meager belongings. What could she leave behind if she had to leave Fannie's mansion today? Where could she go? She hoped her parents would allow her to move back into her childhood bedroom, but that would cause a huge change in *their* lifestyle as well as her own.

In contrast to Hattie's fevered thoughts, Jack was completely relaxed. He twiddled his thumbs, his mind blank. Jack's job today was simple: to do nothing but be present. He would prefer to be at the beach with his family, but all things considered, he was happy to lend his support to his melancholy sister. Or run interference for her, if that became necessary.

Safely behind the closed door of his private office, sweat dampened the DeValcourts' lawyer's crisp white shirt. His shirt had been purchased especially for this meeting. For months he'd known this meeting was inevitable, only a matter of time. He'd asked one of his partners to deal with the matter, but that ploy hadn't worked, and now he hooked a finger inside his shirt collar to hold its limp starchiness off his neck. Even so, he was finding it difficult to swallow.

His office window was the largest in the entire building, and he faced it trying to compose himself, blind to the beauty of the graceful ancient oak. This usually was a view he favored, but today his thoughts were on other things.

The muscles of his jaw worked, grinding his molars in obvious distress—surprising in an attorney who regularly confronted difficult circumstances. His fingers raking through previously combed thick blond hair, he steeled himself against the discomfiture to come. His plan was to fake a relaxed persona for as long as the meeting took.

Should he remain seated when Hattie DeValcourt was shown into his office? Or should he approach her? Yes, that would be the mannerly Southern thing to do, so he would do it, self-protection be damned.

A decision typical of the courtly, handsome man.

His secretary's warning rap came as she opened his door and stepped aside, which allowed Hattie and Jack to enter the well-appointed office. The secretary closed the door softly behind them.

Karl Schmitzer was surprised to see Hattie with an escort. Based on their startled expressions, this meeting with his former fiancée was going to be even more awkward and uncomfortable than he'd anticipated.

He came around his desk with a sigh and a tentative smile. A citrusy whiff of Hattie's familiar light scent wafted into the room with her. He recognized the cologne as the same she'd worn when they were an engaged couple.

Hattie halted abruptly at the sight of Karl, her exclamation so sharp she choked, coughing. Following his sister closely, Jack bumped into her back, pushing her into Karl's outstretched hand. Karl laughed and grabbed Hattie's arm to steady her.

Slight creases at the corners of Karl's hazel eyes crinkled deeper with amusement. His warm smile was as endearing as ever, with his low laugh defusing the tension.

Hattie risked a glance at Karl in time to see a wistful expression cross his face that left him awkward. Otherwise, she liked what she saw. His jawline was more defined, even more appealing now than it had been before she'd steamed away to France. The old relationship they had shared had been one of complex sensuality, and she felt the same old attraction. She shook herself to the present, but wondered whether Karl noticed any changes in her.

Saving the two former sweethearts from additional embarrassment, Jack extended a hand around Hattie's back.

"Be darned—Karl Schmitzer. An unexpected pleasure." The men were happy to see each other over Hattie's hat. They had known each other most of their lives, but Jack was mystified at these circumstances.

He tugged his jacket cuffs, and asked, "Why on God's good earth didn't you tell us it was you that called this meeting?"

Baffled, Karl answered as he gestured to guest chairs set in front of his desk.

"You didn't know? Why, what did my secretary say? Who did you think it would be?"

Hattie had the distinct disconcerting sensation that she floated somewhere above the men. When Jack looked at her, she returned to her body and stammered an answer.

"I'm not sure. Karl… I'm sorry…" His name felt foreign on her lips. It had been so long since she had allowed herself to utter it. It dropped heavily between the former sweethearts, all its edges rough. The tall, muscular man who stood before her woke emotions that Hattie had fought to keep dormant. It had been more than a dozen years since they had seen each other.

"Please don't fuss at the person who called me," said Hattie. "She must've thought I expected her call. She did talk a bit fast, but I was so surprised by the call. I was worried, too."

For good reason. Her emotions had been volatile lately and now she could feel her nose beginning to prickle. She rummaged in her purse for a hanky, but Karl thrust a neatly folded, clean handkerchief at her. She remembered that he'd always had a snowy square tucked in a pocket.

She glimpsed his thin gold wedding band before she accepted the initialed cloth. That quickly extinguished her grateful smile and she continued, "The woman identified herself and reeled off several names.

"I didn't catch everything she said, but I didn't ask her to repeat herself. I caught the address, but I didn't catch your name, Karl," adding to herself that she hardly thought she would have missed that particular detail.

Karl's raised eyebrows, had they been able to speak for themselves, would've said, *like I couldn't tell.*

"No, *I'm* sorry, Hattie. Your surprise threw me for a loop." He reached out to her, then quickly withdrew his hand. He didn't have the right to touch her. That had come to an end years ago when his ring showed up in the mail.

He cleared his throat and decided to become more formal, as though Hattie were just another client. Maybe that way he could get past the emotional turmoil of seeing her again.

"Dr. and Mrs. DeValcourt have told me over the past few years that you've had enough trauma for a lifetime, Hattie. You don't need any new surprises, and I don't want you to feel wrong-footed today. After you leave today, I'll ask my secretary to speak more clearly from here on out." He grimaced. "That's too late today, of course."

Hattie and Jack still stood just inside his office. Venturing a hesitant touch, Karl took Hattie's elbow and guided her to a chair.

His warm hand caused Hattie another struggle with her composure. Widowed for three years, a man's touch, except for Jack's or her father's, felt entirely too foreign. Jack intuited her discomfiture, patted her shoulder, and pulled his chair protectively close to hers.

They heard a great deal of information, not the least of which was that Hattie no longer had anything to worry about financially.

The more Karl read of Fannie's last will and testament, the more their eyes widened. Hattie's gentle, kind mother-in-law had made sure Hattie would never have a worry about where to live. Far from it. With the exception of several sizeable bequests to Hôtel-Dieu and to the faithful DeValcourt household staff, Hattie had inherited the bulk of an enormous fortune and a great deal of real estate. Everything now belonged to Hattie without any stipulations.

To her chagrin, Hattie realized she had smothered herself in self-pity after Luke died. She hadn't had the faintest idea that Luke's parents had cherished her that much. Perhaps their affection had been as deep as her love for them. She was grateful to know that, but she felt guilty she hadn't done more to show it.

At the meeting's conclusion, Karl ended by saying, "The estate's total value—"

But Hattie jumped in and interrupted with her graceful hand raised.

"Stop!" She covered her ears. "Don't tell me the value. I loved Abner and Fannie for themselves, not for their money. I don't want to know. It's enough to know they loved *me,*" and added, "Your office handled all the household expenses and salaries, and managed the entire estate, do I have that right?"

Karl nodded, an elbow propped on the arm of his chair, two fingers against his mouth. If Hattie could've read his thoughts, she would've blushed to see how wonderful Karl believed her to be.

Hattie asked, "Are you willing to continue in that role... manage all the investments and pay the salaries and expenses?"

"Of course. That's the backbone of my law practice. We manage such things for many clients."

"Then that's what I'd like to do, for now. Another time you can tell me the dollars and cents. Do I have to sign anything? I can do that now."

"Can you wait less than an hour? Otherwise, we'll have to set another appointment."

Hattie couldn't wait, late for her afternoon patients at Hôtel-Dieu already. Dizzied by her good news, she clutched Jack by the arm as they walked out of Karl's building and emerged into the midday September warmth of New Orleans.

The DeValcourts' generosity overwhelmed Hattie, though she remained unsure she deserved such largesse. In her will, Fannie stressed the deep appreciation she and Abner had for Hattie's thoughtfulness and unstinting care for Luke and for her new family elders. Before his death, Fannie and Abner discussed how their wills might be adjusted.

It was clear that the DeValcourts understood the importance of the tangible things they would leave behind, but Fannie's will declared they both considered Hattie their daughter, and that she was as much loved as their own son. When Abner died before Fannie, his will was not read, his share of assets becoming Fanny's.

They had been a remarkable couple, Hattie thought. She stood under the blinding autumn sun on the bustling Lee Circle sidewalk, missing the days she could hug Luke's parents. She wished she could plump Fannie's bed pillows for her just one more time. It *was* the bright sun that was making her blink, wasn't it?

Through Hattie's love of Luke's parents, she had developed a deeper, more objective appreciation for her own Maman and Papa. All she wanted was to ease the pain others felt, and that started with the members of her family. It didn't occur to her to remember those days as a child when she was sure the world revolved around her and she thought only of herself.

Those three years she'd spent in the DeValcourt household, they had never once mentioned that Karl Schmitzer was their lawyer. His name never came up, and in that way, the discreet couple protected Hattie from unnecessary discomfort.

Noisy traffic churned around Lee Circle outside Karl's office building. Hardly any vehicles were new, the military having absorbed the nation's iron and steel for the war. Many older vehicles were dilapidated. She and Jack waited in companionable silence on the sidewalk for the taxi that would return him to the station to board the afternoon train to the Mississippi coast.

Jack ran his tongue across his upper teeth, cleared his throat, and offered, "I can stay another night if you want me to. Today had to be quite a shock."

Hattie squeezed his arm. "Thank you, but no. I needed you today more than I thought I would, and in a way I didn't expect. My mind is whirling and it'll take me a while to think about all this. It would be a big help if you'll please tell Maman and Papa everything. I want to be sure they know how generous their friends have been, but they'll have so many questions. Will you run interference for me?"

Jack nodded, accepting his assignment just as a dingy taxi pulled up, its brakes squealing. Hattie hugged her brother goodbye, and he slid into the cab's back seat and waved as the taxi pulled into traffic.

Hattie, who could now afford the cost of a chauffeured limousine, elected to board another streetcar for a swaying ride. There was hardly enough time to think about Karl or her changed circumstances before the hospital stop. She stepped from the streetcar and briskly walked the remaining two blocks to the clinic.

Not many mornings later, Hattie waved away the housemaid and answered the house telephone herself. Once again, Detective Breaux was on the line. She learned that Marie Chennault had evaded arrest. Hattie's cynical thought was, *That's no surprise.* Detective Breaux warned her she might be at risk. Hattie answered, "I see," with a "goodbye" that bordered on rudeness. Slamming the receiver down, she left for work.

PART SIX

EVERYONE, INCLUDING THE DuMonds, the DeValcourts, and most of their social circle in the insular Uptown area of New Orleans, knew that Karl Schmitzer and Hattie were engaged when she'd left for Paris several years earlier.

Hattie's departure had interrupted the couple's story, but Karl's marriage to another woman created a small seismic upheaval of its own in Uptown society, followed by the aftershock of Hattie being marooned in France and in mortal danger.

Powdered and perfumed old biddies fluttered and clucked half-informed gossip when one of the old ladies saw Luke and Hattie upon their return to Uptown as a married couple. How refreshing, how delightful that there was something new about which to scratch and peck. It was the dramatic concluding episode to the DuMond-Schmitzer broken engagement of a few years before. Admittedly, though, it hadn't topped the impossibly hot gossip fires ignited when Hattie and Karl first got engaged.

The flames that briefly flared when the two young doctors returned to Uptown fizzled quickly with Luke's death. Then their venerated Dr. Abner DeValcourt died and Hattie was more or less forgotten, the group focusing on their conjecture that Dr. DeValcourt died of a broken heart, having lost his only son.

Uptown gossip reignited with Fannie DeValcourt's murder, reaching its peak when the police handcuffed and arrested the lovely Hattie for Fannie's death.

Hattie's life became salacious entertainment for the old Uptown women. They waited early each morning for the thunk of the Times Picayune newspaper against their doors, hoping to find news about her.

After her release, Hattie's fame grew, as did her medical practice. Matrons clamored to see the woman doctor at Hôtel-Dieu, for no other reason than to say they'd shared a conversation with her. When the police determined that a seductive French Mata Hari was the real killer, the murmurs fizzled, the coals merely banked. But then the Beauvais woman evaded capture, and the flames of gossip leapt higher.

To think there was a female murderer on the loose in New Orleans—what was the world coming to? Who would have imagined that New Orleans doors had to be locked?

Only if this Jeanne Beauvais person was caught and convicted and locked away for life in a women's state prison as tough as Angola, only then would New Orleans be safe again.

Hattie and Karl faded from conversation and separately they slowly became "normal" people again, until... until someone dusted off Karl's invisible wife. However, the wife wasn't someone people knew much about.

What was her name, again—Ellen? Eileen? Eleanor Schmitzer? Gossip trod lightly around the wife, unwilling to rock the local society boat. Meanwhile, Karl had become an accommodating escort for many single women on the New Orleans society scene. He accompanied newly single women of all ages to balls, concerts, and charity events, those needing an arm to lean on.

Was Karl really even married? Where was his wife? In the absence of answers, Uptown decided to play matchmaker, and dinner hostesses often placed Hattie DeValcourt next to her old beau.

One wonders what the old biddies hoped might happen.

Hattie's brother Jack was delighted that his sister had reconnected with Karl, and he said that in exactly those words. Jack had been Luke's best friend, but Jack didn't feel the least bit disloyal. He knew Luke would want Hattie to live a normal and happy life.

The two siblings lounged at a small table in their parents' back yard, slouched comfortably against the woven rattan backs of Maman's patio chairs. Sheltered by the tree they had hidden behind as children, dappled shade played across their faces. Above them on the branches, foraging birds clung and burrowed, seeking a meal in the ubiquitous swaying moss.

They conducted their desultory conversation in the melodic conversational French that was slowly losing its hold in Louisiana.

"How many times do I have to tell you, Jack? We have *not* reconnected," glowered Hattie. "We meet *seulement parce-que*, only because, we have business to talk about." Possible reconnection made her feel strangely uncomfortable and disloyal to Luke.

"You think I don't know he sits with you at dances and parties? People talk. Luke would want you to be happy. He would be delighted that Karl is in your life. You loved Karl first, before you fell in love with Luke," he said, then sputtered a cough. He wiped his mouth and laughed at Hattie's shocked expression. "Okay, that didn't come out right."

Hattie shrugged in a charming Gallic habit picked up from her years in France, as though unaffected, but she squirmed. Jack's comments hit too close to the thoughts that she'd recently had about Karl.

She protested, "Wrong as usual. Karl is married and you know it. He has a big, obvious ring on his finger. *I* noticed, even if you didn't and I'll thank you to stay out of my personal life."

Jack smirked, as if to say, *"Sounds like you looked."* He hadn't noticed the ring. But even so, he went on the attack.

"Ha! Then why are you so defensive. It just shows you checked him out. I *knew* it. So I guess he's off the romance board, but still, it's not good you're alone. I'll get Angela to host a dinner party and we'll play matchmaker."

"But I married Luke and I don't want to remarry."

Hattie was ready to change the subject. A gust of wind pushed fallen leaves across the yard and she held out her hand, palm up, checking for rain.

"Now, see?" Jack said. "What you just said—you're what? Thirty years old? And that worries me. You're young, and you've stuck yourself into two tiny rooms in that big house like you're punishing yourself. Even when you were taking care of Luke's parents, I didn't understand why you lived like that."

"I don't care what you think. It's none of your business. I'm fine living like that." She added to herself that *those* rooms, *that* bed, reminded her of Luke.

"But here's a news bulletin for you. Someone wants Fannie's house and I'm ready to sell. This morning over coffee, I asked Maman and Papa if it's all right to move back home. I didn't say they need help, but they do, and you're busy with your company and your own family. I can keep an eye on them at night."

Jack asked, "That would take a load off my mind, but you're plenty busy yourself. How—"

Without warning, a gusting downpour made them scramble inside. Fat raindrops pattered against the patio bricks and on parched flowers. The whispering plops forced Hattie and Jack into Maman's kitchen, which had been recently updated to more modern 1944 standards. Wiping her wet shoes on a coir doormat, Hattie gave Cook, now bent and ancient, a robust hug and kiss, and picked up the conversation where she'd left off.

"I have plenty of free time after I see clinic patients and make hospital rounds, when I'm not babysitting for you and Angela.

"Maman, Papa, and I, we settled everything. All you need to say is thank you. They're coming to the mansion Saturday to choose whatever they'd like to have. And I want y'all to join us. Fannie has beautiful, meticulously collected furniture. She would be happy that we cherish her things. I'll keep a few of my favorite things, too."

She turned to Cook. "Do you think our kitchen needs anything from there?" When Cook demurred, Hattie turned back to Jack.

"After this weekend, I'll invite Fannie's friends over. Then the buyer will have a chance to purchase what's left, and the rest goes to the Salvation Army."

Jack was astonished, his voice envious when he said, "Already? You sold the mansion? I didn't know it was on the market—not that I could afford a place like that."

Hattie nodded unhappily. "Sad, isn't it? But it's the right thing to do, and you're right. I rattled around in that place like one solitary BB in a Red Ryder gun. I spend more time on the patio than inside.

"The buyers are nice. I felt much better when they hired Fannie's housemaids and cook. That was what worried me.

"One thing I did do. I asked the gardener who doubled as Fannie's chauffeur, if he'd move here to Octavia Street, and he accepted. A builder is coming here tomorrow. We'll build a garage plus a workshop in the backyard, and a small apartment for him. That way, neither Maman nor Papa—or you and I—have to worry about them driving. Things are working out."

Before she moved back home, Hattie organized a crew to update and repaint her old bungalow bedroom in a sophisticated French color scheme of aubergine and smoky beige, accented with jewel-like turquoise and aqua throw pillows and upholstery.

Karl Schmitzer handled the sale of the DeValcourt mansion from beginning to end as Hattie's financial advisor, but she refused to let him tell her the purchase price. She was feeling guilty enough to be selling Fannie's treasured home. How much worse would it be to feel like a mercenary taking advantage? She had Karl add the money to the assets already administered on her behalf.

Hattie was delighted to be home. Maman had showcased a few of Fannie's gorgeous antiques, including the pale Biedermeier foyer chest she had always greatly admired.

Both DuMond women enjoyed thinking of Fannie as they used her lovely things, not that they needed furniture to remember her sweet face and gentle, loving personality.

Settling on Octavia Street was an easy choice for Hattie. During her years with Fannie, the two often joined Hattie's parents and Jack's young family on Octavia Street for the evening or a special occasion.

That Hattie chose to live with Maman and Papa DuMond spoke volumes about their daughter's maturity and selflessness and her close relationship with her parents. Certainly it was not a matter of finances, though perhaps many thought so. No one outside of Hattie's family had any idea of her new wealth. In 1944, as in earlier times, money, religion, and politics were not considered polite topics for conversation.

Hattie organized her routines for efficiency and tranquility. She finally lived her life on an even keel, except for the glaring, uncomfortable disaster of the police search for the murderer, Marie Chennault.

Of necessity, Hattie remained vigilant, expecting Marie to mount an attack on her or someone special in her life. The treacherous spy couldn't be found. Unaccounted for, Marie was the one dangling thread, the lone flaw in Hattie's life.

Maman relinquished oversight of the creaky Octavia Street bungalow to her daughter, who proved that her mother's lessons hadn't been in vain. The house and surrounding yard blossomed under Hattie's creative, energetic guidance. She became an excellent *chatelaine* in a long line of DuMond *chatelaines*.

"Bungalow" was a relative term when describing the Octavia Street place. Through the generations, the house had grown, built on land grant property far more expansive than the lots of newer homes on the street. The home had been built by modest French immigrants more than a century earlier on isolated acreage in a quiet rural area. The original DuMonds were farmers who raised livestock and chickens, grew vegetables, and tended fruit trees.

New Orleans sprawled until it encroached on, then encompassed the comfortable DuMond farm, and a streetcar line was laid that extended past the family property. That allowed the city to incorporate outlying suburbs, and these new "city dwellers" commuted to work on an electric rail flanked by colorful oleander blooms. Urban density penetrated Octavia Street, and the DuMonds sold bits of the farm over the years until the street became a neighborhood.

Hattie and Maman stared out of the parlor window one Saturday, their shoulders touching, and watched men scrub the walls of the house next door, washing off dust and mildew. When they finished, the unimposing white structure reflected the sun.

Hattie stated the obvious. "We have new neighbors." It was the weekend and Hattie was still at home for a change. She would make today's routine hospital rounds later in the day.

Maman said, "I'll have Cook bake cookies. Will you take them over?" She sat on her rocking chair with a tiny groan and reached for her needlework. "After your rounds, I mean."

"Of course. Good idea, Maman."

Later that afternoon, Hattie mounted two immaculate steps and crossed a clean porch to ring the doorbell. A harried-looking, statuesque woman opened the door in a way that looked defensive. Her voice was brusque.

"Can I help you?" With those not particularly gracious words, she waited impatiently for Hattie's response.

She looked to be about Hattie's age, and had obviously been interrupted mid-chore. A colorful bandana lay over the woman's hair, knotted at the nape of her neck, holding back a riot of dark curls about to burst their confinement. Pastel yellow linen sleeves were rolled to her elbows, exposing a pair of strong, capable hands and dark, creamy skin.

Taken aback, Hattie stuttered, "Why, yes, thank you. May I speak to the lady of the house?"

The woman frowned. She rested her fisted hands on her slender hips and eyed the dish in Hattie's hands.

"That would be me." She clearly enunciated her words and jutted her chin, making no move to invite Hattie into her home.

Off guard, Hattie apologized. "Sorry. I didn't realize…"

"What?" Hattie's new neighbor interrupted, her tone sullen. "Don't think people who look like me should be living here? In this swanky neighborhood? Wake up and smell the roses, lady. It's a new world."

Hattie flushed, her face a mottled red, thinking nothing was new about the world. She retorted, "Madam, you haven't the slightest idea what I'm thinking."

Truthfully, she was ashamed of her reaction. The years in France had taught her to treat everyone the same way. She had a new perspective when she returned to New Orleans, one that made her cringe at some of the local attitudes. She wanted to stomp away, but wasn't willing to alienate this new neighbor.

She ventured, in a pleasant tone, "Let's start over, please. I'm your neighbor." She nodded toward the bungalow and juggled the cookies so she could extend her hand.

"Welcome to the neighborhood. I'm Hattie… Hattie DeValcourt. The cookies are for you and your family. Can I help you with anything?"

Her neighbor looked at Hattie's white hand with suspicion, but grudgingly clasped it. "No, thank you. I can manage. I'm Odette… Odette Landry," and accepted the cookies Hattie thrust at her.

With obvious pride, she added, "My husband is a river pilot. He was called back to work yesterday and left me to finish here."

Odette talked to Hattie, standing in the doorway. It seemed she preferred to keep her distance. That was fine with Hattie, who understood how extraordinary it was to integrate a New Orleans neighborhood in 1946. She had a different outlook compared to many people. Her years in colorblind France had taught her otherwise.

Odette was lonely with her husband away much of the time, and with no family nearby, she allowed herself to be enticed into Hattie's life with invitations to sip wine on the Dumond patio in the evenings. She gradually relaxed, not having expected to experience such acceptance.

Hattie again stood beside the open door of the DuMond mausoleum in Metairie Cemetery. A year had passed, and now she was faced with another death. Her eyes were swollen as she laid her mother to rest. Odette was there and Karl Schmitzer stood beside her. Their presence was a comfort.

In six short years, Hattie had seen her family completely dismantled by death, and now she had only her brother Jack to turn to. She held on to the good fortune that she'd been able to care for her parents in their last years.

Maman never recovered from Papa's death and grew smaller and grayer until the day Hattie brought her to the cemetery to lie beside him again.

Usefulness gave Hattie purpose that she chose to leaven with a cheerful, lighthearted sense of humor. Her work with patients fulfilled the destiny she had wished for in her teens, but she could've done without the reversals that caused her so much pain.

Much as she liked being needed and appreciated, she had to agree with Jack that something was lacking in her life.

Months later, Hattie noticed Odette's house had been locked up and dark for several days. When she returned, Odette wept when she told Hattie her riverboat captain husband had drowned when a runaway barge hit his boat and knocked him from its bridge.

"Oh, I'm so sorry, Odette. I worried about you," Hattie said. She reached over to clasp Odette's hand. "I would've gone with you to the funeral, had I known."

"No, indeed, Hattie. Captain Landry," she called her husband that, "his family would've been uncomfortable. I decided not to go back to that place. I'm going to stay here. I love my house and that's what Captain Landry would want. That's what I want, too."

Twittering birds fluttered into the tall trees to settle on the branches as two months later Hattie complained to Odette that she saw much too much death—not just at the hospital, but in her family life, too. She ticked off her personal losses on her fingers.

"Like you, I lost my husband." Down bent Hattie's first finger. "My husband's father died under my care," and she bent a second finger. "Luke's wonderful mother, Fannie, was murdered," and her voice quavered as the third finger followed the first two.

"My goodness!" Odette gasped. "Did the police catch the man who killed her?"

"No. It was a woman, and she's still out there somewhere." Hattie's harsh words carried a sharp, hard edge. She neglected to mention she was the one who'd exposed Marie Chennault as a Nazi spy, and that the crazy woman had killed Fannie just to hurt Hattie. She continued to enumerate her losses.

"I moved home and less than a year later, Papa died in his sleep. And now Maman.

"Maman was younger than Papa, and she would always say to him, 'You did well by us, my darling. We love you.'" Hattie smiled at the memory.

Odette, by that time Hattie's dearest friend and her confidante, said, "You realize what you did?"

"What do you mean?"

"You started with a complaint, remember? But you ended with a smile. Lots of folks don't get past the pain, but you managed quite well."

"Thank you, Odette. I must have learned that from Annette, the woman I lived with in France. Her husband died at the start of the war. She mourned him, but took enormous pleasure in being alive herself. I was searching for my husband back then, but I wanted to be like Annette. She taught me emotional maturity."

Money management became the unexpected adhesive that cemented a renewed connection between the lovely Hattie DeValcourt and Karl Schmitzer.

"It's nonsensical to move Fannie's assets to a new money manager simply because Karl and I were once involved," she protested to Jack.

"First of all, the assets are *yours*." Jack raised his eyebrows, his lips pursed against a smile that begged to burst free. *And second*, Jack thought, *Karl's interest seems as much personal as fiduciary.*

Hattie continued, "So what, if we have to meet from time to time. So? I can handle that. It's not like we're lovers." As she said the words, her cheeks colored. Her eyelids fluttered, the words prompting a feeling she refused to identify.

"Whatever." Jack grinned, pulled out his car keys and walked to the door. "See you later, sis."

Unaware he was a topic of discussion, Karl went about his business days. An excellent lawyer and a certified public accountant with a superb reputation, his practice continued to grow. His clients knew Karl was financially conservative in general, but aggressive with the right opportunity. And, when Hattie managed to be honest with herself, she admitted she enjoyed his company.

The friendship between the two former sweethearts had become somewhat of a charged camaraderie after years of meetings. On the days of their appointments Hattie paid special attention to her clothes and makeup.

For this particular meeting, Hattie wore a sophisticated new dusty rose faille suit that accentuated her trim waist, rounded backside, and full breasts, but she refused to admit she'd bought the suit for those very reasons. The chaste, demure Hattie DeValcourt and Karl Schmitzer had been tiptoeing around each other for some time, reluctant to damage their fragile friendship.

Swiping rosy lipstick onto her lips and touching cologne behind each ear, Hattie left the house. She had an inkling she was sometimes being watched, but not on that particular morning.

As he greeted her, a vertical line appeared between Karl's dark eyebrows. He nibbled at the full lips that Hattie had always thought luscious, wholeheartedly wishing he could lock the door to his office and hold her close. Instead, he escorted her to a chair.

Outside, the rising crescendo of a fire truck rushing down the street echoed the tumult in Karl's heart.

He touched the back of his head and felt the stitches from the wound he'd suffered earlier that morning.

When leaving his condominium, he realized he'd forgotten a file and turned back to retrieve it. Without warning, jabbing pain at the back of his head pushed him sideways into the door. His hand flew to the back of his head and came away wet with blood. He spun to find his attacker, but saw only a trousered leg whisk around the corner, followed by the bang of the fire door. Off kilter, he blinked, grimacing, and saw the glint of a sharp knife blade half imbedded in the door frame. Karl broke out in a sweat. Had he not forgotten his file and turned back, the knife would have struck him in the face. As it was, the nasty gouge had staggered him. He left the knife where it was and went back inside to grab a towel. With trembling fingers he stanched the blood that ran down his neck and back.

His body was trembling when he cautiously opened the door a second time. There was no one and nothing to see. He'd talk to the police, but Karl wasn't about to waste his morning waiting for the cops. He carefully pulled out the knife, protecting any fingerprints with a wad of paper towels.

Back inside, Karl retrieved the forgotten file that saved his life, grabbed a fresh shirt to wear later, and headed for his doctor's office. The visit turned out to be more than he'd bargained for—stitches, a tetanus shot and a second shot of antibiotics, and some good advice. He took everything but the advice.

"Go home and rest," said Karl's doctor, a friend of long standing. "This could've been much more serious. Did you find the weapon?"

Karl nodded, wincing at the burst of pain caused by his nod. "Yes. It was stuck in the door frame."

"Somebody wants you hurt, my friend, so be careful. You're a rare man—one who pays his doctor on time!"

Karl laughed, tucked in his fresh shirt, tied his tie, and clapped his friend's shoulder. Then he made his way to the office.

He intended to tell Hattie about the incident. He had no idea who attacked him, or why. She might have a few suggestions. An earth-toned bandage over his stitches blended with his blond hair, but he ripped it and a few hairs off, yelping, and dropped it in the trash when his secretary announced Hattie's arrival.

When Hattie walked in, she looked exceptionally beautiful and Karl promptly forgot about his injury, thinking, how did I find you in a world full of people? A thrumming pulse made itself felt under his jaw. His wounded head felt flushed.

"Thank you. This is terrific." Hattie pushed away the stack of paper filled with columns of numbers that sat in front of her on the little table.

"You read through that pretty quickly. Did you assimilate it that fast?" She gave Karl an uncomfortable sidelong glance, then quickly looked away.

"I have some questions."

Her strained words ran together—ihavesomequestions—and she kept her eyes directed at the gleaming surface of Karl's conference table.

Odette idly ran a feather duster around the window frame that faced the side of Hattie's bungalow from across their two yards. She missed her husband. Shaking off her sadness and taking a deep breath, she wondered about Hattie's meeting. Something seemed to be up with her. Seeing movement next door, she wondered if Hattie had already returned. The movement seemed out of place and Odette leaned toward the window pane.

No, this wasn't Hattie. It was someone else and she frowned. A short, skinny man walked back and forth, pouring something from a heavy can on the ground along Hattie's raised foundation. Setting the can aside, the figure dug in a pocket and retrieved a box.

Alarmed prickles ran up her spine, and Odette thought, *are those matches? Matches!*

She ran to the phone and called the fire department, then snatched up the bat she kept for protection by her front door and headed to Hattie's house on a dead run.

Karl knew his emotions were scarcely hidden by a spotless white shirt and dark navy jacket. As usual, they lurked just below the surface where Hattie might perceive them should he not remain carefully professional. On the days they were together, he imagined only he knew there was no reason to meet. A secret to be carefully guarded.

That Hattie had questions threw him off balance, and Karl blinked, for a moment unable to speak. She waited for him to say something—anything—as emergency vehicles continued to pass on the street outside, the sounds of their blaring sirens swooshing through the windows and into the corners of the room.

"Uh, what don't you understand?" Karl's office was too warm, suffocating him.

"Not these." She flicked the papers with fingernails polished a dusty rose, dismissing them as unimportant. "These I understand. What I really want to know—"

Karl's door burst open. He and Hattie flinched when it banged against the wall. His unflappable secretary's eyes were wild, and she rushed in without knocking as she usually did. Karl's already frayed nerves tightened.

"Sorry, sir," she squeaked, but hesitated as if detecting something unusual in the air. Then she wrung her hands and turned to Hattie.

"Mrs. DeValcourt, a Mrs. Odette called to say your house is on fire!"

Hattie shot up with a scream, her hat askew. Papers cascaded to the floor. Karl jumped up almost as quickly and ran around his desk to grab Hattie's hand.

"Come on, darling. My car is downstairs. Hurry!"

Karl's secretary's mouth hung open. *Darling?*

Odette was a heroine. Her quick call to the fire department saved Hattie's bungalow from much greater damage, but it was her actions after the call that were the most important. She had subdued an intruder in the act of committing a crime.

The foolish arsonist had no idea that gasoline fumes would burst into violent flames if someone close by struck a match. The arsonist, however, proved not to be a man but a woman, and rather a weak one at that. Odette had no difficulty subduing the injured woman. Imagine Odette's surprise when she later learned she had apprehended the person responsible for the murder of Fannie DeValcourt.

Marie Chennault, also known as Jeanne Beauvais, had found herself instantly aflame in the heart of a ferocious fire. By the time Odette approached, the licking flames crackling high and hot had greedily ignited her clothes and hair. She stumbled and fell to the ground next to Hattie's house, fully engulfed and screaming so loud the neighborhood dogs howled.

For an instant, Odette was torn. Should she do nothing or try to save this pitiful arsonist trying to burn down her friend's house? Her humanity won out.

Odette dropped her bat to grab one of the Croker sacks Hattie used to protect rooting plants and ran toward the writhing woman. She beat at the arsonist's burning clothes, gagging at the awful smells of burning hair and flesh. As her hands and arms were scalded by heat, Odette fought the flames. She tried her best, not wanting to stand aside and watch death occur.

Firefighters arrived. Two quickly extinguished the flames on the arsonist. Others doused fire that had begun to lick up the bungalow wall. Exhausted, Odette ran home and called for Hattie at Karl Schmitzer's office.

Marie Chennault was admitted to the hospital's burn ward unconscious and severely injured; her prognosis was guarded. If she survived, she would be a grotesque caricature of a woman, without beauty or elegance, perhaps the worst possible punishment for such a vain woman.

Hattie felt sorry for Marie, though the woman had meant to destroy her home—and Hattie, too, if she'd been home. But she would never be able to forgive her for killing Fannie.

It seemed Marie would never answer for her war crimes, but she would spend the rest of her miserable life in prison for Fannie's murder.

Odette was frazzled and on the verge of tears. It was the most devastated she'd felt since the day she learned her husband died. She hated the feeling. Her hair stood out from her head as if she'd been hit by lightning. Her clothes, and especially her shoes, were ruined. Her legs up to her knees were covered in muddy ash. Her smoky clothes would go into the trash, no big thing. She salved her few burns. She needed to get back to bustling around, she thought.

She barely remembered being introduced to Karl Schmitzer. She spoke with Karl and Hattie for only a moment before going home to shower. Hattie could stay with her, she thought, until the cleaners and painters refreshed the bungalow. Knowing of Hattie's plans to renovate and expand the bungalow, she chuckled to herself. *That girl always lands on her feet.* She'd have no reason to delay the project now.

Later that day, Odette's big brown eyes widened when Hattie told her Karl had offered a temporary roof over her head.

She'd turned it down, but blushed and ducked her head, saying, "I was sure it was the right thing to do, but it was hard to refuse his offer. I think I'm in love with him, Odette."

After the firefighters left, Hattie and Karl sat at the table in a smoky kitchen. The clothing they had carefully chosen that morning reeked with noxious smoke, too. They agreed that things would've been much, much worse but for Odette's alert intervention.

Hattie was determined not to waste her courage, and so renewed the conversation she and Karl had been having in his office before it was interrupted by news of the fire.

"I want to know about you and your life, Karl, not your numbers."

"My life?" A drop of sweat slid down Karl's back.

She nodded. Her question was more like a blunt demand, one that created an unexpected galvanic response in Karl. Twin ruddy spots appeared on his cheeks and he squirmed in his smoky suit.

"Yes, Karl, your 'life.' I'm rude, I know," said Hattie, "and I don't care. I've asked everybody about you. People say you're married, but no one knows your wife or has even seen her. One person suggested that you're homosexual."

Karl snorted an "as if" snort. That gave her pause, then she kept going.

"I asked if you had children, but only got 'who knows' shrugs. Nobody knows anything about you, who you really are, other than you're a great dancer."

He tried to sidestep, "What about being a good lawyer?"

But Hattie held up a forefinger and kept talking.

"Other mysteries are where you live and what you do for fun. Do you have a good life, Karl, or do you at least *think* your life is a good one? That's what I want to know. That's only fair, don't you think? You sure know *my* life… and don't try to tell me you don't."

Karl sighed, vaguely pleased that she had invested so much time asking about him. He rose and turned his back on Hattie to look out the kitchen window at the tree they had sat under so often all those years ago. The tree had flourished, its girth greater and its canopy much larger now, but as welcoming as ever. The swing they once shared was long gone, and the tree looked lonesome.

Karl's inner struggle—whether he should share the shattering circumstances of his earlier life—didn't show. His decision made, he turned to Hattie, but she had left the table, offended by his long silence. Halfway to the door, she was ready to abandon him to the rank, smoky kitchen.

Taking a long stride, Karl grabbed Hattie's arm and pulled her to him.

"Don't walk away. I'll need a drink if I have to tell you my story. Let's go somewhere else."

Hattie and Karl, in their smoky clothing, settled at a petite table in one corner of a small Uptown bistro, grateful there were few other customers. Their Bloody Marys with skewered pickled okra and celery sticks were quickly set on the snow-white, cloth-covered table. Soft cocktail jazz trickled from an overhead sound system, encouraging them to unwind.

Karl removed the vegetables from his drink, putting them in a dish before he took a sip. He tasted the tart tomato of the refreshing drink and glanced at the impatiently waiting Hattie. He stared into the table's tiny flickering candle flame and reached for her hand as he began his story.

"The last thing I knew about you was the letter that broke our engagement. I was studying for my bar exam at the time. That letter didn't just break our engagement, it broke my heart. It's still broken, worse now, I think, than ever."

He looked up, his glistening eyes reflecting his torment. Hattie mumbled an apology, then looked down.

She berated herself for making him relive his pain, and said, "Stop, Karl. You don't have to put yourself through this." Her voice might have quavered. Her teeth pinched the corner of her quivering lower lip.

"No," Karl answered, his voice husky. He shook his head. "I *want* you to hear what I went through.

"In your letter, you thought you would probably die at the hands of the Germans. And I thought that's what happened, because it was a full year before

I heard your name again. Even then, it was just gossip and conjecture, but everything, all the news about the invasion, was horrific.

"Hitler's 'scorched earth policy' destroyed everything in his path—fields, houses, and families. We all thought you were dead, even your parents. Many nights I prayed for you, that you'd died quickly, that you'd not suffered the atrocities and brutality so many others didn't escape."

Her hand crept under his palm, and she laced her fingers in his.

"I couldn't help it, Hattie. I did worry about you, but I was young. And in those days, it was really all about me and my feelings." Karl pounded his chest.

"The two catastrophes—losing your love and thinking you were dead—threw me into a depression that I forced myself to climb out of every day. I was a CPA by then, and I'd been practicing law for a while. My conscience wouldn't let me neglect my clients. It was my work that saved me. "

The pain and depression that Karl described—not just his, but that of Hattie's parents, too—dismayed her. Guilty tears sprang to her eyes. She had been such a self-absorbed girl during those years, oblivious of everyone but herself.

Her hand settled on Karl's arm without conscious thought other than to ease his discomfort. Just as unconsciously, his own warm hand covered hers, in imitation of a familiar gesture from decades earlier.

His story continued.

"Do you remember my parents? They never understood my feelings and said it was my fault for letting you go. Had I known how they would react, never in a blue moon would I have said anything, because it opened me up to their ridicule.

"I sought out a girl who had been a law school student with me. Back then, Eleanor was kind. Her apartment became my refuge, a place to lick my wounds. She offered the affection I needed but couldn't find anywhere else. She stayed in New Orleans and joined a large firm after she passed the bar exam, but soon realized practicing law wasn't nearly as entertaining as studying it. She thought about quitting.

"Truly, I thought I would grow to love her. I was wrong about that and so much else. When the government began drafting single men from my age group into the army, it changed everything."

Torment and disgust vied in Karl's face. His eyes probed Hattie's before he dropped them and picked at an invisible speck on his coat sleeve. He resumed the thread of his story before she could interrupt.

"Hang on. Eleanor's behavior didn't help. I'm going to make this fast. I married her to avoid the war in Europe and the war with Japan. Marriage was Eleanor's suggestion. My friends were being forced into the army, losing their jobs and careers. In the beginning, married men had automatic deferrals. That changed later, of course.

"We married in a civil ceremony at City Hall with thirty or forty other couples. No fanfare. No celebration. No nothing.

My brothers and sisters and I had each inherited decent money by that time. My folks caught a virulent flu and passed away within a week of each other. I personally think what Hitler was doing to Germany and our German relatives made my parents question whether life was worth living. My brothers and sisters are far away; I'm the only member of our family left in New Orleans. I wrote to tell them I was married. I'm alone, Hattie, really alone."

Karl spread his hands wide. His agitation increased as he tore his cocktail napkin to shreds.

Hattie slowly shook her head, trying to derail Karl's obvious despair.

"Did you move into your parents' house?"

His hand returned to Hattie's. His grip tightened and his knuckles turned white. His back bowed, as if weighted down. She had asked Karl about his parents' house only to break up his intensity, not to cause him additional pain, but she decided to say nothing.

"Yes. Their house needed a lot of work and we were planning to renovate it, before Eleanor's friend Abigail became a fixture in our lives.

"She had a job, too, but evenings she always got to the house before we did. She was a great cook, and a hot meal was always waiting for Eleanor and me when we got home. I thought she was pretty nice, in the beginning. I didn't know …."

He swung his lowered head in distress, mortally wounded, a man waiting for the *coup de grâce* to end his suffering. Hattie felt his anguish.

"The two of them, Eleanor and Abigail, they were intimate. They had an affair right under my nose and I never suspected a thing. It would've kept going indefinitely if Eleanor hadn't forced a change.

"I was the only one hurt. Not even me, really, because I didn't love Eleanor. I was just embarrassed. Not that anyone outside the house knew what was going on. Eleanor made a unilateral decision and told me, very bluntly, how things stood and what was going to happen.

"Not long after that I got home one night and Eleanor and Abigail were gone. They took everything in the house that was valuable—my dad's gold watch, Mama's jade earrings—and left. I learned they took a train for the far west. Maybe they're still together, who knows. Every month, Eleanor withdraws funds from an account I set up for her.

"She didn't want to get divorced, maybe for convention's sake—you know how people can be—but she needed money. What was I supposed to do, say no? I can afford to support her, so I do."

He couldn't look at Hattie, but talked down at their interlaced fingers. Neither had noticed that the ice in their Bloody Marys had melted.

"Hardly anyone knows my story. Yes, I *am* married, but my wife left me to be with her girlfriend." He glanced up for only a second, addressing his next sentence to his hands.

"I had to move. That was a house of horrors. I sold it fast as I could, then bought the top floor of a condominium on the Avenue. Been there ever since.

"I certainly don't miss Eleanor, but I'm stuck in limbo."

Karl peeked at Hattie, then dragged his eyes away. One closed fist hit the tabletop, so that the few afternoon customers craned their heads to check the fuss. *A lovers' quarrel, maybe?*

"Sad, isn't it? I'm alone a lot. I *do* have work and a few hobbies and friends who give my life meaning." Karl stopped, aware his hand had covered Hattie's again. The background of soft conversations, low laughter, and the sharp clinks of glasses and silverware cocooned the pair, each absorbed in contemplative silence.

Hattie shook her head and leaned across the table, saying, "I have to ask you another question, Karl. The stitches on the back of your head. What happened?"

He'd almost forgotten. He flinched and hissed when he brushed against the sore wound, then shrugged.

"I'm not quite sure why it happened, or even who was responsible." He recounted the incident, still puzzled. Hattie became progressively more upset, until she interrupted, her eyes flashing.

"See, that *had* to be Marie. She's determined to do whatever she can to hurt me, by hurting the people I care most about."

Hattie's remark about *people she cares most about* caught Karl's attention for a moment, but he merely said, "What do you mean?"

"I'm glad to know where she finally is, though what she could've done to you frightens me. Did you get a tetanus shot? He nodded, grimaced slightly and held up two fingers.

Shaking his shirtsleeve, Hattie said, "I'm happy we don't have to worry about that hateful woman any longer." Karl hardly heard her words, loving the play of candlelight on little crinkles at the corners of her eyes.

Hattie continued, "That… *bitch*… struck at me any and every way she could. I believe her evil heart wanted to kill everyone I love, and save me for last. Thank goodness she's nearly killed herself. If she lives, she'll go to prison."

Karl heard only, "everyone I love," and his heart soared.

Their solicitous waiter approached, interrupting their discussion with the bill. They stood, caught up with emotion. Karl dropped a few bills on the table, extended his hand to Hattie, and without another word escorted her out the door to a nearby streetcar stop.

The pair waited, silent, sheltered by exuberant, purple-blooming oleanders in the neutral ground that divided St. Charles Avenue and housed the streetcar line. It was a companionable quiet. They stood nearly motionless, close enough for each to imagine they felt the other's body heat, while their two powerful brains analyzed the day.

Before Hattie climbed aboard for the return to the smoldering ashes on Octavia Street, they merely air kissed and said a simple goodbye.

Shaken that he'd revealed his shameful secret, Karl trudged the short distance to his office and climbed the stairs with more than the usual difficulty. He shut his office door and isolated himself in his handsome, private space, leaning for support against his desk. It had been a relief to share his terrible story, especially with Hattie, but examining that painful time exhausted him and he was afraid Hattie would think less of him now.

He whispered to himself, "Not much scares me, but the thought you can never love me terrifies me, Hattie."

Karl and Hattie were present in the courtroom when Marie's callow young public defender entered her guilty pleas for the murder of Fannie DeValcourt and the arson at Hattie's home.

A few weeks later, Hattie interrupted her third floor hospital rounds at the Hôtel-Dieu clinic to watch Marie's departure. She had no sympathy for the woman. As alert as a sentinel, Karl stood outside the hospital entrance. It was there he saw the ruined, melted face of the formerly beautiful woman and the fingers of her hands fused into mitts by the ferocity of the fire.

Marie's ambulance was taking her to the Women's Prison to serve a life sentence without parole. She would initially stay in the prison infirmary. When her health allowed, she would be transferred to a cell in the general population.

For several months more, Karl and Hattie's meetings focused on business, hardly the stuff of a personal relationship. When they worked together, time passed quickly, in the bat of an eyelash. Otherwise, time was more like an insect mired in resin, pinned for an eternity in the sticky sweetness of amber honey.

Hattie spent her daylight hours with patients and on hospital rounds. Helping the sick recover their health gave her tremendous satisfaction. Hôtel-Dieu valued her work ethic and skills, dangling offers of additional responsibilities and a career path to become Chief of Staff, the position once held by her well-loved father-in-law, Dr. Abner DeValcourt.

She spent lonely evenings mulling Karl's marital dilemma. He yearned for her, but she wanted him as a husband, not a lover. Not that she'd ever told him that, she never would. He had to be divorced from his problem wife before she would entertain a closer relationship. Although inexperienced in such legalities and the emotional complexities, Hattie was smart enough to know Karl wouldn't want her to interfere.

Loneliness threatened to sink her into depression, but the laughter and good humor Odette supplied kept bad days to a minimum. She rekindled old school friendships, which helped, but the lack of a loving mate was a constant tug in the stream of her days.

When she reviewed her life, Hattie realized that every wish granted in life had brought not only satisfaction and fulfillment, but also unexpected burdens and loss. This was true of her small wishes (such as continuing her education at a school with an attractive school uniform that turned out to be uncomfortable) as well as large ones, like marrying Luke to escape the Nazis, before she truly loved him.

Hattie's professional life was happy, but it was not enough. There was a vast, yawning hole in her gut. She would never regret the love she experienced with Luke, and she wanted to experience that again. Now she'd let herself fall in love with Karl a second time. And if she read the signs right, Karl loved her, too.

After months of status quo, Hattie decided to ramp up their relationship.

Far down St. Charles Avenue from Octavia Street, past the stately mansions under their mossy oaks, a diligent attorney concentrated on a complicated file.

Karl enjoyed helping others find comfort in life, at least financially. And he'd learned he could distract himself from thoughts of Hattie by staying busy. Except in the evenings, on those rare nights when he had no social obligation.

His reputation was secure, both socially and professionally. He looked forward to his workday, though with mixed feelings when meeting with Hattie. These he dreaded and anticipated in equal measure. And he'd scheduled another unnecessary update on her finances in an hour.

He stood at his window, his hands in his pockets, as the beautiful love of his life strode toward his office building. Her movement created sublime music in his imagination. Disturbed pigeons fluttered from the grit in her path.

It had become one of Karl's favorite pastimes to study Hattie from head to toe. She was dressed today in a sleek, belted and buttoned, rust suede dress that looked soft even from this height. He would give all he had to unfasten every button and hold her softness close.

With a spark of jealousy, Karl watched Hattie bestow a radiant smile on a passing pedestrian. Her olive skin glowed dewy soft, and experience from so many years ago gave assurance that the lightly tanned oval face with the fortunate freckles scattered across the nose would be even lovelier up close. A tumble of short, dark auburn tresses stirred in the breeze, unfettered by a hat in these more casual days.

Hattie, Hattie… what am I going to do about how I feel?

Karl cursed his marriage. It would flout convention, but he had decided to petition the courts for a divorce and end the charade once and for all. During their appointment today, he would tell Hattie he was in love with her and ask her to marry him.

His heart was light, relieved of its unwelcome burden. He took a deep breath, anticipating the intoxication of Hattie's cologne.

Karl jerked his hands from his pockets. Stunned, he watched Hattie stop, turn, and rapidly walk away, and wished he could yell out and beg her not to go.

"I'm calling at the last minute, I'm so sorry." Hattie paused, the receiver at her ear. She listened for a moment, then nodded as she twisted the cord with her free hand.

"Please offer Mr. Schmitzer my apologies." She paused, then added, "If he's free tonight, I'd like to apologize over dinner. My home at seven. If it's not too much trouble, I'll stay on the line for his response."

She waited, her eyes checking her newly painted and furnished living room. She missed her mother with an unexpected ferocity, still bowled over by her absence, but she couldn't afford to get melancholy. So many of the people she loved were gone—her parents, Luke's parents, Luke. Hattie pursed her lips when she realized she had tacked her husband's name to the end of her list of the dead for the first time. His loss was becoming a little easier for her to bear, though it thrummed like a second heartbeat right beside her own.

Karl's secretary came back on the line to say her boss accepted Hattie's invitation. He would be there at seven. Hattie's voice trembled when she offered her thanks and disconnected, never guessing that Karl's secretary smiled as she lowered her receiver, wishing the best for these two darling people.

Hattie turned to the kitchen and wondered if Maman would approve the wild idea of a home-cooked meal as part of her plan.

Karl showed up with a bouquet of roses and daisies for Hattie.

He wore an odd expression that confused Hattie when she greeted him at the door. Instead of "welcome," she immediately asked, "What's wrong?"

He gestured behind him at Hattie's exuberantly blooming garden, then pushed his nosegay of hothouse flowers into her hand.

"These puny flowers just got embarrassed by your gorgeous garden."

"Silly, thank you for the pretty bouquet. Come in." Hattie stepped back inside and Karl followed through the familiar Octavia Street front door, now painted a sophisticated black with a burnished new bronze handle.

Bemused, Karl looked around, impressed by Hattie's changes. In their youth, he'd thought only of her, not paying any attention to the house she lived in. He wondered how much of what he now noticed was new at all. Had the oversized gas lights he'd seen on either side of the entry door been added? He hadn't a clue. He hadn't noticed such things as a younger man, not that he was all that old now at thirty-six.

They exchanged awkward polite pecks on the cheek. With Karl's delighted moan of "Everything smells delicious," Hattie relaxed. She laughed when he spun on his heel, saying "I hope that's my *stomach* I hear growling at me."

"You're *that* hungry? In that case, let's skip the cocktails and go straight to the table. Dinner's ready and I uncorked a good burgundy. We'll start with a glass of that."

She took Karl's arm and walked with him to the dining room, freshly painted and cured of smoke damage. He recognized the same table, the entire room, in fact. Papa and Maman DuMond's treasured book collection had been lost. Smoke had left those unredeemable, unfortunately. That was the biggest change.

This was where Karl and Hattie had spent so many hours studying together. He was in college, coming by streetcar from Tulane after classes, Hattie still in high school. They'd talk for hours and hold hands under the table, her mother in her rocker with her knitting gently overseeing them from the other end of the room.

Hidden by the tabletop, they'd slipped off their shoes and touched each other's feet, hormones crazily skittering. His knees buckled under the weight of his memories, and he grabbed the back of a chair.

"Please take a seat, Karl, and I'll get the food. Cook has the afternoon off, so I'm both chef *and* server. And would you pour yourself a glass of wine? Pour some for me, too?"

Karl's ears perked. His eyes widened and he thought, *so we're alone?*

At the table, Karl looked around the room. It had probably changed since his days of youthful ardor, though he couldn't be sure. He'd concentrated on Hattie most of that time—her looks, how soft she was, how good she smelled. Come to think of it, he was doing the exact same thing right now. He laughed at himself, so giddy he had to shake his head.

Hattie returned, pushing a butler's table, then transferred the dishes to the dining table under a dimmed chandelier. Aromas tantalized Karl's taste buds as Hattie served the food. Succulent roast beef was stuffed with fragrant onion, garlic, and other seasonings. Heaping spoonfuls of perfect rice and gravy followed. A graceful finger pointed out the savory side dish and hot homemade bread between them on the table.

"Serve that yourself, please, Karl. And eat as much as you want. Whatever we don't eat will go to waste."

Karl's mouth was watering, but he knew better than to take a bite before the hostess lifted her fork, good manners in this twentieth century. Invited guests understood they had to be on their best behavior if they wanted repeat invitations to society's tables.

Karl begged, "Hattie, please pick up your fork. Everything smells so delicious, and I'm starving."

She chortled and raised her fork like a baton, saying in a very French accent, "You may begin." Karl wasted not a second, taking a bite of the roast.

"God, this is good, Hattie. Please compliment your cook."

"My goodness, Karl! Didn't you hear me? *I'm* the cook." She laughed and clinked her glass to his, then poured them both more wine.

"What can I say? The food is even more delicious than I thought it would be." *She can cook, too?* "Where'd you learn to cook like this?"

"Maman and I made a deal. She'd let me go to fifth grade and wear a fancy uniform, but I would have to learn to cook. So, there was that. And then, when I lived in Vierville with Annette, I learned more wonderful dishes from her. Annette could have taught *Cordon Bleu* to a Parisian *Chef de Cuisine*. She was an excellent chef, and she did it with very few choices during the war."

They laughed a lot during the meal. The conversation sparkled, wonderful and convivial. The first bottle of burgundy was excellent, so Karl uncorked a second, which proved just as good.

"You have beautiful art, Hattie. Are they new pieces?" She looked at him, giving Karl a chance to notice that her eyes were burnished bronze in the candlelight.

"Well," Hattie drawled, "After the fire, I painted the house inside and out. Changed some colors here and there, but these are the same ol' paintings. You don't recognize the *da Vinci*? Been in the family forever. I'm surprised at you. We spent enough time in this room."

They looked at each other for a moment. Karl blushed, his eyes wide, and Hattie broke the spell with a peal of laughter before returning to her meal.

It was on the tip of his tongue to tell her what he did remember, but he was his usual circumspect self and thought better of it. Karl loved Hattie's sense of humor.

After a moment, they continued their conversation, unconsciously assessing each other's voices, intellects, and physical attributes. They each passed muster.

Karl finished his meal and his apple tart dessert, then watched Hattie place her fork on her untouched tart, too full to eat another bite.

Hattie invited Karl to join her on the patio, carrying the second bottle of wine. He followed with two fresh goblets. The freshness of autumn had arrived, but early October days were long in the South. The shadows were long, too, and the warm breeze gentled and cooled them.

Karl's hopeful breaths vibrated with decades of anticipation. He barely restrained his ardor when he pulled out Hattie's chair. She wore a tissue-thin, lime green voile dress that fluttered in breezy eddies perhaps fanned by the movement of birds' wings. Slightly tipsy, he yearned to be like that fabric, lucky enough to cover and warm Hattie's body.

Somehow he managed to speak, his voice rough and husky to his ears. He caught an edge of Hattie's voile hem and played with it, rubbing it between his fingers.

"This dress is so delicate. It's like a… a cloud of butterflies has covered you. Lucky butterflies."

She blushed, but didn't move away. She filled his goblet, giving it to him. Her forefinger gently stroked his hand as he took it from her. He quivered, and his eyes closed, wanting her to touch him forever.

"I never imagined anything could improve your handsome face, Karl. Didn't think it was possible, but I think you're better looking now," Hattie teased, before turning serious.

Setting down her wine, she clasped her hands tightly.

"Here goes—"

Her words and change in attitude shook Karl back to reality. His forehead furrowed and his anticipation evaporated. His heart plummeted.

"What do you mean by that?"

She looked up from beneath her lashes. "Did you think I don't know our meetings are unnecessary? Just a connivance to get us together?"

"Well…"

Hattie shook her head. "Don't deny it, Karl. Truth is, I *want* to be with you." She was finding it more difficult to be the aggressor than she'd thought. She forced herself to continue. "Truth is, I want *more* than to sit at some dumb table with you."

Karl's heart soared into the stratosphere. His grin was wide and happy and he reached out a hand, limp with the great release of tension. Until her next statement sent him back to frustrated despair.

"You're married, Karl, not that I give a fig *why* you are. But you are a married man, and I won't be part of an illicit romance."

He tried to interrupt, but she held up a finger and said, "I plan to hug you and kiss you tonight—but only once."

Karl coughed a painful breath. How long could he make that hug and kiss last?

"I won't ever hug or kiss you again until you end your marriage. That's all I have to say, and you know I always mean what I say."

"But—"

"No buts, Karl. I'm more stubborn now than I was as a child, and I was pretty stubborn then. I won't change my mind." Hattie's voice had begun to shake, so she stopped speaking. She disguised her distress by taking a large swallow of wine.

Karl's emotions had ping-ponged back and forth from anticipation to despair. But this confrontation was not completely unexpected. He chugged down the rest of his wine and stood, grabbing the empty bottle to take inside.

In his deepest, most determined voice, he held out his hand for hers, and said, "Well, come on. Time's a-wasting. Let's get on with this hug and kiss so I can go home and lick my wounds."

Hattie followed him to the door. Devastated by Karl's brusque response, she moved hesitantly. Half-drunk with wine and raging hormones, now at evening's end she no longer knew what to expect.

His hug was strong and his warm hands pressed her bare back into his body. His one hungry kiss lasted only long enough to stir up powerful memories. He thanked her for the meal, turned, and walked out without another word.

Her plan had failed. She slumped against the door, then felt it open a crack. Karl thrust his nose into the crack.

"I'm going to get a divorce. We'll work on it together."

He slammed the door and grinned all the way to his car. His heart was light and happy.

That night Hattie drowsed in the dark of her bedroom. Her mind skipped from one subject to another as she wound down. Her last thought as she snuggled under the covers before sleep captured her was of her new yet old romance. *If fate meant for us to be together,* she thought, *why all the heartbreak?*

She slipped off the sleep cliff, hearing Fannie's soft, kind voice. Or was it Luke's?

In a dream, she heard her Maman say, "There's nothing to regret, darling. Had life not knocked you this way and that, you wouldn't be the strong woman you are. You'll have your reward soon, and it will be sweet."

I'll remember that in the morning, Hattie told Maman. Smiling in her sleep, she rested better than ever before.

##

ACKNOWLEDGEMENTS

IT WAS A lucky day when Sabrina Flynn, a fellow Sisters in Crime author, recommended that gifted Tom Welch might agree to copyedit my debut novel *Keep Me Safe*. He burnished the novel into a gem, which makes it no surprise I asked him to work his magic on *Nothing To Regret*. Lightning has struck twice, thanks to this brilliant and truly nice man. That combination turned the tough job of editing into one I enjoyed.

The cover design is the work of exemplary 100 Covers artists who also designed the cover of my first novel, Keep Me. Safe.

I must thank our good friends, Anita Hughes and Dan Hughes, who provided enthusiasm and encouragement that kept my hands on the keyboard and my brain in gear.

And, not least, our beloved family that understand the diligence needed to keep creative juices flowing and who helped support me as I worked. I love them all and appreciate everything they do.

Most important is my wonderful, smart, and funny husband who picks up the slack when I'm in a dither. Because of that, and all of his other adorable habits, he'll never be rid of me.

www.ingramcontent.com/pod-product-compliance
Lightning Source LLC
Chambersburg PA
CBHW051639260626
47170CB00004B/1240